PENGUIN BOOKS
THE GREEN MAN

Kingsley Amis, who was born in South London in 1922, was educated at the City of London School and St John's College, Oxford. At one time he was a university lecturer, a keen reader of science fiction and a jazz enthusiast. His novels include *Lucky Jim* (1954), *Take a Girl Like You* (1960), *The Anti-Death League* (1966), *The Alteration* (1976, winner of the John W. Campbell Memorial Award), *Jake's Thing* (1978), *Russian Hide-and-Seek* (1980), *Stanley and the Women* (1984) and *The Old Devils*, winner of the 1986 Booker Prize. Among his other publications are *New Maps of Hell*, a survey of science fiction (1960), *The James Bond Dossier* (1965), *Colonel Sun*, a James Bond adventure (1968, under the pseudonym of Robert Markham), *Rudyard Kipling and His World* (1975) and *The Golden Age of Science Fiction* (1981). He published his *Collected Poems* in 1979 and his *Collected Short Stories* in 1980. Many of his books are published in Penguin. He has written ephemerally on politics, education, language, films, television and drink. Kingsley Amis was awarded the C.B.E. in 1981.

D0887834

BY THE SAME AUTHOR

Fiction

Lucky Jim
That Uncertain Feeling
I Like It Here
Take a Girl Like You
One Fat Englishman
The Anti-Death League
I Want It Now
Girl, 20
The Riverside Villas Murder
Ending Up
The Alteration
Jake's Thing
Russian Hide-and-Seek
Stanley and the Women
The Golden Age of Science Fiction (editor)
Collected Short Stories
The Old Devils

Verse

A Case of Samples
A Look Round the Estate
Collected Poems 1944–79
The New Oxford Book of Light Verse (editor)
The Faber Popular Reciter (editor)

Non-fiction

New Maps of Hell: A Survey of Science Fiction
The James Bond Dossier
What Became of Jane Austen? and other questions
On Drink
Rudyard Kipling and His World
Harold's Years (editor)
Every Day Drinking
How's Your Glass?

With Robert Conquest

Spectrum I, II, III, IV, V (editor)
The Egyptologists

Kingsley Amis

THE GREEN MAN

PENGUIN BOOKS

to Sargy Mann

Published by the Penguin Group
27 Wrights Lane, London W8 5TZ, England
Viking Penguin Inc., 40 West 23rd Street, New York, New York 10010, USA
Penguin Books Australia Ltd, Ringwood, Victoria, Australia
Penguin Books Canada Ltd, 2801 John Street, Markham, Ontario, Canada L3R 1B4
Penguin Books (NZ) Ltd 182–190 Wairau Road, Auckland 10, New Zealand

Penguin Books Ltd, Registered Offices: Harmondsworth, Middlesex, England

First published by Jonathan Cape 1969
Published in Penguin Books 1988

Copyright © Kingsley Amis, 1969
All rights reserved

Made and printed in Great Britain by
Richard Clay Ltd, Bungay, Suffolk

Contents

1 : The Red-haired Woman

FAREHAM, Herts　　　　　　　　**THE GREEN MAN**
½ mile off A595　　　　　　　　　　Mill End 0043

No sooner has one gone over one's surprise at finding a genuine coaching inn less than 40 miles from London—and 8 from the M1—than one is marvelling at the quality of the equally genuine English fare (the occasional disaster apart!). There has been an inn on this site since the Middle Ages, from which parts of the present building date; after some 190 years of service as a dwelling its original function and something of its original appearance, were restored in 1961. Mr Allington will tell its story to the interested (there is, or was, at least one ghost) and be your candid guide through the longish menu. Try the eel soup (6/-), pheasant pie (15/6), saddle of mutton and caper sauce (17/6), treacle roll (5/6). Wine list short, good (except for white Burgundies), a little expensive. Worthington E, Bass, Whitbread Tankard on draught. Friendly, efficient service. No children's prices.

Cl. Su L. Must Book L; F, Sa & Su D. Meals 12.30–3; 7–10.30. *Alc main dishes* 12/6 to 25/-. *Seats* 40. *Car park. No dogs. B & B from* 42/6.　　　　　　　　　　　　　　　　　**Class A**

App. Bernard Levin; Lord Norwich; John Dankworth; Harry Harrison; Wynford Vaughan-Thomas; Dennis Brogan; Brian W. Aldiss; and many others.

The point about white Burgundies is that I hate them myself. I take whatever my wine supplier will let me have at a good price (which I would never dream of doing with any other drinkable). I enjoyed seeing those glasses of Chablis or Pouilly Fuissé, so closely resembling a blend of cold chalk soup and alum cordial with an additive or two to bring it to the colour of children's pee, being peered and sniffed at, rolled round the shrinking tongue and forced down somehow by parties of young technology dons from Cambridge or junior television producers and their girls. Minor, harmless compensations of this sort are all too rare in a modern innkeeper's day.

In fact, most of my trade did come either from London or the twenty-odd miles from Cambridge, with a little more from the nearest Hertfordshire towns. I got the occasional passer-by, of course, but not as many as my colleagues on the A10 to the east of me and the A505 to the north-west. The A595 is a mere sub-artery connecting Stevenage and Royston, and although I put up a sign on it the day I opened, not many transients ever bothered to turn off and try to find the Green Man in preference to using one of the pubs directly beside the main road. All right with me, that. About my only point of agreement with John Fothergill, the buckle-shoed posturer who had the Spread Eagle in Thame when I was a boy and founded a reputation and a book on being nasty to his guests, is lack of warmth towards the sort of people who use two halves of bitter and two tomato juices as a quadruple ticket to the lavatories and washbasins. The villagers from Fareham itself, and from Sandon and Mill End, each of the two about a mile away, were obviously a different matter. They put back their pints steadily and quietly in the public bar, filling it at week-ends, and had an agreeable short way with dinner-jacketed seekers after rustic atmosphere or the authentic life of the working class.

The locals, with some assistance from the various hearty young men who came in to dine, got through plenty of beer, as much as a couple of dozen tens of bitter a week in the summer. Whatever might be said about its prices, the wine too went quickly enough. Refusing, as I have always done, to offer any but fresh meat, vegetables and fruit, poses a daily transport problem. All this, together with keeping up stocks of salt and metal-polish, flowers and toothpicks, takes a good deal of arranging. One way and another, I used to spend a good two or three hours of almost every day out of my house. But this could be less than a hardship to a man with a newish second wife, a teenaged daughter by a first marriage and an ancient and decrepit father (apart from a staff of nine) to be variously coped with.

Last summer, in particular, would have taxed a more hardened and versatile coper than me. As if in the service of some underground anti-hotelier organization, successive guests tried to rape the chambermaid, called for a priest at 3 a.m., wanted a room to take girlie photographs in, were found dead in bed. A party of sociology students from Cambridge, rebuked for exchanging obscenities at protest-meeting volume, poured beer over young David Palmer, my trainee assistant, and then staged a sit-in. After nearly a year of no worse than average conduct, the Spanish kitchen porter went into a heavy bout of Peeping Tom behaviour, notably but not at all exclusively at the grille outside the ladies' lavatory, attracted the attention of the police and was finally deported. The deep-fat fryer caught fire twice, once during a session of the South Hertfordshire branch of the Wine and Food Society. My wife seemed lethargic, my daughter withdrawn. My father, now in his eightieth year, had another stroke, his third, not serious in itself but not propitious. I felt rather strung up, and was on a bottle of Scotch a day, though this had been standard for twenty years.

One Wednesday about the middle of August reached a new level. In the morning there had been trouble with the repatriated voyeur's successor, Ramón, who had refused to pile and burn the rubbish on the grounds that he had already had to do the breakfast dishes. Then, while I was picking up the tea, coffee and such at the dry-goods warehouse in Baldock, the ice-maker had broken down. It never performed with much conviction in hot weather, and the temperature most of that week was in the upper seventies. An electrician had to be found and fetched. Three sets of hotel guests with four young children between them, no doubt under orders from anti-hotelier HQ, turned up from nowhere between 5.30 and 5.40. My wife succeeded almost totally in blaming this on me.

Later, having settled my father in front of the open drawing-room window with a weak Scotch-and-water, I came out of our apartment on the upper storey to find somebody standing, back turned to me, near the stairhead. I took this person for a women in an evening dress rather heavy for a humid August evening. There was no function in the banqueting chamber, the only public room on that floor, until the following week, and our apartment was clearly marked as private.

With my best offensive suavity, I said, 'Can I help you, madam?'

Instantly, but without a sound, the figure turned to face me. I vaguely saw a pale, thin-lipped face, heavy auburn ringlets and some kind of large bluish pendant at the throat. Much more clearly than this, I sensed a surprise and alarm that seemed disproportionate: my arrival on the landing could hardly have been inaudible to one only twenty feet away, and it was obvious enough who I was.

At that moment my father called to me, and without thinking I looked away.

'Yes, Father?'

'Oh, Maurice ... could you send up an evening paper? The local one will do.'

'I'll get Fred to bring one up.'

'Soon, if you would, Maurice, and if Fred's free.'

'Yes, Father.'

This took no more than a dozen seconds, but when they were over the landing was empty. The woman must have decide to cut short her display of heightened sensitivity and pursue her search on the ground floor. No doubt she was more successful there, for I saw nothing of her as I came down the stairs, crossed the few feet of hall and entered the front bar.

This long, low room, with small windows revealing the thickness of its outer wall, and normally cool and dry in summer, was stickily oppressive that evening. Fred Soames, the barman, had the fans going, but as I joined him behind the counter and waited for him to finish serving a round of drinks, I could feel sweat trickling down under my frilled shirt and dinner-jacket. I was uneasy too, and not just in my habitual unlocalized way. I was bothered by something about the appearance or demeanour of the woman I had seen on the landing, something it was now too late to define. Even less reasonably, I felt certain that, when my father called to me, he had changed his mind about what he wanted to say. I could not imagine what his original thought had been, and, again, I would not now be able to find out. His memory in such cases extended over seconds only.

I sent Fred off with the paper, served, in his absence, three medium sherries and (with concealed distaste) a lager and lime, and took a party of early diners through the menu, pushing the rather boring salmon and some incipiently elderly pork a little less gently than the *Good Food Guide* might have approved. After that, a visit to the kitchen, where David Palmer and the chef had everything under control, including Ramón, who assured me that he was not now desiring to return to Espain. Then, a call at the tiny office under the angle of the main staircase. My wife was listlessly working her way through the bills, but lost some of her listlessness (she never seemed to lose quite all of it) on being told to forget all that crap for now and go up and change. She even gave me a hasty kiss on the ear.

Returning to the bar by way of the still-room, where I swallowed down a very large Scotch put there for me by Fred, I did some more takings-through the menu. The last of the batch was an elderly couple from Baltimore, on their way to Cambridge in search of things historical and breaking their journey at my house to take in a few of the same, or similar. The man, a retired lawyer, had evidently been doing his homework, not a testing task in this instance. Periphrastically but courteously, he inquired after our ghost, or ghosts.

I went into the routine, first piously turning down a drink. 'The main one was somebody called Dr Thomas Underhill who lived here in the later seventeenth century. He was in holy orders, but he wasn't the parson of the parish; he was a scholar who for some reason gave up his Cambridge fellowship and bought this place. He's buried in that little churchyard just up the road, but he nearly didn't get buried at all. He was so wicked that when he died the sexton wouldn't dig a grave for him, and the local rector refused to officiate at his funeral. They had to get a sexton from Royston, and a clergyman all the way from Peterhouse in Cambridge. Some of the people round about said that Underhill had killed his wife, whom he used to quarrel with a lot, apparently, and he was also supposed to have brought about the death of a farmer he'd had trouble with over some land deal.

'Well, the odd thing is that both these people were murdered all right, half torn to pieces, in fact, in the most brutal way, but in both cases the bodies were found in the open, at almost the same spot on the road to the village, although the murders were six years apart, and on both occasions it was established beyond doubt that Underhill was indoors here at the time. The obvious guess is that he hired chaps to do the job for him, but they were never caught, nobody even saw them, and the force used on the victims, they say, was disproportionate for an ordinary commercial killing.

'Anyway, Underhill, or rather his ghost, turned up quite a few times at a window in what's now part of the dining-room, peering out and apparently watching something. All the witnesses seem to have been very struck by the expression on his face and his general demeanour, but, according to the story, there was a lot of disagreement about what he actually looked like. One chap said he thought Underhill was behaving as if he were terrified out of his wits. Someone else thought he was showing the detached curiosity of a man of science observing an experiment. It doesn't sound very consistent, does it? but then...'

'Could it not be, Mr Allington, could it not be that this ... apparition was engaged, if one might so put the matter, in ... surveying the actuality of the crimes, or the, the shadow of the actuality of the crimes he had brought to pass, and that the various observers were witnessing successive stages in his reaction to the spectacle of brutal violence, from ... clinical disinterest to horror, and it might be, agonized remorse?'

'An interesting point.' I did not add that it had occurred, in a less Jamesian form, to almost everybody who had heard this story. 'But in that case he was standing at the wrong window, facing away from the spot where the murders were done towards a patch of woods. Nothing has ever happened there as far as I know, nothing to do with this business anyway.'

'I see. Then let me turn to another consideration. In the latter part of your strange and fascinating tale, Mr Allington, that concerning the figure of ... the revenant, I noticed that you employed the past tense, thereby ... implying that these manifestations are also a thing of the past. Is that, would that be correct, sir?'

The old lad's brain could evidently work a little faster than his organs of speech. 'Quite correct. Nothing has been seen since I took over the house seven years ago, and the people I bought it from, who'd had it for much longer, had never seen anything either. They had heard that an elderly relative of a predecessor had been frightened by what could have been Underhill's ghost when he was a boy, but that must have been in Victorian times. No, I'm afraid if there ever was anything, it's all over now.'

'Just so. I have read that this house has known *at least one* ghost, which would seem to ... indicate the possibility, at least, of another.'

'Yes. Nothing was ever actually seen of him at any stage. A few people said they used to hear somebody walking round the outside of the house at night and trying the doors and windows. Of course, every village must have two or three characters who wouldn't be averse to a bit of burglary at a place of this size if they could find an easy entry.'

'Did nobody take the obvious course of looking out to see ... what there might have been to see?'

'Apparently not. They said they didn't like the noise whoever it was made while he was going round. He rustled and crackled as he moved. That's as much sense as I've been able to make of it.'

'And this ... person also no longer visits the scene?'

'No.'

I spoke a little shortly. I usually enjoyed telling all this, but tonight it seemed silly, fully vouched for by written evidence and yet at the same time a blatant piece of stock-in-trade. My

12

heart was beating irregularly and uncomfortably and I longed for another drink. My clothes were glueing themselves to me in the damp heat, which seemed to be increasing as the evening advanced. I did my best to listen to further inquiries, mainly about the documentary basis for my story. These I checked by saying, untruthfully, that I had nothing of the sort in my own possession, and that all the stuff was in the county archives in Hertford town. The last stages of the conversation were lengthened by my guest's habit of pausing frequently in search of some even more roundabout way of expressing himself than the one which had first occurred to him. Finally, a party at the other end of the bar reached the menu stage, and to them, after receiving a couple of paragraphs of thanks, I moved away.

By the time I had got the new party off, dashed into the still-room thirsty and out refreshed, done a brief tour of the dining-room in modified orderly-officer style, agreed hypocritically that a *sauce vinaigrette* for avocado pears had too much salt, been lavish about making this good (the tasted pears would go very nicely into the chef's salad at tomorrow's lunch), turned down on the office telephone a request for a double room that night from a drunken Cambridge undergraduate or sociology don and given my wife, downstairs again in a quite good sort of silver dress, a glass of Tio Pepe, it was nine twenty. We were to dine, as usual when no major function was in the book, at ten o'clock in the apartment. I was expecting two private guests, Dr and Mrs Maybury. Jack Maybury was the family doctor and a personal friend, or, more precisely, somebody I could bear to talk to. Among that tiny proportion of humanity more entertaining than very bad television, Jack stood high. Diana Maybury made television seem irrelevant, dull; an enormous feat.

They arrived when I was behind the bar again, being very candid with a London museum curator about the third most expensive claret on the list being the best value for money. Jack, a shock-headed, bony figure in a crumpled suit of biscuit-coloured linen, waved briefly and strode off, as usual, in the direction of the office to tell the local telephone exchange where he was. Diana joined my wife in the small alcove beside the fireplace. Together, they made an impressive, rather erective sight, both of them tall, blonde and full-breasted, but so different in other ways that they might have been chosen for some textbook illustration showing the width of divergence among basically similar physical types, or, more to the purpose, an X-certificate Swedish film that would fall a long way short of sticking to straight sex. Dull would he be of soul that would pass up the chance of taking the pair of them to bed. Their visible differences—Diana's slim build, light-tawny hair-colour, hazel eyes, tanned skin and nervous demeanour alongside the strength and roundness, the yellow and blue and pale rose, the slow, steady movements of Joyce, my wife—suggested that there were others to be discovered, no less striking. In the past few weeks I had made some progress towards a vital part of this objective: persuading Diana to come to bed with me. Joyce knew nothing about this, nor about the more ambitious plan; but as I watched them exchange a kiss of greeting in the alcove, it was clear to me that they had always shown a subdued sexual feeling towards each other. Or was it not really clear at all, not true, just attractive as a fantasy?

The museum curator, having taken my advice and saved eleven shillings on his claret, not quite unexpectedly ordered a half-bottle of Château d'Yquem (37/6) to go with his sweet course. I bowed approvingly, told Fred to pass the word to the wine-waiter, mixed Diana a gin and bitter lemon, her invariable pre-dinner drink, and carried it over. I tried for her mouth when I kissed her, but got the side of her chin instead. There was a pause after that. Not for the first time, the idea of chatting to these two seemed altogether less attractive than what I had been thinking about a minute before. Jack reappeared while I was still exploring the topic of the heat and humidity. He kissed Joyce as unceremoniously as he had waved to me on arrival, then moved me aside. He was supposed to be a great hammer of his female patients, but, like most men of whom that sort of thing is said, he had on the whole a disinclination for female society.

'Cheers,' he said, raising for a short space the glass of Campari and soda Fred would have served him. 'How's everybody, then?'

Coming from one's family doctor, this query went beyond mere phatic communion, and Jack always managed to get a slight air of hostility into it. He was inclined to be snobbish about health, implying that the lack of it sprang from some vulgar shortcoming, to be accepted as distastefully inevitable if not actually deplored. This probably served quite well as a form of pressure on his patients to get better.

'Oh, all carrying on all right, I think.'

'How's your father?' he asked, probing one of the several

weak spots in my defences, and lighting a cigarette without taking his eyes off me.

'About the same. Very piano.'

'Very what?' Jack just might not have heard me against the alcohol-fired roar of other voices in the bar, but more likely he meant to rebuke me for using frivolous diction in a solemn context. 'What?'

'Piano. You know. Subdued. Not doing or saying much.'

'You must realize that's to be expected at his age and in his condition.'

'I do, I assure you.'

'And Amy?' asked Jack vigilantly, referring to my daughter.

'Well ... she seems to be okay, as far as I can tell. Watches television a lot, plays her pop records, all that kind of thing.'

Jack stared into his drink, not what I would have called a very meaningful move on the part of somebody drinking what he was drinking, and said nothing. Perhaps he felt that what I had said was condemnatory enough without assistance from him.

'There's not much for her to do here,' I went on defensively, 'and she hasn't had time to make any real friends round about. Not that she'd have much in common with the village kids, I imagine. And it's the holidays, of course.'

Still Jack said nothing. He sniffed, not altogether at physical need.

'Joyce has been a bit sluggish. She's had a lot of work to do these last weeks. And there's this weather. In fact it's been a pretty tiring summer for everybody. I'm going to try and get the three of us away for a few days at the beginning of September.'

'What about you?' asked Jack with a touch of contempt.

'I'm all right.'

'Are you, by God. You don't look it. Listen, Maurice, I won't get a chance later—you ought to see yourself. Your colour's bad—yes, I know all about your not getting much of a chance to get out, but you ought to be able to manage an hour's walk in the afternoons. You're sweating excessively.'

'Indeed I am.' I wiped with my handkerchief the saturated hair above my ears. 'So would you be if you had to charge around this damn place trying to keep your eye on half a dozen things at once, and in this weather too.'

'I've been charging around too, and I'm not in the state you're in.'

'You're ten years younger than I am.'

'What of it? Maurice, what you have is alcoholic sweating. How many have you put down already this evening?'

'Just a couple.'

'Huh. I know your couples. Couple of trebles. You'll have another half a couple before we go up, and at least a couple and a half after dinner. That's well over half a bottle, plus three or four glasses of wine and whatever you had at midday. It's too much.'

'I'm used to it. I can take it.'

'You're used to it, yes. And you've got the remains of a first-class constitution. But you can't take it the way you could in the past. You're fifty-three. You've come to one of those places where the road goes sharply downhill for a bit. It'll go on going downhill if you carry on as you are. How have you been feeling today?'

'I'm all right. I told you.'

'Oh, come on. How have you really been feeling?'

'Oh ... Bloody awful.'

'You've been feeling bloody awful for a couple of months. Because you've been drinking too much.'

'The only time I can be reasonably sure of not feeling bloody awful is a couple of hours or so at the end of a day's drinking.'

'You'll get less sure, believe me. How's the jactitation?'

'Better, I think. Yes, definitely better.'

'And the hallucinations?'

'About the same.'

What we were referring to was less disagreeable than it may sound. A form of jactitation, taking place round about the moment of falling asleep, is known to almost everybody's experience: that convulsive straightening of the leg which is often accompanied by a short explanatory dream about stumbling, or missing the bottom stair. In more habitual and pronounced cases, the jerking movement may affect any muscles, including those of the face, and may occur up to a dozen times or more before the subject finally attains sleep, or abandons the quest for it.

At this level of intensity, jactitation is associated with hypnagogic (onset-of-sleep-accompanying) hallucinations. These antecede jactitation, taking place when the subject is more fully awake, or even wide awake, but with the eyes closed. They are not dreams. They might be described as visions of no obvious meaning seen under poor conditions. Their nearest, or least distant, parallel is what happens to people who have spent much of the day with their eyes fixed on a scene that varies only within certain fixed limits, as when travelling by car, and who find, when they close their eyes for the night, that a kind of muted version of what they have been looking at is unrolling itself against the inside of their eyelids; but there are large differences. The hallucinations lack all sense of depth of frame, and there is never much in the way of background, often none. A piece of a wall, a corner of a fireplace, a glimpse of a chair or table is the most that can be made out; one is always indoors, if anywhere. More important, the hallucinatory images are invariably, so to speak, fictitious. Nothing known ever presents itself.

The images are, on the whole, human. Out of the darkness there will appear a face, or a face with neck and shoulders, or part of a face, or something that cannot be precisely described, but resembles a face more closely than anything else, perhaps seeming to move slowly or changing its expression. Also commonly seen are other parts of the body, a buttock and thigh, a whole torso, a solitary foot. In my case, these are often naked, but this may be the product of my own erotic tendencies, not a necessary feature of the experience. The strange distortions and appendages that, much of the time, accompany the recognizable naked forms tend to diminish their erotic quality. I am not myself sexually moved by a breast divided into segments like a peeled orange, or a pair of thighs that converge into a single swollen knee.

From all this, it might be thought that the hypnagogic hallucination is something to be feared. To an extent this is so, but (in my case) the various images, though frequently grotesque or puzzling, have not much power to terrify. And, as against the times when an unremarkable profile suddenly turns full face and glares in lunatic rage, or becomes quite inhuman, there are the rarer times when something beautiful shows itself clearly, in a small flare of soft yellow light, before fading into nothing, into the state of a vanished fiction. What is most unwelcome about these visions is the expectation of the jerks and twitches, the joltings into total wakefulness and the delaying of sleep, which they always portend.

I looked briefly ahead now to this prospect as Jack and I stood talking in the bar, which had begun to fill up with the first guests out of the dining-room and people from the nearer places who had driven over for the later half of the evening. I said to Jack,

'I suppose you're going to tell me all that stuff is due to drink.'

'There's a connection all right.'

'Last time we talked about this you said there was a connection with epilepsy. You can't have it both ways.'

'Why not, if it is both ways? Anyway, the epilepsy thing is a technicality. I can't tell you you'll never have an epileptic fit, any more than I can tell you you'll never break your leg, but I can tell you there's no sign of it at the moment. Another thing I can tell you, though, is that there's a bloody sight more than a technical connection between your drinking and your jumps and faces. Stress. It's all stress.'

'Alcohol relieves stress.'

'At first. Look, come off it, Maurice. After twenty years on the bottle you don't need me to lecture you about vicious circles and descending spirals and what-not. I'm not asking you to cut it out completely. That wouldn't be a good idea at all. Knock it off a bit. Try keeping away from the hard stuff until the evening. You'd better start that soon if you feel like seeing sixty. But I don't want you sitting there upstairs like a death's head at the feast, so forget about it for tonight. Go and throw down another of your specials and then trot round the dining-room apologizing for the bits of dogshit in the steak-and-kidney pudding while I chat up these birds.'

I did approximately as I had been told, finally getting away rather later than expected by reason of a full-length oral review of my cuisine, delivered at the speed of one addressing a large audience of high-grade mental defectives, from my Baltimore guest. After hearing this out, and responding in appropriately rounded periods, I took my departure and went up to the flat.

The sound of an authoritative and rather peevish male voice, speaking with a strong Central European accent, was coming from my daughter's bedroom. Thirteen-year-old Amy, tall, thin and pale, was sitting bent forward on the edge of her bed with her cheeks in her hands and elbows on knees. Her surroundings expressed her age and station with overdone fidelity: coloured photographs of singers and actors cut from magazines and Scotch-taped to the walls, a miniature lidless gramophone in pastel pink, records and gaudy record-sleeves, the former seldom inside the latter, fragments of clothing, most of them looking too narrow for their purposes, a great many jars and pots and small plastic bottles grouped on the top of the dressing-table round a television set. On the screen of this, a hairy man was saying to a bald man, 'But the effects of these attacks on the dollar will not of course immediately be apparent. And we must wait to see which will be the remedies adopted.'

'Darling, what on earth are you watching this for?' I asked.

Amy shrugged her shoulders without otherwise altering her position.

'What else is there on?'

'Music on one of them—you know, with all violins and things—and horses on the other.'

'But you like horses.'

'Not these ones.'

'What's wrong with them?'

'All in lines.'

'How do you mean?'

'All in *lines*.'

'I don't see why you feel you've always got to watch something, no matter what it is. You can't possibly ... I wish you'd read a book occasionally.'

'But you must understand that this in the first place is not a matter for the International Monetary Fund,' said the hairy man with contempt.

'Sweetheart, turn that down, will you? I can't hear a thing ... That's better,' I said as Amy, her eyes still on the screen, put one long-fingered hand to the remote-control box at her side and reduced the hairy man's voice to a far-away shout. 'Now listen: Dr Maybury and his wife are here for dinner tonight. They'll be coming up here in a minute. Why don't you slip your nightdress on now and clean your teeth and run in and chat to them for a little while before you go to bed?'

'No thanks, Daddy.'

'But you like them. You're always saying you like them.'

'No thanks.'

'Well, come and say good night to Gramps, then.'

'I have.'

As I stood there for a moment by the bed, wishing I knew how to give my daughter a life, I happened to notice the photograph of her dead mother in its place on the wall beside the window. Why I did so I had no idea, and I thought I had made no movement, but Amy, apparently without having glanced aside, knew what I had seen. She shifted her legs slightly, as if in discomfort. I said suddenly, trying to sound enthusiastic,

'I know what: I've got to go into Baldock again tomorrow morning. What I've got to do won't take more than a few minutes, so you could come in with me and we could have a cup of ... You could have a Coke.'

'Okay, Daddy,' said Amy in a placatory voice.

'Now I'll be back in fifteen minutes to say good night to you and I expect you to be in bed by then. Don't forget to clean your teeth.'

'Okay.'

The hairy man having had his hour, it was the recommendation of a shampoo, delivered in the tones of somebody in mid-orgasm, that filled the small room before I had shut the door after me. Amy was not yet a woman, but, even when much younger, she had developed the totally female habit of behaving coolly, or coldly, to a degree that must have a reason, while denying to the death not only the existence of the reason but also the existence of the behaviour. I had not given her the chance just now of doing any denying, but I had not needed to. I was intimidated by the behaviour, and now and then appalled by the reason, while avoiding the question of what it was. Amy and I had never discussed Margaret's death in a street accident eighteen months previously, nor her leaving me, taking Amy with her, nearly three years before that, nor Margaret herself; beyond necessities, we had barely mentioned her. In the end, I would have to find a way of doing something about that, and the behaviour, and the reason. Perhaps I could make a start on the trip to Baldock in the morning. Perhaps.

I went down the sloping passage and into the dining-room, a broad, rather low-ceilinged affair with a beautiful seventeenth-century heraldic stone fireplace I had uncovered behind Victorian brickwork. Here Magdalena, Ramón's wife, a tubby little woman of about thirty-five, was laying bowls of chilled *vichyssoise* round the five places at the oval table. The windows were open, the curtains undrawn, and when I lit the candles their flames swayed slightly without breaking. A breeze from the Chilterns was just managing to reach as far up as here. The air it brought seemed no cooler. When Magdalena, muttering quite amiably to herself, had departed, I walked to the widow at the front of the house, but found little relief.

There was nothing to see, only the empty room reflected in the large square pane. My pieces of statuary stood in their places: a good copy of a Roman terracotta head of an old man on a pedestal beside the door, a pair of Elizabethan youths looking vaguely towards each other from rectangular niches in the far wall, busts of a naval officer and of a military man of the Napoleonic period above the fireplace, and a pretty bronze of a girl, probably French and of the 1890s or just after, on another pedestal in front of the window at my left, placed so as to catch the morning sun. As I stood with my back to the room I could not make out much of her, but from all the others that oddly exact balance between the animate and the inanimate, constantly maintained when they were viewed direct, seemed to have departed. In the glass of the window they looked newly empty of any life. I turned round and faced them: yes, once more human as well as mineral.

With the A595 just too far off for individual vehicles to be heard, and no one, for the moment, moving about in the forecourt, everything seemed quiet until I listened. Then the murmur of voices became audible from downstairs, but, again, none could be distinguished from the rest. I said to myself that if a minute went by without any sort of separate sound emerging, I would go to the cupboard in the bedroom and give myself another drink. I began counting in my head: one—thousand—two—thousand—three—thousand—four—thousand ... The thousand business helps one to attain the correct rhythm, and by using it over the years I have reached the point at which I can guarantee an accuracy of within two seconds per timed minute. This is a useful accomplishment in such situations as having to boil eggs without the aid of a watch, but usefulness is not really the end in view.

I had reached thirty-eight thousand in this count, and was preparing to congratulate myself on entering the last third of the course, when I heard a clearly differentiated and half-expected sound from the drawing-room across the passage, a mingled groaning and clearing of the throat. My father, having heard Magdalena's departure, but not wanting to have it thought that he was acting directly on this signal, had decided that it was time for him to stir himself and come to table. He had deprived me of my drink, but there was a case for saying that that was just as well.

I heard his step, slow and steady, and after a moment the door opened. He said something wearily unfriendly as he found he was being preceded over the threshold by Victor Hugo, who got under his feet even more than most people's.

Victor was a blue-point Siamese, a neutered tom-cat now in the third year of his age. He entered, as usual, in vague semi-flight, as from something that was probably not a menace, but which it was as well to be on the safe side about. Becoming aware of me, he approached, again as usual, with an air of uncertainty not so much about who I was as about what I was, and of keeping a very open mind on the range of possible answers. Was I potassium nitrate, or next October twelvemonth, or Christianity, or a chess problem—perhaps involving a variation on the Falkbeer counter-gambit? When he reached me, he gave up the problem and toppled on to my feet like an elephant pierced by a bullet in some vital spot. Victor was, among other things, the reason why no dogs were allowed at the Green Man. The effort of categorizing them might have proved too much for him.

My father shut the door firmly behind him and gave a neutral nod in my direction. I rather take after him physically, being quite as tall as he and as little inclined to run to fat, and his dark-red hair-colour, still vivid in places among the white, is mine too. But his large high nose and broad hands, as powerful as a pianist's, have in me been replaced by something less assertively masculine from my mother's side.

The neutrality of the nod he had given was a none-too-usual alleviation of the unspecific discontent with which he nowadays looked as if he regarded the world. Here was somebody else whose life I did not understand. The weekday routine, mitigated by a lie-in on Sunday mornings, was a tight one: whatever the weather, off at ten sharp into the village 'to have a look round' (though whatever there was to be seen there never varied, at least to a townsman's eye like mine or his), pick up a packet of ten Piccadilly and *The Times* (which he would not have delivered to the house) at the corner shop, into the Dainty Tea-rooms for a coffee, a chocolate biscuit and a thorough read-through of the paper and along to the Queen's Arms at midday precisely, there to drink two Courage light ales, make a start on the crossword puzzle and chat to 'one or two old buffers' about topics I had found it hard to define when I, on an occasional slack morning, accompanied him on his round. Back to the Green Man at one fifteen on the dot for a cold lunch in his room, and then an afternoon dozing, finishing, or trying to finish, the crossword, and reading one of the crime-and-detection paperbacks I would have got for him in Royston or Baldock. By six or six thirty—here a little latitude was permitted—he would be in the drawing-room, ready for the first of two drinks before dinner, and ready for conversation too, I suppose, because he never took anything in there with him, not even the crossword. But Joyce and Amy and I all had other things to do than go and talk to him, and he would fall back on sending for the evening paper, as tonight, or on gazing at the wall. Whenever I happened to look in and found him like this, again as tonight, I would feel slightly defeated: I could not force him to read, set him acrostics to solve, demand that he learn Latin or take up mechanical drawing, and he would less soon watch television than, in his own phrase, have a lump of vegetable marrow shoved into his skull instead of a brain.

He looked round the dining-room now with a more directed frown than usual, on the point, conceivably, of establishing just what it was about his environment that he found most disagreeable. His eye fell on the dining-table and moved along it.

'Guests,' he said with unlooked-for tolerance.

'Yes, Jack and Diana Maybury are coming in. In fact, they've already——'

'I know, I know, you told me this morning. Funny sort of rooster, isn't he? I mean peculiar. All this I'm the most responsible and efficient general practitioner in the whole bloody country and a great friend of everybody's and that's all there is about me. I don't think I like him, Maurice. I wish I could say I did, because he's been very good to me, I mean as a doctor, I've no fault to find with him there. But I don't think I really like him as a man. Something to do with how he treats that wife of his. There's no love lost there, you know. Understandable enough. That way of hers of going on as if how bloody marvellous you are considering you've got no arms or legs. Well, at my age I more or less expect that style of thing, but she does it with everybody. Oh, very attractive, of course, I can see that. You're not, uh, by the way...?'

'No,' I said, wishing I had a drink. 'Nothing like that.'

'I've seen the way you look at her. You're a bad lad, Maurice.'

'There's nothing wrong in looking at her.'

'In your case there is, because you're a bad lad. Anyway, don't touch it, if you want my advice. That sort of little bitch would be more trouble than she's worth. There are other things to a woman than taking her to bed. And that reminds me—I've been meaning to have a chat with you about Joyce. She's not happy, Maurice. Oh, I don't mean she's miserable, nothing like that, and she does throw herself into the life of the place—you're very lucky there. But she's not really happy. I mean she doesn't really think you'd have gone as far as marrying her if you hadn't wanted somebody to be a mother to young Amy. And that side of things isn't working out as well as it might because you're leaving it to her to do it instead of helping her to do it and doing it with her. She's a young woman, Maurice. I know you've got a lot to do running the pub, and you're very conscientious. But you mustn't hide behind that. Take this morning, now. Some rooster was kicking up a fuss because Magdalena had spilt a few drops of tea into his breakfast marmalade, if you don't bloody well mind. Joyce dealt with him all right, and then afterwards she said to me . . .'

He stopped, as his ear, no less quick than mine, caught the sound of the outside door of the apartment opening. Then, hearing expected voices, he got up from the dining-chair where he had settled himself, so as to be on his feet by the time the door opened. 'Tell you later,' he mouthed and whispered.

The Mayburys and Joyce came in. I went over to the sideboard to see about the drinks for dinner, and found that Diana had followed me. Jack had started being as tolerant as ever to my father, who he seemed to feel could not reasonably be expected to maintain impeccable physical trim at the age of seventy-nine. Joyce was with them.

'Well, Maurice,' stated or queried Diana, managing to turn even that short utterance into a fair sample of her unnaturally precise enunciation. She also implied by her tone that she had effortlessly removed us both to a level far different from the plodding to-and-fro of ordinary converse.

'Hallo, Diana.'

'Maurice . . . do you mind if I ask you a question?'

There, again in small compass, was Diana for you. It was tempting, and would have been near the truth, to answer, 'Yes, I do, by God, if you really want to know, very much indeed,' but I found that I was looking at or near the low top of her serpent-green silk dress, where there was a lot more of Diana for you, and merely grunted.

'Maurice . . . why do you always look as if you're trying to escape from something? What makes you feel so trapped?' She spoke as if helping me count the words.

'Do I? Trapped? How do you mean? As far as I know I'm

not trying to escape from anything.'

'Then why do you look as if something's after you all the time?'

'After me? What could be after me? There's income tax, and next month's bills, and old age, and a few things like that, but then we're all——'

'What is it you want to get away from?'

Sidestepping another tempting retort, I glanced over her smooth tanned shoulder. Jack and my father were talking at once, with Joyce trying to listen to them both. I said in a lowered voice, 'I'll tell you another time. For instance tomorrow afternoon. I'll be at the corner at half-past three.'

'Maurice . . .'

'Yes?' I said, not altogether, I hoped, through my teeth.

'Maurice, what makes you so incredibly persistent? What is it you want from me?'

I felt an individual globule of sweat well up out of the skin of my chest. 'I'm persistent because of what I want from you, and if you don't know what that is I can soon show you. You will be there tomorrow, won't you?'

Exactly then, Joyce called, 'Let's start, shall we? You must all be starving. I am, anyway.'

Not bothering to conceal her triumph at the way events had brought her the prize of quasi-legitimately leaving my question unanswered, Diana moved off. I uncapped my father's pint of Worthington White Shield, picked up one of the bottles of Bâtard Montrachet 1961 the wine-waiter had opened half an hour earlier and followed her. In the last five seconds it had become almost overwhelmingly unlikely that she would meet me the following afternoon, because she was now in the uncommonly rewarding position of being able to stand me up without incurring the odium of having actually broken an arrangement. On the other hand, she was very much capable of following this line of argument and so going along to the agreed corner to find me not there, which would shove me back to the wrong side of square one, not to speak of the questions about why I was so changeable and so selfish, and did I think it was because I was so insecure, that I would have to sweat through as part of the shoving. And, being Diana, to have got that far would mean she would know, without having to think about it, that I would have got as far as it, too. So I would have to turn up anyway. But I had been going to do that all along.

By this time I had poured the drinks and taken my place in my walnut Queen Anne carver, which, though I had one or two older things in the house, is much my favourite piece. I had Diana on my right with my father on her other side facing the door, then Jack, and Joyce on my left. As we ate the *vichyssoise,* my father said,

'All sorts of people seem to be wandering about the house these days. I mean up on this floor, where they've no business to be when there's no banquet affair going on. Not half an hour ago there was some rooster clumping up and down that passage outside as if he owned the place. I was on the point of getting up and going to see what he thought he was doing when he buggered off. It's not the first time in the last few days, either. Can't you put up a notice or something, Maurice?'

'Outside the main door here there's a——'

'No, no, I mean something at the foot of the stairs, to keep them off this floor altogether. The place is turning into a madhouse. Haven't you come across this sort of thing yourself, Maurice? You must have, surely.'

'Once or twice.' I spoke listlessly, my mind and the edge of my vision on Diana. 'Now you mention it, there was a woman hanging about at the top of the stairs earlier on.' I realized for the first time that I had not subsequently seen that woman in the bar or the dining-room or anywhere round the house. No doubt she had found the ladies' lavatory on the ground floor, and left while I was busy standing in for Fred. No doubt. But I half-saw Diana put her spoon down and begin taking stock of my face. I could not stand the prospect of being asked, in those separated syllables, why I was so this, or what had made me so that, or whether I realized that I was so the other. I got up, said I was going to say good night to Amy and went off to do so, ringing for Magdalena on my way out.

Amy's appearance and posture had changed to the minimum degree consistent with her having been Amy sitting on bed before and being Amy sitting in bed now. On the television screen, a young woman was denouncing an older one who was keeping her back turned throughout, not so much out of inattention or deliberate rudeness as with the mere object of letting the audience see her face at the same time as her accuser's. For a moment I watched, in the hope of seeing them do a smart about-turn at the end of the speech, and wondering to what extent real life would be affected if there were to grow up a new convention that people always had to be facing the same way before they could speak to each other. Then I went over to Amy.

'What time does this finish?'

'Nearly over now.'

'Mind you put it off the moment it is. Have you cleaned your teeth?'

'Yes.'

'Good girlie. Don't forget we're going into Baldock in the morning.'

'No.'

'Good night, then.'

I bent over to kiss her cheek. At the same time, there came a succession of sounds from the dining-room: a shout or loud cry in my father's voice, some hurried words from Jack, a sort of bumping crash made by a collision with furniture, a confusion of voices. I told Amy to stay where she was, and ran back to the dining-room.

When I opened the door, Victor rushed past me, his tail swollen with erected hair. Across the room, Jack, with some assistance from Joyce, was dragging my father, who was completely limp, to a near-by armchair. At my father's place at table there was an overturned dining-chair and some crockery and cutlery on the floor. Some drink had been spilt. Diana, who had been watching the others, turned and looked at me in fear.

'He started staring and then he stood up and called out and then he just sort of collapsed and hit the table and Jack caught him,' she said in a jumbled voice: no elocution now.

I went past her. 'What's happened?'

Jack was lowering my father into the armchair. When he had done this, he said, 'Cerebral haemorrhage, I should imagine.'

'Is he going to die?'

'Yes, it's quite possible.'

'Soon?'

'Quite possibly.'

'What can you do about it?'

'Nothing that'll prevent him dying if he's going to.'

I looked at Jack, and he at me. I could not tell what he was thinking. He had his finger against my father's pulse. My body, I myself, seemed to consist of my face and the front of my torso, down as far as the base of the belly. I knelt by the armchair and heard slow, deep breathing. My father's eyes were open, with the pupils apparently fixed in the left-hand corners. Apart from this he looked quite normal, even relaxed.

'Father,' I said, and thought he stirred slightly. But there was nothing to say next. I wondered what was going on in that brain, what it saw, or fancied it saw: something irrelevant, perhaps, something pleasant, sunshine and fields. Or something not pleasant, something ugly, something bewildering. I imagined a desperate, prolonged effort to understand what was happening, and a discomfort so enormous as to be worse than pain, because lacking the merciful power of pain to extinguish thought, feeling, identity, the sense of time, everything but itself. This idea terrified me, but it also pointed out to me, with irresistible clarity and firmness, what I was to say next.

I leant closer. 'Father. This is Maurice. Are you awake? Do you know where you are? This is Maurice, Father. Tell me what's going on where you are. Is there anything to see? Describe how you feel. What are you thinking?'

Behind me, Jack said coldly, 'He can't hear you.'

'Father. Can you hear me? Nod your head if you can.'

In slow, mechanical tones, like a gramophone record played at too low a speed, my father said, 'Maur—rice,' then, less distinctly, a few more words that might have been 'who' and 'over by the . . .' Then he died.

I stood up and turned away. Diana looked at me with the fear gone from her face and stance. Before she could say anything I went past her and over to Joyce, who was looking down at the serving table. Here a tray had been placed with five covered plates and some vegetable dishes on it.

'I couldn't think what to do,' said Joyce, 'so I told Magdalena to leave it all here. Is he dead?'

'Yes.'

At once she started to cry. We put our arms round each other.

'He was awfully old and it was very quick and he didn't suffer.'

'We don't know what he suffered,' I said.

'He was such a nice old man. I can't believe he's just gone for ever.'

'I'd better go and tell Amy.'

'Do you want me to come with you?'

'Not now.'

Amy had turned off the TV set and was sitting on her bed, but not in her previous posture.

'Gramps has been taken ill,' I said.

'Is he dead?'

'Yes, but it was all over in a second and it didn't hurt him. He can't have known anything about it. He was very old, you know, and it might have happened any day. That's how it is with very old people.'

'But there was so much I meant to say to him.'

'What about?'

'All sorts of things.' Amy got up and came and put her hands on my shoulders. 'I'm sorry your father's dead.'

This made me cry. I sat down on the bed for a few minutes while she held my hand and stroked the back of my neck. When I had finished crying, she sent me off, saying that I was not to worry about her, that she would be all right and would see me in the morning.

In the dining-room, the two women were sitting on the window-seat, Diana with her arm round Joyce's shoulders. Joyce's head was lowered and her yellow hair had fallen over her face. Jack handed me a tumbler half-full of whisky with a little water. I drank it all.

'Amy all right?' asked Jack. 'Good. I'll look in on her in a minute. Now we'll have to get your father on to his bed. You and I can do it, or I can go and fetch someone from downstairs if you don't feel up to it.'

'I can do it. You and I can do it.'

'Come on, then.'

Jack took my father under the arms and I by the ankles. Diana was there to open the door. By holding him close against his chest, Jack saw to it that my father's head did not loll much. He went on talking as we moved.

'I'll get young Palmer up here as soon as we've done this, if you approve, just to put him in the picture. There's nothing more that needs doing tonight. The district nurse will be in first thing in the morning to lay him out. I'll be along too, with the death certificate. Someone will have to take that in to the registrar in Baldock and fix things up with the undertakers. Will you do that?'

'Yes.' We stood now in the bedroom. 'What are you looking for?'

'Blanket.'

'Bottom drawer there.'

We covered my father up and left him. The rest was soon done. All of us managed to eat a little, Jack rather more.

David Palmer appeared, listened, said and looked how sorry he was and went. I telephoned my son Nick, aged twenty-four, an assistant lecturer in French literature at a university in the Midlands. He told me he would get somebody to look after two-year-old Josephine and come down by car with his wife, Lucy, the next morning, arriving in time for a late lunch. I realized with a shock that there was nobody else to inform: my father's brother and sister had died without issue, and I had neither. By eleven thirty, a good three-quarters of an hour before the last non-residents would ordinarily have been out of the place, word of the death had spread and everything was quiet. Finally, the Mayburys and Joyce and I stood at the doorway of the apartment.

'Don't come down,' said Jack. 'Fred'll let us out. Have a good long sleep—Joyce one of the red bombs, Maurice three of the Belrepose things.' Speaking neither briskly nor with emotionalism, he added, 'Well, I'm sorry he's gone. He was a decent old boy, with plenty of sense. I expect you'll miss him a lot, Maurice.'

This mild show of commiseration and its accompanying glance, which carried sympathy of a depersonalized sort, were Jack's first non-utilitarian responses to what had happened, nor did he enlarge on them. He said good night in a high monotone, as somebody like Fred might call it across the bar, and led the way towards the stairs. After kissing Joyce and glancing in my direction, but not directly at me, Diana followed. She did not, I was almost touched to see, do any of this with the air of imparting by her silence a message more eloquent than any mere words could have conveyed. The same had been true of her earlier restraint of manner. I felt it was uncharitable of me to wonder how long this uncharacteristic behaviour of hers would last, but wonder I did. Nothing short of physical handicap has ever made anybody turn over a new leaf.

'Let's go to bed straight away,' said Joyce. 'You must be absolutely whacked.'

I was indeed utterly tired out in body, as if I had been standing all day in the same position, but had no inclination for sleep, or for lying down in the dark waiting to go to sleep. 'One more Scotch,' I said.

'Not a giant one, Maurice. And only one.' She spoke pleadingly. 'Don't sit up drinking. Bring it into the bedroom.'

I did as she said, first looking in on Amy, who was lying

asleep quite unemphatically, so to speak, without the parade of concentration or abandonment I have seen in grown women. Would my father's departure leave much of a hole in her world? I could not imagine any of the things she had said she had meant to say to him: his attitude to her had been one of uncertain geniality, she had behaved to him with something not far from a child's version of this, a brightness that had been absent-minded and self-regarding at the same time, and they had never, so far as I had noticed, talked together much. But he had been about the place every day of the year and a half since she had come to live here after her mother's death, and I could see that no sort of hole in a small world could really be a small hole.

'Was she all right?' asked Joyce when I carried my whisky into our bedroom, the next along the passage from Amy's and no broader from window to door, but with more length. Standing in this extra space, she popped one of her red sleeping-pills into her mouth and gulped water.

'Asleep, anyway. Have you seen the Belreposes?'

'Here. Three sounds rather a lot, doesn't it? With you drinking as well, I mean. I suppose Jack knows all about it.'

'They're not barbiturates.'

I chased the white tablets down with whisky, watching Joyce as she kicked off her shoes, pulled her dress over her head and hung it up in the wall-cupboard. The small moment in which she stepped away and turned to go down the room was enough for me to take in the fine swell of her breasts under the spotless white brassière, in unimprovable proportion with the breadth of her shoulders and back and the spreading fullness of her rib-cage. She had not taken three paces towards the bed before I had put my glass down on her dressing-table and caught her round her naked waist.

She held me against her with a quick firmness that belonged to somebody comforting somebody. When, as she very soon did, she found that it was not comfort I was after, at least not in the ordinary sense, her body stiffened.

'Oh, Maurice, not now, surely.'

'Especially now. Straight away. Come on.'

I had only once before in my life felt such a totally possessing urge to make love to a woman, with the mind sliding into involuntary dormancy and the body starting to set up on its own several stages earlier than usual. That time had been as I was watching a mistress of mine cutting bread in her kitchen while her husband laid the table in the dining-room across the passage, so that my mind and body had had to return to normal working with the minimum of delay. It was not going to be at all like that tonight.

Joyce was quite naked, I only selectively so, when I dragged the quilt aside and pushed her down on the bed. By now she was responding in her long, slow rhythms, breathing deeply at no more than a marginally quickening rate, clasping her powerful limbs round me. I was just about aware of an urgency that had a way of seeming infinitely postponable. It was not really, of course, and at some imperceptible signal, a distant traffic noise or a memory or a new movement from one or the other of us or a thought about tomorrow, I took us both to the point, once and then another time or so. Very quickly after that, the facts of the last hour presented themselves as if until now I had only heard of them through some distant and inarticulate intermediary. My heart seemed to stop for a moment, then lurched into violent motion. I got out of bed at top speed.

'Are you all right?' asked Joyce.

'Fine.'

After standing still for a moment, I finished undressing, put on my pyjamas and went to the bathroom. Then I looked into the drawing-room and saw the evening paper neatly folded on a low table by the place where my father had always sat, into the dining-room and saw the armchair where he had died. The triteness of these images calmed me for the moment. Back in the bedroom, I found that Joyce, usually ready for a chat at this stage, was lying with the bedclothes pulled up over her face. This went to confirm my suspicion that she was feeling ashamed, not of having made love on the night of my father's death, but of having enjoyed it. However, when I had got into bed she spoke in a wide-awake voice.

'I suppose it was natural, doing it like that, like an instinct. You know, Nature trying to see to it that life goes on. Funny, though, it didn't feel like an instinct. More like something you read about. The idea, I mean.'

I had not thought of this side of things until then, and was faintly irritated by her shrewdness, or what might have seemed shrewdness to an outsider. Still, it was very consoling that I was having to deal with Joyce here, not Diana, who would have been thrown into ecstasies of needling speculation.

'I wasn't faking it,' I said. 'A man can't fake.'

'I know, darling. I didn't mean that. Just how it might sound.' Her hand came back behind her and caught mine. 'Do you think you can sleep?'

'Yes, I think so. Could you just clear one thing up? Won't take a minute.'

'What?'

'Then I can forget about it. Tell me exactly how it happened in there. I shall always sort of wonder about it if I don't know exactly.'

'Well, he'd just been saying something about people had the right not to be disturbed in their own private houses, and then he stopped and got up, much more quickly than he usually does, and he was staring.'

'What at?'

'I don't know. Nothing. He was looking towards the door. Then he called out, and Jack asked him what was the matter and was he all right, and then he fell against the table and Jack caught him.'

'What did he call out?'

'I don't know. It wasn't a word or anything. Then Jack and I, we started moving him and then you came back. He didn't seem to be in any pain. He just looked very surprised.'

'Frightened?'

'Well . . . a bit, perhaps.'

'Only a bit?'

'Well, a lot, actually. He must have been feeling it coming on, you know, the cerebral thing.'

'Yes. That would frighten you all right. I see.'

'Don't worry about it.' Joyce squeezed my hand. 'You couldn't have done anything about it even if you had been there.'

'No I suppose I couldn't.'

'Of course you couldn't.'

'I forgot to tell Amy where . . . that he's in his room.'

'She won't go in there. I'll see to it in the morning. I'll have to go to sleep now. These bombs really knock you out.'

We said good night and switched off our bedside lamps. I turned on to my right side, towards where the window was, though nothing could be seen of it. The night was still very warm, but the humidity had fallen off a good deal in the last hour. My pillow seemed hotter than my cheek as soon as the two touched, and formed itself into a series of hard ridges and irregular planes. My heart was beating heavily and moderately fast, as on the threshold of some minor ordeal, like going into the dentist's surgery or getting up to make a speech. I lay there waiting for it to make one of the trip-and-lurch movements it had made ten minutes earlier and perhaps a couple of dozen times during the day and evening. I had mentioned this phenomenon to Jack, who had said, condescendingly rather than impatiently, but in any case quite emphatically, that it was not significant, that my heart was merely giving itself, every so often, an extra and premature signal to beat, so that the beat after that was delayed, and might seem stronger than normal. All I could say (to myself) was that at times like the present the bloody thing certainly felt significant. After a minute or two of waiting, there came the expected quiver, followed by a pause prolonged enough to make me draw in my breath, and then a small punch against the inside of my chest. I told myself it was all right, it was nerves, it would go off as it always had, I was a hypochondriac, the Belreposes would be taking over any minute, it was natural, it was egotistical. Yes: already calmer, easier, steadier, more comfortable, cooler, slower, quieter, drowsier, vaguer...

What was before my closed eyes was the usual shifting pall of dark purple, dark grey and other dark that was never quite different enough to be given the name of any other colour. It had been there all along, of course, but now I started looking at it, knowing what would happen when I did, but unable not to, because it was simply the next thing. Almost at once a dim orange-yellow light came up. It illuminated something that had the smooth, rounded and tapering qualities of a part of the human body, but without any guide to scale it was impossible to tell whether I was looking at leg or nose, forearm or finger, breast or chin. Soon a greyish male profile, nearly complete, its expression puzzled or brooding, drifted diagonally in front of this and blotted most of it out. The upper lip twitched, grew suddenly in size and began drifting slowly outwards, swelling at a reduced rate until it was like a thick rope of intestine. Another orange light flared up irregularly in the lower part of my field of vision and played on the intestine-like form from underneath, showing it to be veined and glistening. The face had tilted away out of existence. When the orange glow had faded, there was a kind of new start: shivering veils of brown and yellow appeared and vanished quickly, to reveal a gloomy cavern of which the walls and roof were human, but in a distant sense. No component was indentifiable, only that unique surface quality, half matt, half sheen, that belongs to naked skin.

These apparitions grew, swirled and evolved for a time I could not measure, perhaps five minutes, probably not more than thirty. Some of them were surprising, but this was always part of their nature, and none, so far, was surprising in a surprising way. They were even beginning to slacken, become constricted and hard to discern. Then a rumpled sheet of brown flesh shook itself convulsively and started to concertina in towards the middle. Longitudinal shreds became distinguishable, turned olive-green in colour and could be seen as the trunk and branches of a young tree, the sort that has many stems growing more or less vertically and parallel. This was a novelty in a hitherto exclusively anthropoid universe, a comparatively soothing one. The tree-shape continued the shaking, twitching motion of the fleshy mass that had given birth to it. Slowly, its limbs and minor appendages coalesced into what—by the lax standards of verisimilitude at present in force—were good approximations to a man's thighs, genitals and torso up about as far as the breast-bone. Higher than this, there was nothing identifiable for the moment. The various members retained their vegetable individuality, continuing as closely-packed amalgams of bough, twig, stem and leaf. I was trying to remember what drawing or painting this structure resembled when I heard a noise, distant but not unrecognizable: it sounded like the snapping of greenery and minor branches made by a man or large animal moving through dense woods. At the same time, a shift of illumination began to reveal an upper chest, a throat and neck, the point of a wooden chin.

I clapped my fingers over my eyes and rubbed them fiercely: I had no desire to see the face that topped such a body. In a flash, literally in a flash, everything was gone, noise and all. I pretended to myself that I had heard something from outside; but I knew that that snapping sound had come from inside, again in the most literal sense. Just as I was never in any doubt that what I 'saw' with my eyes shut was not really there, so I knew that what I had just 'heard' was not real either. Tomorrow I might feel appalled at the prospect of a regular, or sporadic, aural addition to these nightly appearances; at the moment I was too tired. When I closed my eyes again, I saw at once that the show was over: all intensity, all potential had departed from the messages of my optic nerves, and the dark curtain before me stirred more feebly with every breath.

I had now come to the outer edge of sleep. As I had known it would, jactitation set in. My right foot, my whole right leg, jerked with a local violence, my head, my mouth and chin, my upper lip, what felt like the whole top half of my body, my left wrist, my left wrist again, moved of their own accord, once or twice with the prelude of a disembodied, watery feeling that advertised their intention, more often quite unexpectedly. I was returned to momentary wakefulness several times by what I assumed to be similar convulsions, though I could not locate them, and once by a triple shaking of the shoulder so like the intervention of one arousing a sleeper that, if I had not quickly remembered disturbances as acute in the past, I might have been alarmed. Finally, images and thoughts and words came from nowhere in particular and were all mingled in some other thing that gradually had less and less to do with me: pretty dress, excuse me you're wanted on the, you ought to realize, very good soup, if there's anything I can, long time ago, be all very dusty, not to agree on the way he, moment she was there and the next, water with it, over by the, darling, tree, spoon, window, shoulders, stairs, hot, sorry, man . . .

2 : Dr Thomas Underhill

At ten o'clock the next morning I was in the office finishing the day's arrangements with David Palmer.

'What about Ramón?' I asked.

'Well, he's done the vegetable dishes—quite good, really, in parts—and I've put him on the coffee-pots. No complaints so far. From him, that is.'

'Watch him over the chef's stuff, won't you? And the ice-cream *coupes*. Explain to him that they've got to look as good as new even though the guests never see them.'

'I have, Mr Allington.'

'Well, explain it to him again, using threats if necessary. Tell him he's to bring them to me personally before lunch. Oh yes —two extra upstairs for that. My son and his wife are driving down. Is that the lot?'

'Just about. There's a bath-towel gone, that Birmingham couple, and an ash-tray, Fred says, one of the heavy glass ones.'

'You know, David, I feel like driving up to Birmingham and finding those people's bloody house and burgling it to get that towel. It's the only way we'd ever see it again. Or putting tea-cloths and old dusters in all the bedrooms in future and making them get rid of their fag-ends in empty baked-beans tins. I don't know why we go on bothering. Well, there's nothing else to do, I suppose. If that's all you've got I'm off to Baldock.'

'Right, Mr Allington.' David's long, very slightly ridiculous face took on a resolute look. 'I just want to say, if there's anything extra or special you want done, I'd be more than happy to do it. You've only to say. And all the staff feel the same.'

'Thank you, David, I can't think of anything at the moment, but I'll be sure to let you know if there is.'

David left. I collected the cash for the bank, found and pocketed the list I had made for the drink supplier, put on my check cap and went into the hall. The char, a youngish, rather pretty woman in jeans and tee-shirt, was crossing towards the dining-room, vacuum-cleaner in hand.

'Cooler today,' she said, raising her eyebrows briefly, as if alluding to how I looked or was dressed.

'But tonight it'll be as hot as ever, you just see.'

She acknowledged this thrust with a diagonal movement of her head, and passed from view. I recognized in her one on whom the lives, or deaths, of others made little impression. Then Amy appeared, looking eager and rather well turned out in a clean candy-striped shirt and skirt.

'What time are we leaving, Daddy?'

'Oh, darling.' I remembered, for the first time that morning. 'I'm sorry, but I'm afraid it'll have to be another day.'

'Oh *no*. Oh, what a *drag*. Oh, *why*?'

'Well . . . I fixed it up with you before . . .'

'Before Gramps died—I know. But what's that got to do with it? He wouldn't have minded me coming. He liked us doing things together.'

'I know, but there are special things I have to do, like registering the death and going to the undertakers'. You'd hate all that.'

'I wouldn't mind. What's the undertakers'?'

'The people who'll be doing the funeral.'

'I wouldn't mind. I could sit in the car. I bet you'll have a coffee anyway. I could look round the shops and meet you at the car.'

'I'm sorry, Amy.' And I was, but I could not contemplate getting through the next couple of hours in any company, however relaxing, and I had long ago faced the fact that I was never quite at my ease with Amy. 'It wouldn't be the right sort of thing for you. You can come with me tomorrow.'

This only made her angry. 'Oh, *yawn*. I don't want to come tomorrow, I want to come today. You just don't want me.'

'Amy, stop shouting.'

'You don't care about me. You don't care what I do. There's never anything for me to do.'

'You can help Joyce in the bedrooms, it's good——'

'Oh, *fantastic*. Huge thanks. *Dad-oh*.'

'I won't have you talking like that.'

'I've talked like it now. And I'll take LSD and reefers and you'll care then. No, you won't. You won't care.'

'Amy, go up to your room.'

She made a blaring noise, halfway between a yell and a groan, and stamped off. I waited until, quite distinctly through the thickness of the building, I heard her door slam. At once, with impeccable sardonic timing, the vacuum-cleaner started up in the dining-room. I left the house.

It was indeed cooler today. The sun, standing immediately

above the patch of woods towards which the ghost of Thomas Underhill was said to gaze, had not yet broken through a thin mist or veil of low cloud. As I walked over to where my Volkswagen was parked in the yard, I told myself that I could soon start to relish the state of being alone (not rid of Amy, just alone for a guaranteed period), only to find, as usual, that being alone meant that I was stuck with myself, with the outside and inside of my body, with my memories and anticipations and present feelings, with that indefinable sphere of being that is the sum of these and yet something beyond them, and with the assorted uneasiness of the whole. Two's company, which is bad enough in all conscience, but one's a crowd.

I was putting the Volkswagen into gear when a dull pain of irregular but defined shape switched itself on in my left lower back, a little below the waistline. It stayed in being for perhaps twenty seconds, perfectly steady in intensity, then at once vanished. It had been behaving in this sort of way for about a week now. Was it sharper this morning than when I had first noticed it, did it come on more frequently and stay for longer? I thought perhaps it was and did. It was cancer of the kidney. It was not cancer of the kidney, but that disease whereby the kidney ceases to function and has to be removed by surgery, and then the other kidney carries on perfectly well until it too becomes useless and has to be removed by surgery, and then there is total dependence on a machine. It was not a disease of the kidney, but a mild inflammation set up by too much drinking, easily knocked out by a few doses of Holland's gin and a reduction in doses of other liquors. It was not an inflammation, or only in the sense that it was one of those meaningless aches and pains that clear up of their own accord and unnoticeably when they are not thought about. Ah, but what was the standard procedure for not thinking about this one, or any one?

The pain came back as I was turning south-west on to the A595, and stayed for a little more than twenty seconds this time, unless that was my imagination. I thought to myself how much more welcome a faculty the imagination would be if we could tell when it was at work and when not. That might make it more efficient, too. My own was certainly unequal to the task of suggesting how I would deal with the situation if my kidney really were under some lethal assault. I had fallen victim to some pretty serious afflictions in my time, but so far they had tended to yield to treatment. The previous summer I had managed to check and even reverse the onset of Huntington's chorea—a progressive disease of the nervous system ending in total helplessness, and normally incurable—simply by cutting down my intake of Scotch. A year or so earlier, a cancer of the large intestine had begun retreating to dormancy as soon as I stopped eating the local greengages and plums, gave up drinking two bottles of claret a day and curbed my fondness for raw onions, hot pickles and curry. A new, more powerful reading-light had cleared up a severe brain tumour inside a week. All my other lesions, growths, atrophies and rare viral infections had gone the same way. So far.

That was the point. Other people's hypochondria is always good for a laugh, or rather, whenever one gets as far as beginning to think about it, just fairly good for a grin. Each case of one's own is hilarious, as soon as that case is past. The trouble with the hypochondriac, considered as a figure of fun, is that he will be wrong about his condition nine hundred and ninety-nine times, and absolutely right the thousandth time, or the thousand-and-first, or the one after that. As soon as I had reached this perception, the pain in my back underlined it elegantly by returning for about half a minute.

I had joined the A507 and was coming into Baldock without noticing anything I had seen on the way or done to keep me on the way. Now that I was about to deal with about the last thing concerning my father that I would ever have to deal with, it was thoughts of him that intervened between me and what I was doing. I parked the Volkswagen in the broad main street of the town and remembered playing cricket with him on the sands at Pevensey Bay in, good God, 1925 or 1926. Once I had been out first ball and he had praised me afterwards for my sportsmanship in accepting this with a good grace. While I waited, then was dealt with, at the registry, I thought about that daily round of his in the village, and wished I had accompanied him on it just once more than I had. By the time I reached the undertakers', my mind was on his first stroke and his recovery from it, and in the bank I tried to imagine what his mental life had been like afterwards, with sufficient success to send me straight across to the George and Dragon at eleven thirty sharp. I had had just enough attention to spare for what I had been doing to notice how trivial and dull everything about it had been, not momentous at all, not even dramatically unmomentous, registrar and undertaker and bank clerk all pretty well interchangeable.

After three quick double whiskies I felt better: I was drunk, in fact, drunk with that pristine freshness, that semi-mystical elevation of spirit which, every time, seems destined to last for ever. There was nothing worth knowing that I did not know, or rather would not turn out to know when I saw my way to turning my attention to it. Life and death were not problems, just points about which a certain rather limited type of mis-conception tended to agglutinate. By definition, or something of the kind, every problem was really a non-problem. Nodding my head confidentially to myself about the simple force of this perception, I left the pub and made for where there was a fair case for believing I had left the Volkswagen.

Finding it took some time. Indeed, I was still looking for it when it became clear that I was doing so, not in Baldock, but in the yard of the Green Man, where I saw I must have re-cently driven the thing. There was a bright dent at the rear offside corner that I was nearly sure I had not seen before. This bothered me to some degree, until I realized that no event that had failed to impede my progress to this place could have been particularly significant. The next moment I was in the hall talking to David Palmer, very lucidly and cogently, but with continuous difficulty in remembering what I had been saying to him ten seconds earlier. He seemed to think that my anxieties or inquiries or reassurances, though interesting and valuable in their own right, were of no very immediate con-cern. Accompanied for some reason by Fred, he saw me to the foot of the stairs, where I spent a little while making it plain that I did not need, and would not brook, the slightest assist-ance.

I made it to the landing perfectly well, but only after a great deal of effort, enough, in fact, to get me on the way to coming round. I had not had one of these time-lapse things at such an early hour before, nor after so few drinks immediately before-hand. Well, today was a special day. I was crossing to the apartment door when the woman I had seen the previous even-ing, almost at this very spot, suddenly came past me—from where, I had no idea—and hurried to the top of the stairs. Without thinking, I called out after her, something quite un-managerial like, 'What are you doing here?' She took no notice, began to descend, and when, after a not very competent pursuit, I reached the stairhead, she had gone.

I got down the stairs as quickly as I could without falling over, rather slowly, that is. David was just approaching the couple of steps that lead down to the dining-room. I spoke his name, louder than I had meant to, and he turned round abruptly.

'Yes, Mr Allington? Is anything the matter?'

'Look, David . . .'

'Hallo, Dad,' said the voice of my son Nick. 'We got here earlier than——'

'Just a moment, Nick. David, did you see a woman coming down the stairs just now?'

'No, I don't think I——'

'In a long dress, with reddish kind of hair? Only, God, ten or fifteen seconds before I started speaking to you.'

David considered this for so long that I wanted to scream at him. I had time now to notice whether we were attracting any attention, but I did not use it. Eventually David said, 'I wasn't conscious of anybody, but I walked straight across from the bar, and I wasn't really noticing, I'm sorry.'

'All right, David, it doesn't matter. I thought it might have been someone who bounced a cheque on me once, that's all. It doesn't matter. Let me know if there are any problems in the dining-room. Hallo, Nick.' We kissed; David went on his way. 'Sorry about that, I just thought . . . Where's Lucy? Did you have a good journey?'

'Fine. She's over in the annexe, having a wash. What's wrong, Dad?'

'Nothing. I mean it's been a bit of a hellish day, as you can imagine, what with all the . . .'

'No, now. You look as if you've had a scare or something'

'Oh no.' I had had a scare all right. Come to that, I was still having one. I did not know whether to be more frightened at the idea that had come into my mind, or at the fact that it had come there and showed no signs of going away. I tried to let it lie without examining it. 'To tell you the truth, Nick, I had a few quick drinks in Baldock, which you'll understand, a bit too quick probably, anyway I very nearly took a bad toss on the stairs just now when I was chasing that bloody woman. Might have been nasty. Bit off-putting. You get the idea.'

Nick, a tall square figure with his mother's dark hair and eyes, looked at me stolidly. He knew that I had not told him the truth, but was not going to take me up on it. 'You'd better have another, then,' he said in the quick tolerant voice he had first used to me when he was a child of ten. 'Shall we go up? Lucy knows the way.'

A few minutes later, Lucy joined Nick and Joyce and me in the dining-room. She came and kissed my cheek with an air perfectly suggesting that, while not for a moment abating her dislike and disapproval of me, she was not, in view of the circumstances, going to get at me today unless provoked. I had always wondered what Nick saw in such a dumpy little personage, with her snouty nose, short-cut indeterminate hair, curious shawls and fringed handbags. Nor had he ever tried to enlighten me. Still, I had to admit that they seemed to get on well enough together.

Amy came in and stared at me until I had noticed the dirty sweater and holed jeans she had exchanged for her earlier get-up. Then, still staring at intervals, she went over and started being theatrically cordial to Lucy, whom she knew I knew she thought was a snob. I told things to Nick while my mind worked away on its idea like an intelligent animal functioning without human supervision, rounding up facts, sorting through questions and wonderings. It went assiduously on while lunch was served.

Joyce had put up a cold collation: artichoke with a *vinaigrette*, a Bradenham ham, a tongue the chef had pressed himself, a game pie from the same hand, salads and a cheese board with radishes and spring onions. I missed out the artichoke, a dish I have always tended to despise on biological grounds. I used to say that a man with a weight problem should eat nothing else, since after each meal he would be left with fewer calories in him than he had burnt up in the toil of disentangling from the bloody things what shreds of nourishment they contained. I would speculate that a really small man, one compelled by his size to eat with a frequency distantly comparable to that of the shrew or the mole, would soon die of starvation and/or exhaustion if locked up in a warehouse full of artichokes, and sooner still if compelled besides to go through the rigmarole of dunking each leaf in *vinaigrette*. But I did not go into any of this now, partly because Joyce, who liked every edible thing and artichokes particularly, always came back with the accusation that I hated food.

This is true enough. For me, food not only interrupts everything while people eat it and sit about waiting for more of it to be served, but also casts a spell of vacancy before and after. No other sensual activity must take place at a set time to be enjoyed by anybody at all, or comes up so inexorably and so often. Some of the stuff I can stand. Fruit slides down, bread soon goes to nothing, and all pungent swallowables have a value of their own that transcends mere food. As for the rest of it, chewing away at the vile texture of meat, pulling bones out of tasteless mouthfuls of fish or encompassing the sheer nullity of vegetables is not my idea of a treat. At least sex does not demand a simultaneous outflow of talk, and drink needs no mastication.

No drinking to speak of went on at this lunch. While I tried to keep my mind entirely on my objections to food, I covered some ham and tongue with chutney and hot sauce and washed the mixture down with a powerful tumbler of whisky and water. It did not look very powerful, thanks to my use of one of those light-coloured Scotches so handy for the man who wants a stronger potion than he cares to advertise to his company. The onions and radishes got me through a small hunk of fresh Cheddar; I had made a good meal. We went on to coffee, that traditional device for prolonging artificially the conditions and atmosphere of food-consumption. I took a lot of it, not in the hope of sobering up, for coffee is no help there and I was already as sober as I could hope to be, but to render myself reasonably wakeful. I wanted to be in some sort of form for later that afternoon.

As soon as Amy had left the table I made up my mind. There is always the chance, when only two people are talking together, that the one may listen carefully to the other and take seriously what he says. No such risk attaches to gatherings of more than two. So I gave up the idea of taking Nick aside afterwards, poured myself more coffee and, addressing him rather than anyone else, said as casually as I could,

'You know, I've been wondering if there mightn't have been something ... slightly curious going on about the time the old man died. I asked——'

'Curious in what way?' asked Lucy sharply, intent on getting this settled before I could switch the conversation irrevocably to football or the prospects for the harvest.

'I was coming to that, actually. According to Joyce, just before he collapsed he stood up and stared in the direction of the door, only there was nothing there. Then, immediately before he died, he said to me, "Who?" and, "Over by the ..." something. I think what he meant to say was, "Who (was that standing) over by the (door)?" That's——'

'I don't see anything very curious about that,' said Lucy. 'He was having a stroke—he might have——'

44

'Carry on, Dad,' said Nick.

'Yes. That's the first thing, or the first two things. Then, he'd been talking a few minutes earlier about hearing somebody walking up and down the passage outside here. I can't think of any actual person that could have been, though it wouldn't be at all significant on its own, I admit. Then, twice, last night and again an hour or so ago, I saw a woman dressed in a, well, it might have been an eighteenth-century ordinary domestic kind of dress, at the top of these stairs. And I think she vanished, both times. I don't really know about last night, but today, when she went down the stairs I followed her, and no one had seen her. If she went out by the front door, Nick would have seen her, wouldn't you, Nick? I'm sorry I spun you that yarn about her, but I was a bit het up at the time. Anyway, did you see anyone like that as you were coming in?'

The relief I had been looking for, that of simply telling somebody about my idea, had destroyed my casual tone, and Nick answered very deliberately.

'Yes, I couldn't have helped noticing, and there wasn't anybody. But so what? Who do you think she was, this woman?'

I found I could not say the word that had been in my mind. 'Well ... you've heard this house is supposed to be haunted. I don't know what it's sensible to say about things like that, but it does make you think. And then there was Victor...' I glanced at him sitting in front of the fireplace with his toes tucked in under him like a dish-cover, the picture of a cat to whom nothing out of the way, almost nothing at all, had ever happened. 'He acted very scared just when my father collapsed. Shot past me out of the room when I came back in. Very scared indeed.'

I could think of nothing more for the moment. All three of my audience looked as if they had been listening for a long time to a recital that, although not in the least strange or unexpected, was embarrassingly difficult to deal with except by straightforward, all-out insult. I felt garrulous, egocentric and very, very silly. In the end, Lucy stirred and said judicially—I remembered that she had taken an upper second in some vaguely philosophical mélange at a 'new' university——

'I take it you're referring to the possible presence of *ghosts*.'

To hear the word spoken took all the heart out of me. I could not even summon up a dab of sarcasm about haunted houses and vanishing women in antique dress often being

45

thought to carry some such association. 'Yes,' I said.

'Well, in the first place it isn't cats that are supposed to be sensitive to paranormal phenomena, it's dogs. There's no way of knowing what your father saw, if anything, and you're making a lot out of what he said, a few disjointed words you may not even have heard correctly. As for the woman you saw, well ... Anybody might have wandered up from the hall and down again. Are you sure she couldn't have gone into one of the rooms on the ground floor, the ladies' for instance?'

'No, I'm not. What about the footsteps in the passage?'

'What about them? You said yourself they wouldn't be significant on their own.'

'Mm.' I drank some coffee.

'I remember you telling us the story about the ghost who's supposed to turn up in the dining-room, but that was a man, wasn't it? Have you ever heard anything about a woman ghost?'

'No.'

Lucy did not actually say, 'Your witness,' but she hardly needed to. Nick looked at me indulgently, Joyce irritably, or with what could have been irritation if she had not recently been reminded that I had lost my father. I searched my brain. This was not altogether easy. Some shift in my metabolism, or perhaps the gill of whisky I had been putting away, had made me slightly drunk. Then, contrary to the odds, something came up. I turned to Lucy again.

'If there had been a story about a woman ghost, dressed as I described, would you have believed that that was what I'd seen?'

'Yes,' she said, confounding me, and showing she knew she had.

'Are you saying you believe in ghosts?'

'Yes. In the sense that I believe that people see ghosts. I can't think how any reasonable person can be in doubt on that score. That's not the same, of course, as saying that you see a ghost in the same way as you see a real person. Ghosts aren't *there*, so you can't take photographs of them or anything. But people see them all right.'

'You mean they think they see them,' said Nick. 'They imagine it.'

'Well, not quite, darling. I would suggest that they see ghosts in something of the same *sort* of way as they have hallucinations or religious visions. We don't say, for instance, that St

Bernadette *thought* she saw the Virgin Mary, unless we're trying to accuse her of misrepresenting what happened, or implying that she was mistaken or deceived. Unless we mean something like that we say she saw the Virgin Mary.'

'Who wasn't really there. I'd call that a hallucination. Same with ghosts.'

'There's a similarity, certainly, but it doesn't go all the way.' Lucy felt in her current fringed handbag, a red-and-white striped object that had no doubt come from somewhere in particular, and took out a packet of menthol cigarettes. She lit one of these as she went conscientiously on. 'Different people see the same ghost, at the same time or at widely differing times. Hallucinations don't seem to work like that. You can make a man have hallucinations by giving him certain drugs, but you can't make him have the same hallucination as someone else. People can see the same ghost as someone else without knowing the other person saw it until later, and they don't see a whole series of all sorts of other things as well, like people with hallucinations. Put a man in a haunted house and he may see a ghost, even if he didn't know it was haunted. Give a man a psychedelic drug and he'll have hallucinations. We don't know *why* in either case, but it's pretty certain the explanations don't coincide.'

'What do you think, Joyce?' asked Nick, who had listened to all this attentively enough, but with no sign of feeling that anything more than the validity of a theory was at stake.

'I don't know anything about it,' said Joyce, 'but I think ghosts are all balls. There can't be any such things. Maurice has been upset, and that's made him, you know, a bit imaginative.'

'That's roughly what I think,' said Nick.

Lucy frowned to herself and fiddled with her cigarette packet, as if pursuing her line of thought internally.

I had been all too right about not being taken seriously—by which I suppose I had meant causing some sort of stir. Accusations of madness or shouts of ridicule would have been preferable to these sober, sedative evaluations of my idea. 'Well, what do I do now?' I asked.

'Forget it, Dad,' said Nick, and Joyce nodded.

Lucy drew in her breath consideringly. 'If this woman turns up again, see if you can touch her. Try and make her speak. It would be quite something if you could, because there are surprisingly few really well-attested instances of a ghost saying anything. Anyway, chase her and find out whether other people can see her. That'd be worth knowing, from your point of view.'

'I don't get the point of all that,' said Joyce.

'Well ... it might be interesting.'

I found myself feeling slightly angry with Lucy. She alone had given me practical advice, which I had already decided to follow, but I disliked her bigoted reasonableness and her air of having already, though nearly thirty years younger than I, accumulated quite enough information and wisdom to deal with anything life might have in store: deal with it better than I could, too. I said in what I hoped was no more than an interested tone,

'You seem to know a lot about these things, Lucy. Have you studied them?'

'Not *studied*, no,' she said, to rebuke me for seeming to suggest that she had taken a university course in ghosts. 'But I have looked at the problem. I was doing a paper on the meaning of unverifiable statements, and it just happened to strike me that saying you've seen a ghost is one of a special class of unverifiable statements. I read a few accounts. Some interesting points of correspondence, I thought. This business, for instance, about the temperature dropping or seeming to drop before a manifestation. It's been claimed that thermometers have registered it, but I'm not convinced. It could be subjective, a concomitant of the person entering the physiological state in which they can see ghosts. Did you feel cold before you saw this woman?'

'No. Hot. I mean there was no change.'

'No. My own view is that there aren't any ghosts around here. At the moment, anyway. But tell me ... Maurice,' said Lucy, giving just a hint of what it cost her to call me by my name, 'would you say you believe in ghosts?'

'God, I don't know.' Until last night's events and today's appearance had taken on their present shape, I would have answered no without thinking about it. But I am not enough of a bloody fool to have bought the Green Man if I had heard any talk of hauntings in living memory. 'Of course, if any more evidence turns up ...'

'Any evidence is how I'd put it. I could be wrong, but according to me you only thought you saw a ghost.'

That was that: the table broke up. Joyce went off to check the bed-linen. I said I would take a short nap and then go and collect fruit and vegetables from a couple of farms in the district. Nick said that in that case, if it was all right, he would ring up John Duerinckx-Williams, the French scholar who had been his supervisor at St Matthew's, and see if he could arrange that he and Lucy should drive up to Cambridge and have a cup of tea with him, returning about six o'clock. I said that sounded a good idea, and we parted.

It was two fifty. I had a shower, put on clean clothing and otherwise prepared myself for encountering Diana. For some reason I could not then discover, I felt sure she would turn up. I combed my hair carefully, then decided it looked too much like a dark-red wig, and worked on making it seem careless but cared for. By the time I was satisfied it was too late for a nap. Not that I could have managed one of any sort: I was too strung up. With me, this is normally an altogether unpleasant state, but fluctuating within it now was a tinge of amorous expectancy. I looked at my face in the glass. It was all right really: on the pale side, a bit red under the eyes, and that ageing division between chin and jaw at least as perceptible as ever; but physically not unpresentable. What I had against it was its sameness and its continuity, always availabe with its display of cheap sternness and furtive worry, always a partner to unnecessary and unavoidable questioning. Timing it just right, my heart gave one of its lurches and, following up dependably, the pain in my back, which I had not thought about since the morning, turned itself on. I retaliated immediately by making a face of maniacal relish at myself and marching purposefully out of the room. I am too old a hand to be put off pleasure by even the certain prospect of not enjoying it. What will have been, will have been.

The pain went. I backed the 8-cwt trade truck out of the garage and drove towards the centre of the village. The engine was not loud enough to drown the horrible roaring and rattling noises from a couple of earth-moving machines that were levelling a slope beyond the back gardens of a dotted line of cottages. Here, perhaps in early 1984 if the present rate of progress was maintained, a row of houses was to be built, though I could not imagine what sort of person was going to be forced to live in them. The village itself looked as if it had been uninhabited for some weeks. A mail van coated with dust stood outside the corner shop, its driver more than just possibly in the arms of the postmistress, a middle-aged spinster people said was a funny sort and who certainly had two illegitimate children as well as an authentic bedridden mother. Everywhere else, if not actually dead, they were brooding about their wheat, dimly contemplating the afternoon milking, hoping on the whole that it would be fine for the Saturday cricket match against Sandon, dropping tea-bags into the pot, playing with the baby, asleep. Rural life is a mystery until one realizes that nearly all of it, everywhere in the world, is spent in preparing for and recovering from short but punishing bouts of the tedium inseparable from the tasks of the land, or rather their failure to give the least sense of achievement, as it might be a lifetime spent washing up out of doors. I have never understood why anybody agreed to go on being a rustic after about 1400.

The Mayburys' house, a genuine-looking stone structure that might have been a converted dames' school or primitive pickle factory, was at the farther end of the village. I drove past it, along a pot-holed road between bramble hedges, turned off and stopped on a patch of bare sandy soil at the corner of a farm track that led between fields of corn, the place where I had met Diana on two previous and unrewarding occasions. It was three thirty-two.

In the middle distance, beyond the crops, a man hunched up on a tractor was slowly dragging some farming implement across a large area of naked earth. From where I was (and I dare say anyone on the spot with a magnifying-glass would have told the same tale), this activity seemed to leave matters as they had been, apart from the multiple ruts being made in the soil. Probably the fellow was getting nerved up, trying to accustom himself to the idea of performing some actual deed of tillage there the following week.

His machinery was making the only audible sound, apart from the song of a blackbird with nothing better to do. I had barely started to hope I would not have time to think about things when I heard a third sound, turned my head and saw Diana approaching on foot—only five minutes late, quixotically early, in fact, by her standards: a good sign. She was wearing a dark-blue shirt and a tweed skirt, and was carrying a folded newspaper. I wondered slightly about the newspaper. When she reached the truck, I leaned across and opened the door on that side, but she made no move to get in.

'Well, Maurice,' she said.

'Hallo, Diana. Let's go, shall we?'

'Maurice, don't you think it's rather extraordinary of you to have decided to come along after all this afternoon?' She said this in full-blooded oral *Chick's Own* style, with tiny hyphens of silence between the syllables of the hard words. To say it all while being seen to do so, she had to bend both neck and knees and also rely on my remaining twisted round in my seat and leaning deeply over towards her.

'We can talk about that when we're on our way.'

'But don't you think so? To be prepared to make advances to somebody else's wife less than eighteen hours after you've seen your father die?'

The lack of hesitancy about the number of hours, evincing previous calculation, had a point to it. I understood now why I had been so sure earlier that she would appear as asked: I had sensed that she would not have been able to resist the chance of such a meaty interrogation-session. 'Oh, I don't know,' I said. 'If you'll get in I'll see if I can explain.'

'I mean, most men who've had that happen to them wouldn't even contemplate that sort of thing. What makes you so different?'

'I'll be giving you a full demonstration of it shortly. Come on.'

As if only then making up her mind, she settled herself beside me. I took her in my arms and kissed her forcefully. She remained passive until I put my hand on her breast, when she promptly removed it. Nevertheless, I was sure she was going to yield that afternoon when she was ready to, and this time understood at the same moment why I was sure. By opening her legs to me today of all days, she would be being strangely responsive to my strange need, finding herself strangely in tune with this strange man—in other words, she could represent herself as an interesting person. But before she got on to being strangely responsive, she was going to exact her full toll by making me put up with her questioning patiently enough, and long enough, for it to seem that I agreed she was an interesting person. Seeming, luckily for me, was all that was going to be required, since she needed no real confirmation of her view of herself. True, but why, then, was there any need for me even to do any seeming? Most likely she was just looking forward to the simple pleasure of watching my antics as I battled to master my impatience.

Diana had opened her newspaper—*The Guardian*, of course —but was evidently not reading it. When, as we approached a corner, an old man sitting in his garden came into view, she hid her face in the middle pages. Good security, and a further good sign, had one been needed, but if she wanted to avoid being seen in my car why had she just now stood by it in the open for a full minute? Other people's priorities are endlessly odd.

'Where are you taking me?' she asked.

'Well, I'm afraid there's nothing in the love-nest line available, but it's a warm day and there hasn't been any rain for nearly a fortnight, so I thought we could manage very nicely out of doors. There's an ideal spot less than a mile from here.'

'Well known to you from previous use for the same general purpose, no doubt.'

'That's it.'

'Maurice, will you be frightfully annoyed if I ask you something?'

'Oh, I shouldn't think so. Try me and see what happens.'

'Maurice, what is it that makes you such a tremendous womanizer?'

'But I'm not. I was fairly active in my youth, but that's a long time ago.'

'You *are* a tre ... men ... dous womanizer. Everybody in the village knows that no attractive female who comes to your house is safe from you.'

'How often do you think an unattached one of those comes wandering in?'

'They don't have to be unattached, do they? What about the wife of that Dutch tulip-grower in the spring?'

'Soil expert. That was different. He passed out in the dining-room, David put him to bed, and she said she didn't feel sleepy and it was a beautiful night. What could I do?'

'But what's at the back of it all, Maurice? What makes you so determined to make love to me, for instance?'

'Sex, I should imagine.'

I knew this would be nowhere near good enough for Diana in her present mood, indeed in the only mood I had ever seen her in in the three years I had known her. Glumly, I tried to run up in my mind a spontaneous-sounding remake of the standard full answer—reproductive urge, power thing, proving one's masculinity (to be introduced one moment and decisively rejected the next), restlessness, curiosity, man-polygamous-woman-monagamous (to be frankly described as old hat but at the same time not dismissible out of hand) and the rest of it, the whole mixture heftily spiked with pornographic flattery. However, I had barely started on this grim chore when Diana herself let me off that particular hook by attending to our route.

'Where are we going? You're taking us back to the village.'

'Just round the edge of the village. We cross the main road in a minute and go up behind the hill, a bit beyond where the new houses are going up.'

'But that's almost opposite the Green Man.'

'Not really. And you can't be seen from there.'

'Pretty close all the same.' A farm lorry came into view ahead and *The Guardian* went up again. From within it she continued, 'Is that part of it, Maurice? Part of the thrill for you? Flaunting it?'

'There'll be no flaunting if I have any say in the matter, and as I said no one can see you anyway.'

'Still...' She lowered the paper. 'Do you know another thing that's been puzzling me dreadfully?'

'What?'

'Why you haven't done anything about me until practically the other day. You and I have known each other jolly nearly since Jack and I moved to Fareham, and you just treat me as a friend, and then you suddenly start making these colossal passes at me. All I'm asking is, why ... the change?'

This was her least dispiriting query so far, at any rate in the sense that I could think of no answer, either then or later. Almost at random, I said, 'I suppose I've realized I'm nearly an old man. I haven't got all the time in the world any longer.'

'That's complete and utter rubbish, Maurice, and you know it, darling. You haven't got a paunch and you've got all your hair and I can't think how you do it when you drink so much but you look about forty-four or -five at the outside, so don't be so silly.'

She had more or less had to say something on these lines, since to declare a fondness, whether sneaking or flagrant, for budding old-age pensioners would have made her seem to herself one of the wrong sorts of interesting person. But it was nice to hear it said just the same.

We duly crossed the main road beside the dilapidated and overgrown churchyard where Thomas Underhill was buried, and climbed a twisting lane where a hazy afternoon sun came down diagonally through a straggle of poplars. Just beyond the crest I drove the truck into a turning so narrow that the hedges brushed the doors on either side. Two minutes later I took us off this into a space almost enclosed by a high bank, a rough semicircle of brambles and a sudden rise in the ground between us and the main road. I stopped the engine.

'Is this it?'

'It's nearly it. There's a splendid little hollow in the ground by those bushes that you can't even see from here.'

'Is it safe?'

'I've never seen anyone up this way. The track peters out in those woods.'

I started kissing her again before she could speculate on the reasons for this or whatever other facts might strike her. The only really good point about the raised hem-line is that a man can put his hand on a girl's thigh a long way from the knee without being said to be putting it up her skirt. I took full advantage of this. Diana responded to it and such moves as enthusiastically as anybody setting out to display a contrast with earlier, unresponsive behaviour. But quite soon, using a moment when my mouth was not on hers, she said, sounding as if she really wanted to know,

'Maurice, don't you think it's important to get some things straight?'

I could not imagine any such things, or any things, but said, perhaps a bit dully, 'Don't let's bother about that kind of stuff for now.'

'Oh, but Maurice, we have to bother, surely. We must.'

In a sense I felt this too, or had done so and would again, but this was not enough to call me back from where I was. What did that was the knowledge, dim but powerful, that she had not yet had her say—her ask, rather—that nothing would make her throw away her present seller's-market advantage and postpone having it until significantly later, and that therefore she had better have it now, not when I had got her on her back. Playing up to her, however revolting in retrospect, would probably shorten the say, or at least cut down the intervals between the various sections of it. Well, worth a try.

'You're right, of course,' I said, releasing her, gripping her hand and staring responsibly past her at the bushes. 'We're two grown-up people. We can't just sail into a thing like this with our eyes shut.'

'Maurice.'

'Yes?' I spoke gruffly, to show how tortured I was feeling.

'Maurice, why have you suddenly changed? One moment

you're seducing me as hard as you can go, and the next you back off and say we ought to worry about what we're doing. You're not having second thoughts, are you?'

'No,' I said rather quickly, 'certainly not, but you said something about getting our ideas straight, and that reminded me of, well . . .'

'But you are absolutely sure you really care?' Her tone was edged with suspicion, and I realized what a mistake it would be to suppose that those who habitually talk insincerely, or for effect, or balls, are no good at spotting others who try the same line. When she went on, 'That sort of thing sounds so funny, coming from you,' I took her point at once: all the balls-talking that afternoon was going to be done by her.

'Well, I . . .' I muttered, and did something in the air with my free hand, 'I was just . . .'

'Maurice,' she said, at her ease again and giving me a wide-eyed hazel stare, 'isn't it wrong to put one's own pleasure before everything else, before other people's happiness?'

'Perhaps. I don't know.'

'Wouldn't you say that one of the most absolutely typical things about the way everybody goes on nowadays is this thing of making up your own rules?'

'There's a lot of truth in that.'

'And what bothers me is can it ever be right. After all, you wouldn't take the line that we're just animals, would you?'

'No.'

'Maurice . . . don't you think sexual attraction is the most peculiar and unpredictable and sim—ply *mad* thing in the world?'

At this, I cheered up a little. Either Diana was semi-consciously groping for the sixty-four-cent question, the ultimate bit of balls which I would pass the test by letting her get away with, or she was just running out of material. 'I've never understood it,' I said humbly.

'But isn't it true that if people don't pay attention to what their instincts tell them then they get jolly closed up and cut off from everything and perfectly awful in every way?'

I was feeling by now as if I had not paid attention to what my instincts told me for weeks, and perhaps never would again, but just then, to emphasize her proposition about its being a bad thing to be perfectly awful, she leaned earnestly forward, and I caught sight of the bare flesh between the base of the mound of her left breast and the lip of the brassière-cup. My concentration slipped; I had it back on full within a couple of seconds, but in that interval I found I had said something like, 'Yes, well let's go and show we're not that sort,' and had started to open the door on my side.

She caught my wrist, pursing her lips and frowning. Even before she spoke I could see that, after mounting a series of short but cumulatively valuable ladders, I had just gone sliding down a major snake. But, as in the substantial form of the game, so too in the version Diana and I were playing, there are certain parts of the board where a single throw can restore everything lost on the previous turn, and more.

'Maurice.'

'Yes?'

'Maurice ... perhaps if two people really want each other it's sort of all right in a way. Do you really want me?'

'Yes, Diana, I really want you. I mean it.'

She stared at me again. Perhaps she thought I did mean it—and, good God, any man who had not only put up with all this without screaming, but was ready for more if need be, must really want her in some fairly ample sense. Perhaps I had merely produced the necessary formula with the necessary show of conviction, nothing more than a piece of sexual good manners. Perhaps, whatever the difference might be between really wanting someone and wanting someone, I had meant it. Anyway, the last snake was behind me now, or so it seemed to me then.

'Let's make love to one another, my darling,' said Diana.

The new problem was to prevent her from making too many remarks in this style until the stage of no remarks was reached. I got out of the truck, went round and helped her down.

'In a summer season,' she said, actually looking up at the sky, 'when soft was the sun ...'

'Well, we can't say we haven't been lucky with the weather,' I babbled, pulling her along beside me. One more really corking cock-crinkler like that one and I would be done for. 'The forecast said rain later, but they're hopeless, aren't they? Just a lot of guesswork. Here we are.'

I preceded her into the hollow and swung her down the three- or four-foot drop. The place was as clean as when I had reconnoitred it the previous day, without even any evidence of courting couples. Probably Fareham couples could not find the energy to court, slipping bemusedly into marriage as they might into debt or senile dementia.

'Maurice, I'm sure it'll all be marvellously beautiful, with the——'

I cut this one off by kissing her. While I was doing so, I finished unbuttoning her shirt and unclipped her brassière. Her bosom was firm under my hand, almost hard. The discovery had the effect of making me begin to draw her with me towards the ground. She freed herself and stepped away.

'I want to be naked,' she said. 'For us, I must be naked.'

She took off her shirt and this once I overlooked her literary style. If she had, after all, wanted me to think she was an interesting person, not just seem to think so, she was going a much better way about it now than at any earlier time. Her breasts turned out to be high as well as full and firm, and heavily pointed, but a few moments later I could see how small-made, how long in leg and body she really was. In the short time it had taken her to strip, her face had changed, losing only now its quick directed glance and tenseness of jaw, becoming heavy-eyed, slack-mouthed, dull with excitement. Slowly, her shoulders drawn back and her stomach in, she sat down on a patch of short turf, and seemed to catch sight of me.

'You too,' she said.

This struck me as a novel and not particularly good idea. A man undressing lacks dignity; more than that, a man undressed in the open feels vulnerable, and with good reason. From an outsider's point of view, a naked woman out of doors is either a sun-worshipper or a rape victim; a man in the same state is either a sexual criminal or a plain lunatic. But I obliged just the same, finding the air pleasantly warm. Diana sat and waited, not looking at me, gently and rhythmically pressing the inward surfaces of her upper arms against the sides of her bosom. It was clear that she had had to be naked not for us, let alone for me, but for her. Here, though, was something in her that was really in her, for narcissists, by definition, do not care whether other people find them interesting or not. There was a paradox here, involving the way Diana went on when she was fully dressed, but I had no time for that now: I agreed too heartily with her about the importance of her body.

As I soon found when I lay down with her, it was the top half of that body that most appealed to her. In some important ways, she had sexual and aesthetic right on her side. However attractive a woman's face may be when she has her clothes on, it is much more so when she is naked; then, sometimes only then, it becomes the most attractive part of her. Throat, shoulders and upper arms, not to speak of breasts, are all individual or at least personal; below the waist, there is a massive lack of detail and a small amount of mere anatomy. I worked on Diana's principle for some time, with her unqualified and often noisy approval. But eventually there had to come the start of the accelerating swing to anatomy and, in every sense, to lack of detail. Diana's pleasure abated at once.

At this point I saw (just) that I had a choice. I could perhaps return as far as possible to what she so obviously enjoyed most, while nearly—but not quite—stopping what I had just started on my own account: a sort of sexual equivalent of uninterruptedly performing a piano sonata and at the same time lunching off a plate of sandwiches. Or, without any effort at all, I could forget about her and, more important, forget about myself. That afternoon, I wanted this release even more than usual, but on the other hand I wanted to end up with a satisfied and grateful Diana—if there was any such thing—more yet. So I chose the first alternative, in fact improved on it by metaphorically playing a demanding coda, full of ornamentation and difficult runs in both hands, that went on quite a long time after the disappearance of the last sandwich. (They had been good sandwiches, anyway, as sandwiches go.)

I moved the minimum distance away. Diana peered at me. Her face was flushed and looked swollen round the eyes and mouth.

'Oh God,' she said, 'lovely. There was so much of it. Wish I could remember it all. I don't know how I felt.'

'You were beautiful. You are beautiful.'

She smiled and looked away, down at herself. Soon she stopped sprawling and lolling, drew in her chin, crossed her legs and pushed herself up into a half-sitting position. When she looked at me again, her eyes were side, the swollen look had almost faded into her familiar expression of faint anxiety touched with pertness.

'Maurice,' she said now, 'that was ab-so-lute-ly terr-i-fic. I don't know *how* ... you do it. Was it nice for you? You certainly deserved it to be.'

'It was splendid.'

I put my arms round her again and briefly ran over some of the main points treated in depth earlier, but this time in a lofty, impartial spirit, just underlining the essential continuity of how I felt about her attractions. After a few minutes, I said,

'Diana.'

'Yes?'

'Diana, have you ever been to bed with more than one person? At the same time, I mean.'

'Maurice, really ... Well yes, I have, actually. Years ago now. Before I met Jack.'

'Was it fun? It was two men, I suppose?'

'*Maurice* ... Yes, it was two men. If you could call them men. I thought I was the one it was going to be all about, but they were only really interested in each other. They went on taking it in turns to be in the middle, and what they wanted me to do wasn't very nice. I got totally and completely bored and simply left them to it. It was all quite ghastly. But——'

'I'm sure it was. But it would be quite different if you——'

'You mean you and Joyce.'

'Well, yes. She's always——'

'Maurice, you're not to be furious with me, because I know you often are, but I must ask you something. What makes you even think of a thing like that? It's all so frightfully unnecessary. Could it be that you really are getting old? I want to ask you something else. Can I?'

'Ask away.'

'Well ... how often do you and Joyce make love? On the average?'

'I don't know. Once a week, perhaps. Sometimes not as much.'

'There you are. You want to sort of spice it all up in a horrid way. You've got a lovely young wife who absolutely adores you, but you have to go for me as well, and even then that's not enough for you. It's like, you know, boots and transparent macks and typing-up and things.'

'Sorry, Diana. Forget all about it. I've made a mistake. I thought you were the sort of person I could ask that. I'm sorry.'

'What sort of person do you mean?'

'Well, eager for new experience, new sensations. Somebody who wants to ... extend their awareness.' (Her head was safely on my shoulder, where she could not meet my eyes.) 'Somebody who's interest*ed* in everything, and also interest*ing* in all kinds of——'

'Maurice, when did I say I wasn't interested? I was just jolly fascinated to know why you wanted to do it. Isn't that what I asked you?'

'Sorry, yes, it was. Of course. And, you know, it wouldn't be like the time with the two chaps. I do exactly what you love having done, don't I?' (Here I made a short allusion-in-action to some of this.) 'Don't I, darling?'

'Oh yes. Yes, you do.'

'And Joyce thinks you're the most stunning creature she's ever——'

'Does she? What does she say?'

'Oh, that she can understand what lesbians are on about when she looks at you, and she'd love to find out if that figure's real, and all that. And you see, Diana darling, you'd be the complete centre of attraction. After all, Joyce and I are used to each other these days, you know what I mean, but with you we'd both——'

'Have you mentioned it to her?'

'Not yet.'

'Well, don't until we've talked about it again. Maurice . . .'

'Yes?'

'What else does Joyce say about me?'

I produced some more exaggerations or inventions—Joyce certainly admired Diana's looks, but the amorous part of that admiration, if any, I knew nothing about. What I said was unmemorable enough but effective. Diana began breathing deeply, then squaring and relaxing her shoulders as she did so. I moved in.

A little later, fully dressed and savouring the relief that this brings in any adulterous circumstance, I obeyed Diana's command to disappear for five minutes and climbed out of the hollow, which I found I had not until then thought of as a place in any full sense. Even the criss-cross pattern of indentations the grass had made on my forearms and knee-caps, noticeable as I put my clothes on, had been no reminder that we had actually been lying on and among grass, and the scene outside, the brambles, the sandy, stony banks and the trees farther off, had been on the edge of non-existence. Now all this, in the duller light from an overcast sky, settled into position. I strolled along the track towards the woods into which it disappeared. The air was thick and sultry, without any breeze. When I had walked a hundred yards, I turned off in the direction of the road, firstly to have a pee, secondly to establish, in an idle, time-filling way, just where I was in relation to my house. I moved up the ridge, skirting the more thickly-grown area, mostly oak and ash with a scattering of holly, hazel and elder, which I took to be the copse that could be seen from the front of the building: I had never wandered up as far as this before.

The going was difficult, with slippery tussocks of grass, patches of crumbling soil and here and there holes in the ground a foot or more deep. As I neared the crest, there appeared the slender chimney-pots of the Green Man, the shallow tiled slopes of the roofs, finally the main body of the house and the outbuildings. The annexe containing the guest bedrooms was hidden by the bulk of the original inn. As I stood there, an inconspicuous figure, no doubt, against the taller hillside behind me, I saw a car approach and turn into the yard (possibly the Cambridge party who had booked by telephone the previous day), and then somebody standing at one of the dining-room windows and looking in my general direction. Whoever it was—one of the waiters, I assumed, in an interval of laying for dinner—could scarcely have seen me, but there was no point in an unnecessary risk. I turned to retrace my steps, then noticed a rough path leading through the wood towards the track. This would take me some dozens of yards out of my way, but would be preferable to the scrambling, stumbling route I had followed a minute before. I started along the path.

Immediately I felt very frightened indeed. At first—if it makes any sense to say so—this did not alarm me. I am well acquainted with causeless fear, with the apparently random onset of all the standard symptoms, from accelerated pulse and breathing to tingling at the nape of the neck and rear part of the scalp, sudden profuse sweating and a strong desire to cry out. Then, as my heart went into a prolonged stumbling tremor, the concomitants of fear, in themselves no more than very disagreeable, seemed to bring fear itself. I halted on the path. For a few more seconds I wondered if I were really about to die, but soon after that I became certain that whatever was going to happen was outside me. What it might be, or where, I could not imagine. Something frightening, yes; something monstrous, so monstrous that the mere fact of it, its coming to pass at all, would be harder to bear than its actual menace to me personally. My head began to tremble uncontrollably. I heard, or thought I heard, a whispering sound like the wind through grasses, saw, had no doubt that I saw, the growth of ivy on a near-by oak ripple and turn its leaves to and fro, as if in the wind, but there was no wind. Just beyond this, I saw a shadow move in a thicket, but I knew there was nobody else in the wood, and there was no sun. This was the place that Underhill's ghost had been seen watching, and what had terrified him was here. With a sharp snap, one of the fronds of a large fern growing beside the path detached itself from its root, turning over and over like a leaf in a squall as it moved fitfully towards the thicket where the shadow had appeared. I did not wait to see if it was still there, but ran headlong down the path, through the wood and out of it on to the track I had walked up five minutes before, and down it again to where Diana sat smoking a cigarette on the edge of the hollow.

At my approach, she turned her head with a display of grace which faltered when she looked at me. 'What's the matter? Why the great gallop? You're——'

'Come on,' I said, panting. I must have shouted it.

'What's the matter? Are you ill? What's the matter?'

'All right. Got to go. Now.'

Diana did no more than look genuinely alarmed while I got us into the truck, turned it unhandily round and drove as fast as possible down the track to the road. There, I turned away from the village. After about a mile, I found a field of pasture with an open gate and parked just inside. I had got my breath back and had stopped trembling, had been frightened only in retrospect ever since leaving that wood. But that was how I felt still. I opened the dashboard cupboard—yes, there was a half-bottle of Scotch, nearly full. I saw in passing that I had thought to mix a bit of water in for reasons of taste. I drank it all.

I realized that I would have to think of something to say to Diana, who had gone on sitting unnaturally quiet beside me, but my mind was a blank. I began to talk in the hope that words would bring ideas.

'Sorry about that. I suddenly felt absolutely terrible. I had to get away from that place. I don't know what it was, I just felt awful.'

'Ill, you mean?'

'Not exactly. No, not ill. Just ... No, I can't describe it, I'm afraid. Some sort of neurotic thing, I suppose. Anyway, it's over now.'

'Maurice.' For once she sounded sincerely diffident about what was to follow her operating call-sign.

'Yes, Diana?'

'Maurice ... tell me one thing frankly. This isn't a way of

letting me know you don't want to have anything more to do with me in this kind of way, is it?'

'A what? How could it be that?'

'Well, you might have decided it made you feel too awful, guilt and so on, and so you piled it on and made it into a sort of dizzy spell as a way of saying it was all too much for you.' (No diffidence now.) 'Because I suppose what you really mean is I didn't do the right things for you or something.'

This, I reflected, from a woman who, three minutes earlier, had been showing every sign of real concern about another person. 'Of course not. Nothing like that, I assure you.'

'Because if you think I'm not good enough for you or something it's better if you say so straight away.'

'If that's what you're afraid of,' I said furiously, 'it must be because I'm not good enough for you, whatever I do. Do you imagine I make love like that every day?'

She blinked her eyes and twitched her mouth and shoulders for a short while as evidence of internal conflict. Then she smiled and touched my hand.

'I'm sorry, Maurice. I suddenly went into the most ghastly panic. I somehow got the idea you didn't like me at all. The most frightful sense of insecurity. Women get that, you know. Well, some women do, anyway. There was simply nothing I could do about it, honestly.'

I kissed her. 'I understand,' I said, and meant it. 'But up there ... you did have a splendid time, didn't you?'

'Mm. Splen ... did.' With her hegemony of sensitivity re-established, she must have felt she could afford to be generous. 'Absolutely splendid.'

'But nothing to what Joyce and I will do for you, I promise you.'

'Maurice, you are completely extraordinary. One moment you're having a dizzy spell and the next you're keeping up the pressure to make me have an orgy with you. What makes you so incredibly sort of changeable?'

On the drive back, I advanced a theory or two about what made me like that, never ceasing to imply that, whatever it might be, Diana and her attractiveness and fascinatingness had a hand in it up to the collar-bone. I said I would pick her up the next day at the same place and time, made her promise to think over the orgy project (I was pretty sure she had already decided in favour of it, but to say so at this stage might have made her seem interesting almost to a fault), dropped her at the corner and went off to pick up my vegetables and fruit.

This last operation took a bare three-quarters of an hour, and would have taken only half as long but for the slow-motion of both the farmers concerned. The older of the two performed as if I had turned up to buy his daughters instead of his lettuces and tomatoes; the younger, whose top incisor teeth lay horizontally on his lower lip and who smelt a lot, treated me like a Tsarist tax official. Throughout, my sexual elation kept being overlaid by unsought memories of what had happened in the wood and by notions that in thinking about my father as little as possible all day I had behaved badly to him. The pain in my back did what it could on this side of the scales by coming up with some unusually firm and authoritative twinges.

By the time I had driven the truck into the yard at the Green Man and sent for Ramón to come and unload it, it was twenty past six and my thoughts had homed in on drink. I had a large one—one only in the sense that I did not allow my glass to become empty before topping it up to an even higher level than before—while I showered and put on my evening rig-out. Then I looked in on Amy, who was watching a TV inquiry into householders' insurance and who was, if anything, rather less polysyllabic than usual. My father's absence made this entire section of the daily routine seem unduly contracted. I had a word with David Palmer and joined Nick, Lucy and Joyce in the bar just after seven, not at all looking forward to a couple of hours of work. We had a drink (I switched to sherry, my standard public potation at this hour), and very soon the first diners had reached the menu-conning stage.

There were no difficulties, none at least that stuck in my mind. By the time I got to the third, or possibly the fourth, party, however, I found I was beginning to encounter the problem I had failed to solve on my return from Baldock earlier that day: continuing to talk constructively without being able to remember, even in outline, what had been said just before. My order-pad was a help here, but not when it was a matter of deciding what to write down on it. The bar became almost empty. Those in search of an earlyish meal had either moved into the dining-room or fled out of the front door at the sight of me. A little later again, I suggested to David that now would be a good time to have a look at the kitchen. I understood him to say that this was of course an excellent idea, but that it might make just as much sense to defer it to a later stage, rather than carry it out so comparatively soon after a previous visit. I wondered just how soon afterwards it was, and whether, while having my look at the kitchen, I had said anything noteworthy, either for its wit or for its insight into the human condition. David's expression gave no help here. Using his special reliable voice, he said,

'Mr Allington, why don't you let me take over now for what's left of the evening? There's only a few late bookings tonight, and you must have had a tiring day, and you'll be handing over to me anyway at ten o'clock. And you agreed with me the other day that I ought to have more solo time.'

'Thank you, David, but I think I'll carry on for a bit. Remember we've got Professor Burgess booked for nine thirty, and I want to see to him personally, after that soufflé disaster when he was here before.'

As regards coherence, this was probably no great advance on what I had been saying for the last twenty or forty minutes; the point was that I knew what I had said, and even what David had said just earlier. I was back in control, or nearly so, without having done anything to earn it in the way of sleep or abstention, a familiar enough experience. Equally familiar would be the experience of sliding out of control again without having done a great deal to earn that, so I made a brief but violent attack on the cheese, biscuits and stuffed olives Fred had put out on the counter, and resolved to drink no more until I was up in the apartment. David got most of this, and shortly withdrew.

Burgess, a caricature of a savant, arrived soon afterwards with his wife, also a caricature of a savant, though of a more purely learned, perhaps more Germanic, type. They had brought along a couple of friends, less discernibly erudite than themselves. As expected, they all went for the grouse—the first of the year to have hung long enough—accompanied by a couple of bottles of the Château Lafite 1955 I kept under the counter for a few people like old Burgess, and preceded by some of the chef's admirable kipper pâté. I ushered them into the dining-room myself; the head waiter, alerted in advance, met us at the doorway. The rather low-ceilinged room, a little over half-full, looked pleasantly welcoming with its candles, polished silver, polished oak and dark-blue leather, and was much cooler than the bar had been. The sight and sound of so much eating and talking daunted me a little, but there was a certain amount of drinking going on as well: not enough to satisfy me, but then there never is.

I had got the Burgesses and their friends settled, and was about to make a round of the other tables when I caught sight of a man standing by the window, perhaps looking out through a chink in the curtains, although he seemed to be in a slightly wrong position for doing this. I was pretty sure he had not been there when I came into the room. For a moment, I assumed this person to be a guest concerned about, for instance, the state of the lights of his car. Then, as my inn-keeper's reflexes sent me across the room with officiously helpful tread, I saw that the figure was wearing a short grey wig and a black gown and white bands at the throat. By now I was no more than six feet away. I halted.

'Dr Underhill?'

It is never true that we speak so entirely without volition as not to realize, even for an instant, that it is we who have spoken. But I had not had the least conscious intention of pronouncing that name.

In leisurely fashion, but without delay, the head turned and the eyes met mine. They were dark-brown eyes with deeply creased lids, thick lower lashes and arching brows. I also saw a pale, indoors complexion scattered with broken veins to what seemed an incongruous degree, a broad forehead, a long, skewed nose and a mouth that, in another's face, I might have called humorous, with very clearly defined lips. Then, or rather at once, Dr Underhill recognized me. Then he smiled. It was the kind of smile with which a bully might greet an inferior person prepared to join with him in the persecution of some helpless third party. It also held a certain menace, as if any squeamishness in persecution would result in accomplice becoming victim.

I turned to the nearest table, where there sat a party of three youngish London lawyers and their wives, and said loudly, 'Do you see him? Man in the black ... Just here, there ...'

Underhill had gone when I looked round. I felt a great weary irritation at the predictability of this. I floundered idiotically on for a bit about his having been there a moment before, and how they must surely have seen him, before I realized that I could not stand up any more. My heart was perfectly steady just then, I was not dizzy or ill, and I have never fainted in my life; it was simply that my legs would not do their job. Somebody—the head waiter—caught me. I heard alarmed voices and scuffling sounds as people got to their feet. Immediately, and from nowhere, David arrived. He put his arm round me, called out a sharp order for my wife and son to be fetched from the bar and steered me into the hall. Here he sat me down in an upright-backed Regency chair by the fireplace and tried to loosen my collar, but I prevented him.

'It's all right, David, really. Just ... nothing at all.'

Nick said, 'What's the matter, Dad?' and Joyce said, 'I'll phone Jack.'

'No, don't do that. No need for that. I just came over a bit dizzy. I must have been drinking faster than I realized. I'm all right now.'

'Where would you like to be, Mr Allington? Can you make it upstairs if we give you a hand?'

'Please don't bother, I think I can make it on my own.' I got up, not all that shakily, and saw that people were watching me from the dining-room and bar door and elsewhere. 'Could you tell anybody who's interested that I've been under severe strain recently, or some such flap-doodle? Everyone'll think I was as tight as a tick anyway, but I suppose we might as well preserve the outward forms if we can.'

'I'm sure very few of them will think that, Mr Allington.'

'Oh well, what of it? I'll be off now. Don't worry, David. If Ramón goes berserk with the meat-cleaver you'd better let me know, but short of that the house is all yours until the morning. Good night.'

None too comfortably, the four of us settled in the drawing-room, so called by my predecessor, though its lack of spaciousness and its pretty unrelieved symmetry made it, for me, a mere parlour or ante-room. I had never much tried to make it more than barely decent, had rather tended to turn it into a dump for the less attractive furniture and a couple of bits of statuary that had started to get on my nerves, a portrait bust of an early-Victorian divine and a female nude in some pale wood, sloppily modernistic in tendency, which I had bought in Cambridge after a heavy lunch at the Garden House and had since been too lazy to get rid of. Only my father had seemed to like the room, or at least had used it regularly. However, we would not be disturbed here.

I told them what I had seen. Nick watched me with great concern, Joyce with concern, Lucy with responsible vigilance, like a member of a team conducting a nationwide survey of drunks who see ghosts. Halfway through, I made Nick fetch me a small Scotch and water. He demurred, but I made him.

Joyce lost her look of concern as I talked. When I had finished, she said, 'Sounds like D.T.s to me, don't you think?' in the interested voice she had used in discussing my father's chances of surviving the current year, and, once, to suggest that Amy's remoteness might be due to mental subnormality.

'Christ, what an idea,' said Nick.

'What's so terrible about it? I mean, if it's that you can deal with it. Not like going mad, after all.'

Nick turned to Lucy. 'Isn't D.T.s little animals and that type of stuff?'

'Very often, yes,' said Lucy dependably. 'Something completely removed from reality, anyway. A man just standing about smiling hardly counts as that.'

This was a small relief, but I rather wished she had not spoken as if what I had seen was on the same level as one of the waiters wearing a dirty collar. 'All right,' I said, 'what was it, then?'

Nick drew back his lips and shook his head earnestly. 'You were pissed, Dad. I don't know whether you realize, but you were really droning away when you were talking to the three of us in the bar just before.'

'I'm not pissed now.'

'Well no, but in the meantime you've had a shock and that does pull people round. But earlier on you were. Oh, you were making plenty of sense, but I know the way your voice goes, and your eyes.'

'But I'd come round after that. I was talking to David … Look, Nick, you go down now and ask Professor Burgess. He'll tell you I was all right. Go on.'

'Oh, *Dad*. How can I go and ask him?'

'Go down and get hold of David and the two of you take some of the regular people aside, David knows who they are, and ask them if they saw somebody standing by the window. I've described how he looked, so they'll be——'

'*Christ*, Dad … Let it drop. Take my advice, honestly. All their bloody tongues'll be flapping as it is. Don't go and make it worse. You don't want it going round that the landlord of the Green Man seems to be seeing things. Don't mind me saying this, just with the four of us, but they all know you're a boozer. And anyway they wouldn't remember seeing anyone, not even taken it in. *Really*, let it go.'

'Nick, go and get David up here.'

'No.' Nick's face went hard in a way I had known for a

dozen years. 'No use keeping it up, Dad. It's not on.'

There was silence. Joyce drew her legs up under her and smoothed her hair, not looking at anyone. Lucy clicked her lighter at a menthol cigarette.

'What do you think?' I asked her unwillingly.

'No investigation, of course. We know that's out. Basically, I agree with Nick. That is, I think you'd been under a certain amount of strain, you had ghosts in your mind, you knew the story about this Underhill character, your judgment was, let's say, impaired by alcohol, and the lighting in the dining-room is subdued, especially over by the window. There was somebody standing there, I'm quite ready to believe, but a real person, a waiter or one of the customers. As before, you thought you saw a ghost.'

'But the wig, and the clothes . . .'

'You filled them in out of your mind.'

'But he recognized me, and he smiled at me.'

'Of course he did. You were his boss, or else his host, and you'd just embarrassed him slightly by calling him by the wrong name.'

'He'd disappeared. When I——'

'He'd moved away.'

Another silence, in which I heard Magdalena enter the apartment and go into the dining-room. I very much wanted to tell the three what had happened in the wood, if only to dissent from Lucy's Q.E.D., but I could think of no innocent reason for having gone there, and anyway I had been under strain, alcohol, etc., then too.

'So I imagined it,' I said, finishing my whisky.

'That's what I think,' said Lucy, 'but it's only what I *think*. I could quite easily be proved wrong.'

'Oh, really? How?'

'I could be proved wrong tomorrow, in fact any moment, by someone else seeing what you see—though it goes without saying that if nobody else sees what you say you see, that's no proof you didn't see it—or if you found out something from a ghost you couldn't otherwise have known about, then that would be not exactly a proof, but it would weigh with me considerably.'

'What sort of thing?'

'Well, supposing you saw a ghost walk through what's now part of a wall, say, but it was a doorway or something in the past, and afterwards you found evidence of the doorway which you'd never have found unaided. Anything like that—something in a book, or behind a hidden panel there was no other clue to, that sort of thing would certainly weigh with me.'

Joyce said, 'I must go and see to Magdalena,' and left the room. Nick was screaming quietly and rocking from side to side.

'Oh, ballocks, darling,' he said. 'What if something does weigh with you? Why don't you leave him alone and let him forget about it? Sorry, Dad, I know you're still here. Nobody wants to see ghosts or think they see them or whatever you prefer. Can't do you any good, even if it is all only in your mind—worse if it's that, in fact. As I said, Dad, drop it. If there's nothing in it there's nothing in it. If there's something in it, nobody with any sense would want to know.'

Putting her hands on her knees, Lucy gave a pedagogical sigh. 'Ghosts can't harm you. They aren't *there*, as I explained earlier.'

'You could get driven, uh, get pretty disturbed by buggering about with that kind of thing.'

'That's up to the person. No ghost can drive anybody out of their mind, any more than a human being can. People go out of their minds because of something about them, inside them.'

I knew, without looking, that Nick was making a face at his wife. Neither spoke. I said I would go and lie down for an hour and then probably reappear for a final drink or two and some more chat, if anybody wanted any. In the passage outside I ran into Joyce.

'Dinner's ready,' she said. 'I was just coming to——'

'I don't want any, thank you.'

'You ought to eat something.' She sounded unconvinced.

'I'm not hungry. I might have a bit of cheese later.'

'All right. Where are you off to now?'

'Going to have a little nap.'

'And then you'll get up about the time I'm coming to bed and go and talk to Nick and then sit on your own with the whisky-bottle until about two o'clock and tomorrow I'll see you at lunch and after that in the bar in the evening with everybody else there and so on like today and yesterday and that's what you and I are going to do tomorrow.'

This was a very long speech for Joyce, and was charged with resentment. I decided not to ask her what of it, and said instead, 'I know. I'm sorry, darling. This is a busy time of the year.'

'Every time of the year is a busy time. That's no reason why we should never see each other.'

I thought how pretty she looked, leaning against the wall of the passage just next to one of my hunting prints—prettier even than Diana, her full but finely proportioned body shown off by her blue silk dress, yellow hair smoothly piled up to reveal her handsome ears. 'I know,' I said.

'Then do something about it I'm your business partner and housekeeper and Amy's stepmother and that's it.'

'Is it? I make love to you too, don't I?'

'Sometimes. And lots of people make love to their house-keepers.'

'I haven't noticed you being a very active stepmother, I must say.'

'I can't be it on my own. You and Amy have got to join in, and neither of you ever do.'

'I don't think this is the time, the right day to start——'

'It's the right day of all days. If you've got nothing in particular to say to me the day after your father dies, what would have to happen to make you talk? I can't remember the last time we ... No,' she said, catching my wrists as I stepped forward and tried to embrace her, 'I don't count that. That's not talking.'

'Sorry. Well, when would you like to have a talk?'

'Talk, not have a talk, and when's no good. Hopeless. There's no time now, anyway. You go and have your nap.' She walked past me.

Some talk was certainly going to be called for, I reflected, not only in order to get Joyce into bed with Diana and me, but as prelude to that conversation. I must start working on that first thing in the morning. Meanwhile there was work (of an unexacting sort) to be done.

I went into the dining-room, where four covered pots of soup stood on the table, and moved over to the bookshelves to the left of the fireplace. Here I kept two or three dozen works on architecture and sculpture, and a hundred or so plain texts of the standard English and French poets, stopping chronologically well short of our own day: Mallarmé and Lord de Tabley are my most modern versifiers. I have no novelists, finding theirs a puny and piffling art, one that, even at its best, can render truthfully no more than a few minor parts of the total world it pretends to take as its field of reference. A man has only to feel some emotion, any emotion, anything differentiated at all, and spend a minute speculating how this would be rendered in a novel—not just the average novel, but the work of a Stendhal or a Proust—to grasp the pitiful inadequacy of all prose fiction to the task it sets itself. By comparison, the humblest productions of the visual arts are triumphs of portrayal, both of the matter and of the spirit, while verse—lyric verse, at least—is equidistant from fiction and life, and is autonomous.

However, the book I had come to fetch lay in none of the categories mentioned. It was Joseph Thornton's massive *Superstitions and Ghostly Tales of the British Folk*, in the second edition of 1838. I took it down from the shelf, poured myself a medium-sized Scotch (say a triple bar measure) and went and sat in my red padded-leather bedroom armchair.

Thornton devotes nearly three pages to Underhill in his chapter on 'Magicians and Conjurors', but the greater part of the passage concerns Underhill's alleged reappearances in supernatural form during the century and a half or so after his death, together with an account of that other being said to have been heard making its rustling, crackling progress round the outside of the house after dark. The treatment of the murders and their aftermath is less full; through lack of time or sheer absence of surviving evidence, as opposed to just talk, Thornton failed to establish any tangible link between Underhill and the two unsolved killings, and had to be content with recording the strength and persistence of the tradition—among people in Baldock and Royston as well as in the surrounding hamlets—that the man had acquired the 'mysterious and evil art' of striking from a distance at those foolhardy enough to cross him, 'of causing his victims to be torn to pieces by hands that were not mortal, so that a villager would not pass his house, by day no more than by night, for dread that the nefarious Doctor's eye would light upon him and find in him a fresh object of fear or hate.'

With no clear idea of what I was looking for, I read inattentively through the four or five long paragraphs, or rather re-read them for the dozenth time. Then, towards the end, I came to a couple of sentences I could not remember even having seen before:

'... Such were the events attending the obsequies of this infamous creature, for such I hold him to have been at the least, whatever be the truth of the copious testimonies to his wizardry. His effects, whether by chance or by malignity, appear to have been dispersed: the greater proportion of his books and papers suffered destruction at a fire on his premises (for which I can find no cause adduced) the second day following his death; some small part, at his own request, was buried with his person; a fragment of a journal survives in the library of his college, All Saints' at Cambridge. Of this relic it should be said, that it is not worth the pain of perusal, save by him whose curiosity in the manners of that still barbarous age may be sufficient to abate his natural aversion from the task.'

I thought I saw something faintly odd about the last part of this. Why should Thornton, normally keen to infect his readers with his own enthusiasms, to the extent of (perhaps too often) exhorting them to go and look up his sources for themselves, have mentioned this bit of journal, together with its location, and then warned them off taking the trouble to 'peruse' it? Well, any mystery here might easily be cleared up tomorrow. If that Underhill manuscript had been in the All Saints' library in the early nineteenth century, there was a good chance that it was there still. Anyway, I was going to drive to Cambridge in the morning and find out. I could not have said why I was immediately so determined to do this.

Between the pages of the *Superstitions* concerned with Underhill, I used to keep a few papers relating to him that had 'come with the house', chiefly Victorian local-newspaper cuttings of no great interest, but including a statement made by a servant at an earlier period. In the past, I had dismissed this too as dull, and had not looked at it for four or five years, but now I felt it was important to me. I unfolded the stained, dry single sheet.

'I, *Grace Mary Hedger*, chamber maid in the service of *Samuel Roxborough, Esquire*, being xlix yrs of age, & a *Christian*, do solemnly avouch and declare, that yesterday evening, the third day of March, A° D. MDCCLX, at about v o clock, I enterd the little parlour [then part of what was now the public dining-room] about my tasks, & there saw a Gentleman standing near the window. His cloathes somwhat like the cloathes of old Revd Mr *Millinship* I saw when I was a young girl. His complection very pale, but scarrd wth red, his nose long & turnd to the side, his mouth like a woman's. He apeard in distress of mind. When I asked him his pleasure he was there no longer, he did not quit the chamber, of a sudden he was not there. I was much affrighted & shreikd & swoond & my mistress came to me. I would not see such a Gentelman again for an hunderd poun. All this I swear.'

Grace Mary had added a careful signature and somebody called William Totterdale, rector of the parish, who had obviously written out the statement, had been a witness. Between them they had put my mind at ease, on one matter anyhow: the three accurately expressed facial details were enough on their own, without the reference to a kind of clerical garb to which the nearest parallel in Grace's experience would have been what she remembered having seen an old clergyman wearing in the 1720s. I drank to her and blessed her for her powers of observation and recall.

Through no fault of hers, on the other hand, her service to me was limited. I could not tell Lucy or anyone else, including myself, that I had not read the affidavit before. It was possible—I disbelievingly supposed it to be just possible—that my earlier couple of readings had impressed the facts on some buried part of my mind, from which something had dredged them up to create an illusion. What that particular something might have been was in itself mysterious, because any thought of Underhill's ghost I had about my mind at the time had also been pretty deeply buried, but that sort of problem is no problem in an unphilosophical age in which lack of total disproof is taken as the larger half of proof.

I had refolded Grace's statement and was about to close the book on it and the other papers, when my eye fell on another passage of Thornton's I had forgotten, more precisely on a single phrase in brackets in the middle of his account of the unseen nocturnal prowler: 'which some suspect to have been the Doctor's agent'. At once I saw what I should have seen earlier, or had seen without knowing what it was I saw. The witness who had disagreed about the expression on the face of Underhill's ghost had not really disagreed at all: they had seen him as he had been in life at different times, separated perhaps by a matter of seconds. He had had a look of clinical curiosity as he waited to find out just what sort of creature he had conjured up out of the wood, and this look had changed to one of horror when it came into his view on its way to tear his wife or his enemy to pieces. And this creature, or its phantom, had somehow not been fully laid to rest at Underhill's death, had from time to time tried to find its way into its former controller's house—for further instructions? And it had made the sound of moving branches and twigs and leaves as it walked because that was what it consisted of. And if I had been able to wait long enough in the copse that afternoon, I would have seen it too; it, or its phantom.

The whole left half of my body, including arm and leg, shook emphatically to and fro four times. My immediate thought was that I had now started to experience jactitation while fully conscious, and this filled me with fear, until I realized that I had merely shivered from fear, the double fear I had already felt at lunch-time, fear both of what had come into my mind and of the fact that it had done so and was going to stay there. I did not know anybody well enough, I could not imagine anybody knowing anybody well enough, to be able to tell him or her a tale like this. Perhaps I would have found this a less unlikely concept if I had not recently passed from being a notorious drunk to being a notorious drunk who had begun to see things, but I doubt it. Anyway, I was going to have to deal with this myself, without any clear idea of what this was or what dealing with it would entail. Thought was going to be necessary: that much could be glimpsed. I tried to do some thinking now, and got to the point of perceiving that the reason why Thornton had found no clear link, almost no link at all, between Underhill and the wood creature was that he had never visited the copse (or, if he had, whatever conditions had been operating six hours ago had been absent then). That was the farthest I could go for the moment. I felt I had had enough of my own company for a bit, whatever the disadvantages of swelling the number. I went to the bathroom, washed briefly, threw some after-shave lotion round my face to vie the fumes of whisky and set off down to the bar.

I was back up again in half an hour, after chatting with a couple of businessmen from Stevenage and a young farmer from round about who was rich enough to be doing his farming on purpose, so to speak. As I remounted the stairs, I found I had forgotten every word of the conversation, not by way of the instant-amnesia process I had had the benefit of twice earlier, but owing to that alcohol-fuelled unmemorability that does something to make middle age less intolerable, however coarsely tuned it may become with use. On the landing I was ready for an appearance of the woman with auburn hair, presumably Underhill's wife, and a tractable spectre by local standards; but she was not to be seen. Then, finally, just at the apartment door, I had a moment of simple selfish joy at the memory of what had happened in the hollow by the wood, and in that moment experienced a genuine hallucination, wonderfully and purely tactile, of Diana's naked flesh against my own. It has never surprised me that some men should try to beat Don Juan's traditional total, only that more do not. Seduction is the unique sensual act; other pleasures, including sex *per se*, are mere activities, durative and repetitive. Each particular seduction is a final and unchangeable thing, a part of history, like a century before lunch or a winning try (few of which carry the bonus of orgasm). And a sculpture can become nothing but a stale grotesque, a poem lose all its edge, but nothing of the sort can happen to what you got up to that night with the princess or the barmaid.

In the dining-room, the three of them were sitting over coffee. No drink had been so much as poured. While they struggled with the silence that had arisen at my entry, I got myself a glass of claret and started on some bread and a piece of Cheddar. In an under-rehearsed way, Nick said casually that, since he happened to have brought a bit of work with him and nothing was going on at the university, he would—if convenient, and only if—welcome the chance of a couple of days off from young Josephine, who was teething again, and stay on for the funeral. Lucy would return for this occasion, if that was all right, but meanwhile intended to go back home the following morning. I said that that and everything else would be all right.

Outside, I could hear men and women coming out of my house, standing about and chattering, getting into their cars and driving away, a series of sounds that always filled me with momentary animation and sadness and unconsidered envy. In the room, tonight as every night, the old Roman, the Elizabethan boys, the French officers and the French girl looked better than by day, more assimilated into the rest of the environment, though no less to be felt as presences. The humidity seemed to have increased again; at any rate, there was sweat on my forehead and at the roots of my hair.

Joyce said, 'Isn't it incredible to think that last night Gramps was just as much alive as any of us?' She was never one to be put off a disturbing remark merely by its obviousness.

'I suppose it is,' I said. 'But it's not the sort of thing anybody spends much time trying to take in, even in a situation like this, where you'd imagine none of us would be able to get our minds off it. That's what's really incredible. And I honestly can't see why everybody who isn't a child, everybody who's theoretically old enough to have understood what death means, doesn't spend all his time thinking about it. It's a pretty arresting thought, not being anything, not being anywhere, and yet the world still being here. Simply having everything stopping for ever, not just for millions of years. And getting to the point where that's all there is in front of you. I can imagine anyone finding themselves thoroughly wrapped up in that prospect, especially since it's where we're going to get to sooner or later, and perhaps sooner. Of course, it's not really true to say that that's all that's going to be in front of you. There are all sorts of other things thrown in, like waiting to see the doctor, and fixing up to have a test, and waiting for the test, and waiting for the result of the test, and fixing up another test, and waiting for that, and waiting for that result, and going in for a period of observation, and being kept in, and waiting for the operation, and waiting for the anaesthetist, and waiting to hear what they found, and waiting for the second operation, and waiting to hear how that went, and being told they can unfortunately do nothing radically curative but naturally all measures will be taken to prolong life and alleviate suffering, and that's where you *start*. A long way to go from there before you get to the first lot of things that are turning up for the last time, like your birthday and going away and going out to dinner, and then the rest of those things, like going out anywhere and going downstairs and getting into bed and waking up and lying down and shutting your eyes and beginning to feel drowsy. And that's where you start, too.'

'It doesn't happen like that to everybody by any means,' said Joyce.

'No, I quite agree for some people it's much worse. And I'm leaving out things like pain. But for most of us it's either what I've said or it's like what happened to my father. With reasonable care and a hell of a lot of luck you might last another ten years, or five years, or two years, or six months, but then of course again on the other hand as I'm sure you'll appreciate trying to be completely objective about the matter you might not. So in future, if there is any, every birthday is going to have a lot of things about it that make it feel like your last one, and the same with every evening out, and after four of your five years or five of your six months the same with most things, up to and including getting into bed and waking up and the rest of it. So whichever way it turns out, like my father or like the other lot, it's going to be difficult to feel you've won, and I don't know which is worse, but I do know there's enough about either of them to make you wish you could switch to the other for a bit. And it's knowing that every day it's more and more likely that one or the other of them will start tomorrow morning that makes the whole business so riveting.'

Nick stirred and muttered. Lucy, after glancing at me to make sure I felt I had done about enough maundering for the moment, said, 'The fear of death is based on not wanting to consult fact and logic and common sense.'

'Oh, in that case I'll pack it up right away. But it isn't exactly fear. Not altogether. There's a bit of anger and hatred, and indignation perhaps, and loathing and revulsion, and grief, I suppose, and despair.'

'Isn't there something egotistical about all those feelings?' Lucy sounded almost sorry for me.

'Probably,' I said. 'But people usually feel bad when they realize they're on one of the conveyor-belts I was talking about. Which makes it natural, at any rate, to feel something of the same when you realize we're all on conveyor-belts to those coveyor-belts from the moment we're born.'

'It's all right, Nick, I'm trying to be helpful, really. Natural, yes. But it's natural to be all sorts of things it'd be better if we weren't. Being afraid of the dark, for instance; that's natural. But that's one we can do something about, by using reason on it. The same with death. To start with, death isn't a state.'

'That's what I don't like about it.'

'And it isn't an event in life. All the pain and anxiety you've been talking about can be very horrible, no doubt, but it all takes places in life.'

'That's what I don't like about life. Among other things, let it be said.'

'I mean you're not going to be hanging about fully conscious observing death happening to you. That might be very bad and frightening, if we could conceive of such a thing. But we can't. Death isn't something we experience.'

'What we experience up to that point is quite bad enough to satisfy me. The ancient Assyrians believed in immortality without heaven or hell or any form of other world. In their view, the soul stayed by the body for eternity, keeping watch. Keeping watch for not a hell of a lot in particular, I suppose, but anyway *there*. Some people seem to think that's a dreadful idea, worse than extinction, but I'd settle for it. Having somewhere to be.'

'But nothing more than be, apparently. How would you

spend the time? I'm sure you'll have realized there'd be plenty of it.'

'Oh yes. Well, thinking. All that kind of thing.'

'I'm going to bed,' said Joyce. 'Laundry in the morning. Good night, Nick. Good night, Lucy.' She kissed them both, then said mechanically to me, 'Don't be too late.'

While she departed, I got myself a Scotch and water. Nick was looking compliantly bored. Lucy seemed to be taking a minute or two off, as between one seminar topic and the next. After pouring herself a careful half-cup-and-no-more of coffee, and adding perhaps a minim-of milk, she said,

'Uh, uh-Maurice, I take it you don't allow any possibility of survival after death?'

'Christ no. I've never believed in any of that crap, not even when I was a boy. To me, it's always been a matter of a sleep and a forgetting, beyond all question. The other thing is egotistical, if you like. And so outré, somehow. Fit for madmen only. Why?'

'Oh, I was just thinking that one of the traditional parts of the case for belief in some sort of hereafter is the existence of ghosts, which usually resemble actual people known when alive, and behave like them too, just as they would if they'd come back from beyond the grave.'

'But according to you earlier on, ghosts don't really exist as entities, and seeing one is seeing something that isn't there.'

'Yes, I'm not changing my mind. I don't believe myself that ghosts are there in that sense, but there's an arguable case that they are. And I have to admit that some ghosts do put on a remarkable show of having momentarily wandered back into our world from some place they went to after they died physically. I don't mean so much the haunted-room sort of ghost, like the ones here; I'm thinking more of the sort that turn up under the most ordinary circumstances, sometimes by day, and speak to someone, often a person they knew well in life. Like the airman who walked into his friend's room one afternoon and said hallo to him five minutes after he'd been killed in a crash and hours before the friend heard about it. Or the woman who'd been dead for six years who appeared on the doorstep of her sister's house at her usual time for coming to see her, only the sister had moved in the meantime, and the new occupant recognized the dead woman from a photograph the sister showed him. And even your friend Underhill ... There's one point in what you say happened in the dining-room tonight that takes him out of the category of the ordinary revenant kind of ghost.'

I judged that Lucy was fully capable of going to her grave without ever saying what this point was unless I prompted her, so I prompted her. 'Namely?' I said, with that sensation of taking part in Armchair Theatre on TV from which I suffered much more often, indeed continually, when dealing with Diana.

'The fact, at least you say it's a fact, that Underhill recognized you. Of course, he might just have mistaken you for someone else, but if he did really recognize you, then there's an obvious case for saying that he is in some sense or other existing in the twentieth century, having died physically in the seventeenth—existing to the extent of being able to perform at any rate one kind of action, involving intelligence, memory and so on: recognition. There's no knowing what else he may be able to do. Not at the moment, that is. But, given your views on death, I should say it's more than ever up to you to try and get in touch with what you believe to be Underhill's ghost.'

Nick had begun to twist about slightly in his seat. 'Oh, *Lu.* Get in touch with a ghost? How do you do that?'

'I was saying earlier, your father could see if he could touch the woman he thought he saw, or really saw—I've never denied that that's a genuine possibility—or try to get her to speak to him if she appears again, and the same applies to Underhill. He seemed to hear his name being spoken tonight. I still don't think it was Underhill, but your father does. In his place, I'd spend as much time as possible sitting in that dining-room while it's not in use and waiting for Underhill to reappear. He might speak next time. From your point of view, that's logical, don't you agree ... Maurice?'

'*Christ*, Lu,' said Nick before I could answer. (I would have answered yes.) 'Dad doesn't want to sit up in the middle of the night waiting to see a sodding ghost. That would be asking for trouble for anyone who was doing it. I tell you, farting about with this type of stuff doesn't do anybody any good. Look at the shags who go in for mediums and séances and psychic phenomena and the rest of it. Raving nuts, the lot of them. And stop being so *interested* in this thing. Dad just feels very low and a bit confused and he's got Gramps on his mind. *Leave* it, Lu.'

'All right, I will. But you think everybody goes by mood because that's the way you work yourself. You're bloody bright, Nick, but on almost everything except Lamartine you muddle up what you think with how you feel. I prefer to take what your father says at face value. But I promise to drop it. I'm off to bed now anyway. See you both in the morning.'

'You mustn't take too much notice of Lucy,' said Nick when we were alone. 'She misses the old cut-and-thrust of academic discussion up there. I'm no good to her on that one, and the faculty wives can't follow two consecutive remarks on any subject. She's all right, actually. I know you can't understand what I see in her, and I'm not sure I can myself, but I love her. Anyway. How are you really feeling, Dad?'

I hesitated. I had not until that moment thought of what I now urgently wanted to say, any more than I had consciously rehearsed a single word of my diatribe about death, which, it occurred to me belatedly, I had delivered as if I had had it by heart. I stopped hesitating. 'I feel I ought to have done more for Gramps. I don't just mean what everybody's bound to feel, about wishing you'd been more considerate and nicer and everything. I could have tried to help him live longer. For instance, perhaps those walks of his were too taxing. I ought to have thought about that, talked to Jack Maybury and so on.'

'Look, to begin with, Gramps wasn't your patient. And Jack's a good doctor; he knew what was best for him. And he was a vigorous old boy; he'd have died a bloody sight sooner, out of misery, if he'd been cooped up in the house all the time. Don't worry about that.'

'Mm. Would you like a whisky, or a beer?'

Nick shook his head. 'You have one.'

While I poured, I said, 'And the stairs here, they're very steep. I ought to have tried——'

'What could you have done? Put in a lift? And I don't think climbing stairs gives you strokes, does it? That's heart, I thought.'

'I don't know.' I hesitated again. 'It made me think of your mother.'

'Mum? What's she got to do with it?'

'Well, I . . . feel responsible for that too, in a way.'

'Oh, Dad. The only people responsible were the chap driving the car, and perhaps Mum herself a bit, for crossing the road without looking properly.'

'I've always wondered whether she stepped out deliberately.'

'Oh, Christ. With Amy holding her hand? She'd never have risked anything happening to Amy. And why should she?

Knock herself off, I mean.'

'That bit's obvious. Thompson letting her down.' Thompson was the man for whose sake Margaret had left me, and who had told her, four months before her death, that he was not after all going to leave his wife and children and set up a home with her.

'That's Thompson's headache, if it's anybody's, which I don't believe.'

'I ought to have tried to stop her going.'

'Oh, balls. How? She was a free agent.'

'I ought to have treated her better.'

'You treated her well enough for her to stay with you for twenty-two years. This is a load of crap, Dad. What's bothering you isn't that you were in any way responsible for her death, but that she died. Same with Gramps. Both those things remind you that you'll be going the same way yourself one of these days. I know you'll hate me taking a leaf out of Lucy's book, but that is egotistical. Sorry, Dad.'

'Okay. You may be right.' He was certainly right about the first part of it—the small but permanent despair, and the illogical feeling of dread, that come from having spent so many years with a dead woman, talked, met people, gone to places, eaten, drunk with her, most of all (of course) made love to her, and had children by her. Even now I woke up three or four mornings a week assuming that Margaret was still alive.

'How's Amy?' asked Nick. 'From the look of her . . .'

I stopped listening as I heard, or thought I heard, a rustling noise at ground level outside the house, near the front door. I jumped up, ran to the window and looked out. The overhead lights were still on, showing walls, flowerbeds, road and verges as colourlessly empty as if nobody had ever been near them. The noise had stopped.

'What's up, Dad?'

'Nothing. I thought I heard someone at the front door. Did you hear it?'

'No. Are you all right?' Nick looked warily at me.

'Of course.' It disturbed me that what I might or might not have heard, and identified, had happened immediately at the mention of Amy. I had no idea why I made this connection. I tried to think. 'There's . . . been some talk of a burglar in the district. You were saying.'

'Did you see anything?'

'No. Go on.'

'All right. I was just wondering how Amy feels about Mum's death these days.'

'I suppose at that age you forget a lot quite quickly. You put things behind you.'

'But has she? What does she say about it?'

'We haven't gone into any of that.'

'You mean you haven't discussed it with her at all? But surely——'

'You try asking a kid of thirteen how she feels about having her mother knocked down and killed in front of her eyes.'

'No, *you* try.' Nick stared at me. 'Look, Dad, for some reason you've got death on the winkle. That's all right with me, as long as you keep it as a sort of hobby. But one can't afford to let a hobby get out of hand, so that it stops you paying attention to what's really important. You must talk to Amy about this business. I'll set it up for you if you like. We could all——'

'No, Nick. Not yet. I mean give me a chance to think about it first.'

'Sure. But I'm going to bring it up again, if that's all right. Or even if it isn't all right, actually.'

'It is all right.'

Nick got up. 'I'm buggering off now. I'm afraid I haven't been much use to you today.'

'Yes you have. Thank you for coming down, and for staying.'

'A breeze. I'm afraid I've spent most of the time telling you what to do and what not to do.'

'I probably need that.'

'Yes, you do. Good night, Dad.'

We kissed and he went. I drank more whisky. The items on my personal agenda seemed impossibly many and varied. For a time I walked about the room and stared at each of the sculptures in turn. They suggested nothing to me, and I found I could not imagine what I had ever seen in any of them, whether as works of art or as quasi-people. I heard a scratching at the door and let Victor in. He bounded past me, impelled perhaps by the fragments of some memory of having been disturbed by Nick's passing within earshot. I stooped down and began to stroke him; he strained against my hand, purring like an old-fashioned and not very distant motor-bike. When I settled in my reading-chair by the bookshelves, he joined me, and made no objection to my using his back as a desk. The book I opened on him was the Oxford text of Matthew Arnold's poems. I tried to read 'Dover Beach', which I had often thought an acceptable, if rather prettified, account of life in general. Tonight I found something too easy in its stoicism, and that

> *darkling plain*
> *Swept with confused alarms of struggle and flight,*
> *Where ignorant armies clash by night,*

supposed such a grim and realistic contrast to dreams of romance, sounded quite an interesting, worth-while area to find oneself in. I made a second attempt at the poem, but this time could not follow its argument for more than a line together.

After a little more whisky, I put the book and Victor down and walked about the room again. Father, Joyce, Underhill, Margaret, the wood creature, Amy, Diana: a novelist would represent all these as somehow related, somehow all parts of some single puzzle which some one key would somehow unlock. As it were. One—thousand—two—thousand—three—thousand—four—thousand—five—thousand—six ... If nothing whatever happened before I reached a hundred, or better say two hundred, or two hundred and fifty would be a nice round number—then Joyce and I would end up with a good marriage and we would both be all right with Amy. How the first part of this hope fitted in, or failed to fit in, with the orgy project—nineteen—thousand—twenty—thousand—twenty-one—thousand—I had no idea, and did not want to have one, and I was not much better informed about what the fulfilment of the second half would feel like. I poured more whisky—thousand—twenty-nine—thousand—thirty ...

... thousand—eighty-seven—thousand—eighty-eight—thousand ... I was slowly but efficiently climbing the stairs up to the apartment. In my right hand was an empty glass, the one I had been using for some time; the little finger of my left hand was pressed against the palm, the other four digits stiffly extended. This meant a total of nearly five hundred thousand, the equivalent of over four minutes, or, assuming I had passed that total and was counting back towards the thumb, seven hundred thousand, or, of course, fifteen hundred thousand (over twenty minutes) or seventeen hundred thousand, or more. I stopped counting. I was going up to bed, but where had I been?

My watch said ten to two. I had been downstairs for a

period I could not after all measure, and could not even estimate as between half an hour or less and about two hours. Altogether, the dining-room was a good bet. I went back, opened its door and turned on the lights. In my late-night wanderings round the house, I remembered having seen it plenty of times like this, and must in fact have seen it more often still: the heavy silk curtains drawn, the tall chairs neatly grouped in their twos and fours and sixes, most of the tables bare, those by the window laid for breakfast, the whole place looking as permanently empty as the exterior view I had had earlier from the upstairs dining-room. However, I felt certain that this was the first time tonight I had seen what I now saw.

Feeling certain of that kind of thing is very far, in cases like mine, from being certain. I went quickly round the tables, examining them, with the self-directed sleuthing technique I had developed over the years, for traces of my own occupancy, like disarranged cutlery or a napkin unfolded to serve as a mat for my glass—I could never be (had so far never been) so drunk as to put it down on polished wood. Everything was in meticulous order, which proved either my absence or my assiduity in concealing my presence, and no more. Had I been here until just now? It seemed probable that I had, but no more probable than when I had thought it on the stairs. Had anything happened here? Yes; I felt certain, I almost was certain, that something had. What sort of thing? Something ... unusual, something not only interesting in itself, but opening further possibilities. Was I ever to know what it had been?

3 : The Small Bird

I had my answer the next morning. The first half-hour of the new day deserved to be forgotten at once. I had slept well enough for five and a half hours, without dreaming; I never dream, have not done so since I was a boy and can hardly remember what it was like. But I woke up with my heart going so irregularly that it seemed to have forgotten its business and to be treating each pulsation as a new problem that must be solved on its merits. The pain in my back lost no time in setting up an accompaniment. As I lay there beside Joyce, who as always made no sound and moved only in breathing, I reflected that neither heart nor back had drawn attention to themselves for several hours before I went to bed, and that Jack Maybury had more than once told me to arrange for plenty of things to be happening in my environment and then see if I was troubled physically. Well, he had a sort of case in point. Now, certainly, lying awake in near-darkness, I was shut up with myself in the smallest possible box.

I embarked on the tedious drills of getting up, all those dozens of actions that seem to carry no more meaning than a religious ritual performed by one who has forgotten its significance. Shaving in the bathroom, I discovered a new pimple at the side of my chin. From time to time, I still suffer one of these unengaging advertisements of the fact that losing the nicer parts of being young—whatever they may be—by no means guarantees the loss of the nastier parts. This particular example, in as flourishing a state as if it had been there for days, was too cunningly deep-seated for me to be able to nick off its top with my razor, nor, of course, could I have squeezed it out except at the price of messing up about a tenth of my face.

'Instructions to a pimple,' I said to myself as I worked on my upper lip. 'One. Acquire head *as slowly as possible*. Exception: if can arrange first appearance after six p.m., reverse this procedure. Prominent head viewed for first time morning after party, etc., valuable aid nullifying in retrospect subject's subtle seduction moves, gay fund of anecdotes, etc. Two. Select site either *where squeezing painful*, e.g. round eye, cheek near nose, or *where skin too soft for efficient squeezing*, e.g. between mouth and chin, at side of neck (if latter, prefer area where shirt-collar will rub). Three. Appear *in combination*, near existing pustule(s). If none, take as focal point patch of broken veins, mole, birthmark, anything a-bloody-tall, in fact' —I was talking aloud now, though not loudly—'which will aid the impression that some major skin disorder is about to break out of its beachhead and overrun every visible square inch up to the hairline, and be sure to pick a day when the poor sod's meeting his girl,' I finished not so not loudly, after a small disjunctive voice in my head had asked me whether I knew I had some frightfully funny sort of *spot* thing on my chin.

Things failed to pick up much in the kitchen, where I stood drinking coffee, eating a piece of toast and listening and looking while the chef told and showed me how badly Ramón had done his cleaning job the previous day. I put David on to that, on to everything else for the next six or eight hours too, and was off, at any rate as far as the office. Here I put a call through to John Duerinckx-Williams in Cambridge. For my present purpose, or indeed for any other I might have there, he was the only possibility among the dozen or so university people I knew otherwise than as guests at my house; I would not have asked any of those I had known as an undergraduate there, back in the mid-1930s, to tell me the time, let alone to help me with what must seem outlandish inquiries.

Despite everything the St Matthew's porter could do, I finally got hold of Duerinckx-Williams, who said he would see me at eleven o'clock. I was just about to go and find Joyce and tell her something of my plans for the day, when I caught sight of the cheap folio notebook in which I, and she and David too, used to scribble down reminders and messages. The left-hand pages were folded round against the back cover; on the topmost right-hand page there was some stuff about meat in David's hand, then, in my own, information in overwhelming detail, almost amounting to a *curriculum vitae*, from a London art dealer who had finally cancelled his booking and rung off abruptly when I told him we had no TV in the bedrooms. But that had been last week, ten days ago. Then I started to read something I thought at first I had never seen before, but soon realized I must have, because I had written it myself, at whatever hour of whichever night and however drunkenly. It ran:

'Accent like west of England with bit of Irish. Voice wrong, artificial. Something funny about movement, as if behind glass.

?no air displacement. Could not touch. Did not see hand going through, was like hand still ~~in front of h~~ between him and me even tho hand stretched out and he less than foot away. ~~Could not ask~~ Still 'injaynious' ? =poss[ess]ed of intelligence. No answer where. *Proof.* Behind head, body about 3″ by 1½, silver, arms out, left hand missing, smiling. ~~Wanted to~~

With what I might term shallow alcoholic amnesia, a man can be quite easily reminded of what he has temporarily forgotten. The deeper sort blots out memory beyond recall. This was the case here: I was prepared to believe that I had conversed with Thomas Underhill's ghost last night, but I would never know what it had been like to do so. I might do better next time; it seemed to me there was going to be a next time. If so, I must try to clear up some obscurities: exactly what, for instance, the 'proof' of Underhill's survival after death was supposed to prove, and also what it might consist of. The idea that he had been carrying or wearing some kind of giant silver brooch 'behind his head' was unhelpfully bizarre; I recognized that, like most of those whose midnight selves write notes to their daytime selves, I had thought some vital points too obvious and memorable to be worth the trouble of recording. At a future meeting, too, I might establish whether my account of trying to touch what I had seen and heard was a brilliant attempt to describe the indescribable or a straightforward result of drunken uncertainty about relative distances. Other questions could be cleared up at once, such as why I had written on a past page of the notebook—to conceal my story from others —and why I had nevertheless propped the book open at that place—not to conceal it from myself: a reconstruction almost too plausible to be likely.

I hurried upstairs and met Joyce on the landing. At first, she put on a not-speaking act, presumably by way of showing me how much she wanted me to talk to her, but soon abandoned this.

'What's happened?' she asked, looking me over.

'Happened? How do you mean?'

'You're all sort of excited. Charged up.'

It was true. Ever since receiving my own message, I had been mounting on a spiral of elation and disquiet, a state I was not used to. I suppose I was equally unfamiliar with the prospect of setting off to do something of which the end was unforeseeable. I could not even remember when I had last felt in any way strung up, as now, for a reason—not a very full or clear reason, certainly, but one with a sense of adequacy about it.

I decided to play all this down. 'Really? I must say I don't notice it particularly. Standard awful to bloody awful is how it feels from here.'

'Oh, all right. What are you going to Cambridge for?'

'To look up some stuff about the house, as I said.'

'How can that take all day?'

'It might not, as I said. It depends how soon I find what I'm looking for.'

'You're not, you know, meeting anybody there, are you?'

'I'm going to see Nick's old supervisor, yes, but not anybody in the sense you mean.'

'Mm. What's Nick going to do all the time?'

'He can please himself. He's brought some of his university stuff along. Or he could do something with Amy.'

'Why don't you take them both with you into Cambridge? There's a lot more there they could——'

'I'd have to hang about waiting for them, and I told you I might be coming more or less straight back. Anyway, I'm going on my own.'

'Oh, all right. You know Lucy's off this morning?'

'She'll be here again tomorrow for the funeral. But say goodbye to her for me if you like.'

'Do you want me to do the wages and stamps and things?'

'Would you? I must be off.'

I took a quick and fairly small nip in the still-room and was soon belting up the A595 in the Volkswagen. It was a genuine hot day, with the humidity down for once and the sunshine unfiltered by haze. Vehicles flashed and glistened as they moved, their bare metal seemingly burnished, their paintwork sheened with oil. They hurtled past me in the opposite direction, swung into and out of corners ahead, pulled aside to overtake as if with an extra dash, like actors conscious of appearing against an advantageous background. Even in the deep shadows of the trees lining the road, individual branches and clusters of leaves and patches of soil reflected light with an intensity, and yet with a depth of colour, that I was used to seeing only in Alpes-Maritimes. In the middle distance, re-fraction-mirages, illusory strips of still water lying across the road, constantly came into view and vanished. Beyond Royston, the confluence of the A10 and the A505 brought heavier traffic, but I kept my average up to forty-five or better. The outskirts of Cambridge rolled by, with the familiar thickening of wayside timber and shrub that suggests the approach to a forest rather than a town. Then this disappeared into the fen-land openness of the place itself, never crowded-looking even at mid-morning in term-time, and the landmarks were there: the Leys School, Addenbrookes Hospital, Fitzwilliam Street (where I had had digs when sitting my scholarship in 1933), Peterhouse, Pembroke and finally, more or less side by side with St Catherine's on the corner of Trumpington Street and Silver Street, the long bitten-off rectangle of St Matthew's, a flat-fronted Tudor structure not too badly restored at the end of the eighteenth century.

I found a parking space only a hundred yards from the main gate. The outer walls bore chalked or whitewashed slogans here and there: COMMUNALIZE COLLEGE ESTATES, NUDE LIE-IN GIRTON 2.30 SAT., EXAMS ARE TOTALITARIAN. First one whiskered youth in an open frugiferous shirt, then another with long hair like oakum, scanned me closely as they passed, each slowing almost to a stop the better to check me for bodily signs of fascism, oppression by free speech, passive racial violence and the like. I survived this, entered and cross the front court (which looked oppressively clean to my eyes), went through a low archway and ascended to the square panelled study-sitting-room that overlooked the long slope of the Fellows' garden.

Duerinckx-Williams, thin and dry-looking, with a stoop and paraded short sight although well over ten years younger than I, got to his feet and smiled at me fixedly. I had met him perhaps a dozen times on occasions involving Nick.

'Salut, vieux—entrez donc. Comment ça va?'

'Oh, pas trop mal. Et vous? Vous avez bonne mine.'

'Faut pas se plaindre.' Then he turned grave, or graver still. 'Nick told me of your loss. May I offer my sympathy?'

'Thank you. He was nearly eighty, you know, and hadn't been well for some time. It was no great surprise.'

'Wasn't it? In my experience'—he made it sound as if this went back to the time of the foundation of the college, give or take a century or so—'these things are never imaginable in advance. But I'm glad to see you're not unduly bowed down. Now, can I offer you something? Sherry? Beer? Port? Tea? Whisky? Claret?'

It was kind and intelligent of him to pretend, as usual, not to understand about drink, and so allow me to choose what I wanted without embarrassment. I said a little whisky would be very nice. While he got it for me, and made further show of incomprehension in pouring out rather more than half a gill, he came up with some amiabilities about Nick. Then, when we were sitting on either side of the splendid late-Georgian fire-place, he asked what he could do for me. I told him only of my interest in the history of my house and particularly in Under-hill, of a reference to his diary in a book I had come across and of my hope that he, Duerinckx-Williams, would telephone the librarian of All Saints' and assure him of my bona fides.

'Mm. How urgent is your desire to see this man's diary?'

'Not at all, really,' I lied. 'It's just that I so seldom get the chance of a day off like this, and I thought I'd take advantage of it. Of course, if it's going to be . . .'

'No no, I'll be happy to do all I can. It's merely that the librarian may not be there at this precise instant. At All Saints' everybody seems to tend not to be there so much of the time. But I can readily establish that. Would you excuse me a moment?'

He telephoned briefly and rejoined me.

'We're in luck, Maurice. He's not only there but also free of entanglements. Would you care for some more . . . of that?' he asked, pretending now to have forgotten what I had been drinking.

'Uh . . . no thank you.'

'In that case we might be on our way. No no, I assure you it's no trouble. Three minutes' walk at the most. As you know.'

Four minutes later we had passed through a carved wooden doorway of great age and were walking down the All Saints' library, a lofty and narrow room in the shape of an immense L, with some good Victorian stained glass in the windows at the angle. There was a characteristic smell, chiefly of dust and ink. The librarian came to meet us with a demeanour that managed to be haughty and deferential at the same time, like that of a West End shopwalker. There were introductions and explanations.

'Underhill,' said the librarian, whose name was evidently Ware. 'Underhill. Yes. Fellow of the college in the 1650s. Yes.' Then he said with great emphasis, 'Never heard of him.'

'Your manuscript collection is pretty extensive, isn't it?' asked Duerinckx-Williams.

'Oh, it's *extensive* all right,' said Ware, a little put out at this irrelevant reminder.

'Then a Fellow's personal papers, found here and inspected

soon after the beginning of the last century, as I understand the case ...?'

Ware relented a little. 'It's possible. There's an autograph catalogue dating from the 1740s, when the libraries first started taking an interest in manuscripts and older stuff generally. We rather led the way there, it seems. Here it is. Or rather its photocopy. Splendid invention. Underhill. Underwood, Aubrey. Several verses upon occasions, with part of *Philoctetes*, an heroical poem after the manner of Mr Dryden. How dreadful. That wouldn't be your man, would it? No. Wrong name, for one thing. Nothing by any Underhill. What a pity. I am sorry.'

'There's no other collection it might be in?' I asked.

'Not relating to the date you gave me, no.'

'But my author saw it in the 1810s or thereabouts.'

Duerinckx-Williams peered at the thin regular handwriting. 'In certain circumstances, such as the loss or detachment of the first leaf or leaves, might not the diary have been entered under some general head referring to anonymous writings?'

'Oh, I don't know about that,' said Ware, momentarily put out again. 'It's possible. Let's see. Yes, under Anonymous, in fact. Anonymous, a tract discovering the vices of Popery, notably its Mariolatrous practice, by a gentleman, never imprinted. Fascinating, but not your quarry, I think. Anonymous, a quantity of sermons, and prayers, and pious thoughts, by the late rector of St Stephen's, Little Eversden. No. Anonymous, of sundry matters, by a man of learning. Not over-informative, is it? A possibility, I suppose. Anonymous ...'

There were no other possibilities. Ware looked at me with gloomy expectancy.

'Could I have a look at those sundry matters?' I asked.

'All these items are kept in the Hobson Room,' said Ware forcefully, but without indicating whether I was expected to give a cry of pure animal terror at this disclosure, or burst out laughing to find my quest so comically and decisively thwarted, or what. I turned to Duerinckx-Williams.

'Which, I believe, is not open to non-Fellows without the written permission of the Master,' he said, 'but in the case of Mr Allington, who is an M.A. of my college and for whom I am happy to vouch, perhaps this requirement could be waived.'

'Of course,' said Ware, impatient now, and with a key already in his hand. Resuming his shopwalker manner, he added, 'Would you come this way?'

The Hobson Room turned out to occupy a whole floor of a tower at the opposite angle of the court, approached by a winding stone staircase and possessing small windows on three sides. It was cool, the first cool place I had been in for what seemed like weeks. Most of the available wall-space was filled with deep oak shelves of Edwardian pattern, and two working-tables and chairs of the same period completed the furniture. On the shelves stood ranks of grey cloth folders, presumably containing manuscripts. Ware began to examine the top outer corners of these like somebody looking through a collection of gramophone records. I could not watch him; I stood and tried to read a framed quarto page of some book that hung among others on the stone wall, but failed to take in a word.

'Here we are,' said Ware. 'Complete with fly-leaf, I see. Thomas Underhill, D.D., *olim Sodalis Collegii Omnium Sanctorum, Universitatis Cantabrigiensis.*'

He had to supply the last part from memory, because I had turned and taken the folder from him. It contained all or part of an octavo notebook shorn of its covers—there were traces of glue and stitching—and, apart from a little foxing, in an excellent state of preservation.

'An odd sort of anonymity, with the man's name plastered all over the front,' said Duerinckx-Williams.

'Thank you,' I said. I had seldom wanted anything as much as I wanted the two of them to go away and let me read what I held in my hands.

Duerinckx-Williams sensed this at once. 'We'll leave you in peace. If you happen to be free at one thirty or so, I'd be delighted to give you lunch at Matthew's. Just the ordinary combination-room stuff, but eatable as a rule. But you mustn't feel bound by that.'

'Perhaps you'd lock up when you leave and return the key to me in the library,' said Ware, handing it to me.

'Yes,' I said. I had the notebook open on one of the decks and a reading-light switched on. 'Thank you.'

There was a short pause while they presumably looked at each other or, for all I cared, went through a complicated mime of impotent fury, and then there was the clank of the iron latch.

Underhill had written a good clear hand, and had not used any private shorthand system: abbreviations were few and immediately understandable. He began, on June 17th, 1685 (he had died in 1691), by boasting to himself about how learned he was and listing and briefly describing the books he had read. Evidently he had had a considerable private library. Most of the works and authors mentioned were unknown to me, but I did recognize references to the Neoplatonist philosophers, who had been contemporaries of his at Cambridge, quite possibly acquaintances: Cudworth's *Intellectual System*, More's *Divine Dialogues* and a couple of others. I remembered from somewhere that More had been part of, or on the edge of, a circle that practised magic, including a sinister-sounding Dutch baron. What had he been called? Never mind—an interesting lead, perhaps, to the scholar, but I am no scholar, and my interest in Underhill was not scholarly.

I read on, found more of the same, together with mystical speculations either unintelligible or trite, and began to get bored. Was this all there was going to be? Then I came to the entry for September 8th:

'My man Gurney, on Instruction, adviz'd me that the Girl-child of Widow Tyler was come to the door, to sell Fruits & Vegetables. When this was done, enquir'd of her, Whether she wou'd take a cup of Chocolate w. mee in my Parlour, the day being so foul? She v. prettily consentg, we talk'd there together about half an hour. Told her of the Wonders I cou'd work, & how I was us'd to reward such as pleas'd me. She listen'd to all, & I warrant beleev'd all. At last, bid her, did she desire a fair Husband & Health, Wealth & Good Fortune all her life long, come to mee the night following at ten of the clock, but privily, & to tell none on pain of losing all her Benefits, for did she but breathe a Word I wou'd most infallibly know of it, thro' my Art. But, says shee, She was afear'd of the Dark of the Night. To wch I reply'd, That she must hold in her hand this Crucifix (givg it to her, a worthless Toy), & she wou'd enpoy the surest Protection, both of our Lord J.C. in Heaven, and of myself on Earth. She ask'd, If I wou'd say a strong Spell for her? My strongest, my Dear (smilg). Then (says she) I will come indeed.

'Of middle stature, good Carriage, full Bosom. Unlike the Country Folk, her Cheek not ruddy, but a fine rose, her Teeth white, her Hand small, a Lady's hand. Of fourteen year. I dare aver, Kg Solomon had not a finer Wench.'

After this interview, Underhill had evidently returned to his reading with the same diligence as ever: that afternoon, a Latin work on anemomancy, or divination by means of observing the strength, direction and steadiness of the wind, by a certain Alanus Candidus; after dinner, a life of another man I had never heard of by a third such. I felt that this detachment boded no good to Widow Tyler's daughter. With dread and fascination I turned on through Underhill's entry for the next day.

'Upon her most punctual arrival, gave my Visitor a Potion, compounded of Claret & Brandy-wine, w. certain Additions, after the Prescription of Jacobus Magus in his De Inductione Luxuriae. Set going my Brazier, & threw thereon an artful Succession of Incenses, Powders, & caet. from my store, thus producg most delightfull & lascivious Perfumes & also strange & many-colour'd Smoaks. When all these had sufficiently work'd upon her, caus'd her to beleeve she heard sweet Musick from many Voices, warblg amorous and wanton Airs. Then, conjur'd up Shapes to appear, at first pleasg, as, Shepheards & Shepheardesses, Nymphs, Gallants, Revellers, Catamites, Masquers, Hero's, Queens of Antiquity, some consortg carnally one w. another. Next, desir'd her to remove her Cloaths.

'Why, Sir, (says shee) you ask me to commit a Sin. Not so, my Dear, (says I) it is not at all sinful to requite w. a show of your Beauties, those who have labour'd to entertain you, & who so labour yet. See, (indicatg a Grecian Youth & a Maid in concourse) what these two are even now about, & solely to make you Sport. Solely? (asks she, slily). In part, you must allow (says I). Why then, (says she) how can I bee less *liberal* (a stroak of wit that delighted me). & at once stript herself to her naked Skin. O quae deliciae!

'Now show'd her Creatures not as attractive, as, Hippogriffs, Apes, Turks, Centaurs, Harpies, Chimaera's, Caribans, Executioners, Worms, all fightg & murtherg & devourg one another. Fill'd her ears w. cries of wild Beasts, & Thunders, & Groans of the Damn'd. She shreik'd without cease, & entreated mee to have done, & to banish these Sights. Shreik as you will, (says I) there is none to hear, my Servants are abroad, & these are no Sights, see how they are all about you & but for mee wou'd rend you in peeces (not tellg her they were mere Apparitions & cou'd not do any thing save affright her). When as I judg'd, she had reach'd the Pitch of Terror, ravisht her upon the Floor, & shortly thereupon drove her from my Presence, throwg her wretched Cloaths after her, & warng her it were best she spoke no word of what had past, else my Devils wou'd pursue her to the Grave & beyond, & she wou'd come to me again whenever I requir'd it of her, & she was mine.

'Took a glass of small Ale to quench my thirst, & retir'd to my Chamber, & open'd Johannes à Ponte upon the Venom of Toads & Serpents, but found the matter phantastick beyond credence, & ill set out, & being much fatigu'd, (tho' in ease of mind) took myself to my Bed.'

The Hobson Room seemed a good deal less cool than at first. I would have to have a drink soon—I had been mad not to bring a flask with me—but I had to put my thoughts in order first, or at least recite them to myself. Not in any order, then: I did not know whether Underhill had really conjured up apparitions and noises and the rest of it, or even what that meant, but I believed that he and the girl thought he had, and the experience seemed to have been quite frightening enough to seal her mouth permanently, for I had never come across the least suggestion that he had gone in for any kind of sexual adventure. I could not remember the date of Mrs Underhill's death, but fancied that it had been later than 1685, so that she had presumably been living in the house throughout this period, but without once being mentioned, not even in the entry I had just read. She must have known better than to interfere when she heard the girl's screams. I understood how Joseph Thornton had been too much of a scholar to conceal the existence and location of Underhill's diary, but too much of a moralist, or human being, not to warn his readers against it, and not to let it remain as hard to find as when he had managed to find it. Similar motives, the desire to preserve alongside the desire to thrust out of sight, must have worked on whoever had catalogued the diary seventy years before Thornton's time. And I would have liked to do something about Widow Tyler's daughter, but she had been dead for two and a half centuries, if not longer.

Ten minutes later, having been out and returned, I was eating a ham sandwich which I had coated with mustard-substitute from a tube, washing the result down with Scotch and bottled soda-water, and going on with the Underhill diary. By the time I was coming to the end of the year 1685, I became aware that the character of this was changing. The reading summaries became briefer, some works receiving no more than the notice that they were or were not useful to some 'purpose' kept in mind. At first, it seemed to me that this purpose had to do with the Tyler girl, who, also briefly, was described by Underhill as having 'return'd to [his] Embraces' every week or so, and/or with another girl called Ditchfield (I hated his way of ignoring their Christian names), aged twelve, whom he drew into his clutches in the first week of December, no doubt by a similar technique, though he was not very explicit about that. What had clearly been more interesting to Underhill at this stage was this long-term purpose of his, or, as it became in the entries for January 1686, his purposes. Maddeningly, just when I would have welcomed full information on the books he was reading, he started to mention nothing beyond authors and titles, often in a shortened form. I could do nothing with, for instance, 'Geo⁹ Verul. : Of spirits, & caet.' beyond concluding that at any rate Underhill's preoccupations had remained constant.

Then, at April 29th, 1686, I came to the following:

'Must cast aside fleshy Delights, & all such Concerns (for the moment.) Have now refin'd my Method, whereby I may cease to take heed to those who trouble mee. The place is fit, (id est, v. dense, horrid, of much Verdure & Timber sufficient.) What I hold een now, w. due words deliver'd, will most assuredly secure me such Power, as never was seen in this Kingdom, not even in it's Gothick or Saxon age, but only in the rude beginnings of our Folk, before the Ministry of Our Lord J.C., when men worshipt only Trees & Bushes, (in their silly Ignorance, or their Knowledge? Mem. to consider curiously upon this, & in time deliver Judgment.) I thank the chance that deliver'd this Engine to mee, & the Talent that empowers me to have learnt its true Employment.

'As to my 2nd, & larger, I mean not larger but INFINITELY GREAT purpose, I will say nothing at the present, but this, *Hee who knows my mind* cannot but know too, & for certain, What is the lastg Repository *where I have hid* what will enable him to aid this purpose &, in process learn the Secret which will render him *Master of Himself*, & who is master of himself is master of every thing (vide Carⁱ Voldemar Prov., Verum Ingenium).'

This almost filled up a right-hand page. When I turned over I found nothing more; the final twenty or thirty leaves of the notebook were blank. I poured more whisky and considered.

Thornton, as I had decided earlier, had not had the experience I had had in the wood above my house, and so had been unable to make anything of the reference to that wood on the last page of the diary. He must then have dismissed Underhill's first purpose as too nebulous to be worth recording, possibly as empty vaunting or delusion. As regards the second purpose, Thornton had not, again, had the benefit of a conversation with Underhill's ghost, as I had had, and could not have been expected to realize that this purpose had had to do with some form of survival after death. If Thornton had deduced the nature of the hiding-place referred to in the closing paragraph, he had no doubt been, as I could very well suppose from my reading of his book, too pious a man to contemplate disturbing the remains of a departed soul, even those of an 'infamous creature' like Thomas Underhill. I had no such inhibitions; and I was going to open that grave and coffin and see what 'books and papers' (as mentioned by Thornton) and other extras were to be found there.

As I sat on the hard scholar's chair with the diary before me, I felt as elated and unsettled as I had done just before setting off today—more so. I see well enough now that a little more prudence would have been in order, but at the time I was revolted by the thought of prudence. Until Diana came along, I had had nothing to be more than trivially imprudent about for years, and never anything on this scale. There might even be something in—anyway, something interesting about—the supposed secret which was going to render me master of myself. I, of all people, could afford to learn that sort of secret. Not that I had forgotten what had become of the promises Underhill had made to the Tyler girl, and presumably to the Ditchfield girl also. These two, in fact, figured somehow in my motives for going on with the investigation, though I could not then have said how or how importantly.

But, talking of Diana ... It was five-and-twenty to three, comfortable time to copy out Underhill's last page, pack up and lock up here, return the key to Ware in the library, leave a thank-you note for Duerinckx-Williams at St Matthew's lodge, drive down to Royston, have a furious argument there with the tiny wizened young man who supplied me with my drink and see to it that he would never again try to sell me pre-tax-increase stock at the increased price, go on to Fareham and the appointed corner and pick up Diana at three thirty.

That was just how it went. Diana's questionings covered some of the same ground as those of the previous afternoon, eventually branching out into the general topic of what it was, or what I thought it was, that made men so different from women, by and large an easier assignment. Then, before we had quite reached the hollow on the hill, she started stripping with creditable speed. Everything was rather different from last time. When she was naked, and I was still stepping out of my trousers, she lay down on her back, stared at me and moved about a good deal on the ground. As soon as I reached her, she made it very clear that what the books used to call fore-play was not needed now; in fact, I had no chance to so much as kiss her until after the main stage of the whole business had been set in vigorous motion. It seemed to go on for hours, with Diana showing incredible energy. Whether this was natural or assumed I did not bother to wonder then, and quite right too. The distinction is in any case a doubtful one: orgasm itself is a reflex, but nothing much that accompanies even orgasm can be called so (let alone what people get up to during other parts of the performance). Nor did I ask myself whether Diana was reaching that point as often as her behaviour claimed, or indeed at all. That is not my way at such times, and even more quite right too. The mystery, the emotional secretiveness, the self-distancing of women, all the luggage of feeling they go about with and expect men to handle for them—these and countless more concrete manifestations start, not from the minor circumstance that women carry and bear and rear children, but from the fact that they do not have erections and do not ejaculate. (And, while we are about it, it is the fact that men do that deprives the passive homosexual's role of any real depth or credibility.)

Ejaculation, as all good mistresses know, is a great agent of change of mind and mood. As, now, I lay beside Diana, it occurred to me first that she had been demonstrating her unpredictability: nothing but receptiveness yesterday, all positive action today. A moment later, perhaps more charitably, though perhaps not, I decided that yesterday she had been too excited not to behave as she really wanted to, whereas today's gymnastics were designed to make me admire her sexual prowess: a move from involuntary narcissism, so to speak, into the purposeful kind. What of it, anyway? Both kinds suited me.

I told her more or less how unpredictable she was, and this went down all right. I was ready with further material of the same sort when she said:

'About your idea that we all ought to go to bed, you and I and Joyce.'

'Yes?'

'I've been thinking about it.'

'Good.'

'Maurice.'

'Yes?'

'Maurice, what would you get out of it exactly? I mean, I can see what I'd get out of it, at least I think I can, but where would you come in? *No*, Maurice, you're not to be horrid and awful. You know what I mean.'

'I think so, yes. Well, seeing that it's so much fun to go to bed with one beautiful girl, it ought to be twice as much fun to go to bed with two, if not more. More than twice as much fun. Worth trying, anyhow.'

'Mm. You want to watch us at it, kind of thing, too, don't you?'

'Yes, I do rather. I've never been able to see anything wrong with the idea of watching people at it, provided that's not all you're doing, and that won't apply in my case, of course. And provided, as far as I'm concerned, that neither of the people is a chap, and that's not going to apply either.'

'I ... *see*. Would you want me to, well, be nice to Joyce as well as Joyce being nice to me?'

'You can do whatever you feel like doing.'

'No, but would you?'

'Well, yes.'

'Oh. Maurice ... Maurice, isn't part of this whole thing doing what you're not meant to do?'

'I expect so, yes. And as good a reason as any, by God.'

'You're not to be cross, but I think that's a jolly schoolboyish view.'

'Ah, so that's why it's got so much appeal.'

'Well, one thing to be said for a threesome is that Jack wouldn't approve,' she said abruptly, so much so that she got to the end of the sentence at about the time she would normally be drawing the first word to a close.

I opened my eyes, on the instinct that tells us that having done so we will be better prepared for whatever may follow, even when the view consists of as little as, in my case, an irreducibly near cheek and part of a nose and chin. 'There is that,' I said.

'I know all doctors screw their patients but he might at least take the trouble to pretend he's not,' she went on, sticking for the moment to her new policy of talking at ordinary human-being speed. Then she reverted to the old one. 'But—that's—nuh—thing, compared to what I've really got against him.'

Silence fell. One of these days I would bury her in an ant-hill up to her neck or feign sleep when she did this to me, but not today. 'What's that?'

'I hate him. I can't bear him.'

'You can't?' I may have sounded less mildly surprised than I felt. Diana so seldom provoked anything more than the merest flicker of reaction (apart from lust and annoyance in full measure) that I had probably got into a habit of overdoing the eyes and teeth.

'Of ... *course* I can't. *Sure*-ly you must know that. He doesn't mind me, because he doesn't mind a single blessed thing one way or the other, but I mind him like mad.'

'What don't you like about him?'

'Oh, everything. I've been trying to make up my mind to leave him for simply ages. But, Maurice, don't you think this is most peculiar?'

'... Isn't what most peculiar?'

'Well. That you've known Jack and I for three years or more, and you've never noticed the absolutely obvious and simple fact that I can't stand him. You really do not have, I suppose? I mean, you're not joking?'

'No.'

'Are you sure?'

'Yes. Yes, I'm quite sure.'

'*Maurice.*' She turned her head, and I saw a tremendous eye looking into one of mine. 'But that is simply the most extraordinary thing I've ever heard. A man like you, whom I've always thought was one of the most sensitive and observant characters one could wish to meet, and it's never struck you that I can't stand the man I'm married to, and you're supposed to be so frightfully interested in me.'

I was sure I had never seen or heard anything to suggest that Diana was on anything but—at worst—tolerable terms with Jack, but could not make out whether all this was aimed at justifying her dealing with me or, more likely but just as merely, constituted one more tactical move in her campaign to show me up as coarser in spirit than some other people round the place—herself, for instance. However, before I could devise some ramshackle confession of emotional inferiority, she had shifted a little away from me, as if to enable us to see each other's faces properly, but with a series of movements that involved her whole body. These continued while I watched her jaw sink and her eyes grow fixed in the doltish look they had taken on the previous afternoon. Arching her back, she said without hyphens,

'All right, let's do it. Whenever you like. I'll do whatever you like.'

I was so excited that it was all over quite soon, but I have never known a woman who did not set a high value on male excitement, and in that short space I was able to produce a compelling pot-pourri of everything that had happened between us before. That is denigrating it a good deal, actually. I cannot imagine ever quite forgetting what it was like, while I can remember anything. And if what set it off was a little impure, in at least two senses, then let it be impure. Alternatively, fuck you. Anybody who feels like saying that a particular sexual act of any ordinary sort, possibly of any sort at all, ought not to have been enjoyable is a monster, large or little.

On the drive back to the corner, Diana was subdued. I wondered whether this was a prelude to her making a bid for a new kind of interestingness by telling me she had changed her mind about the orgy project, but I could not wonder very hard or for long at a time because I was thinking how best to put another proposal to her, one just as tricky in its way. Finally I said,

'Diana, there's something else I want to ask you.'

'What, you and me and David Palmer?'

'No, quite different. I think I've found out about a place where there may be some buried treasure. Would you give me a hand looking for it?'

'Maurice, how frightfully exciting. What sort of treasure? How did you find out about it?'

'I came across some old papers to do with the house, just saying where the stuff had been put, nothing about what it consisted of. Of course, there may be nothing in it.'

'I see. Where is it?'

'Apparently, uh, it's in that little graveyard just up the road from the Green Man.'

'In a grave? In someone's coffin?'

'That's what the papers said, yes.'

'You're proposing to dig up a grave and open someone's coffin?' She was getting the idea fast.

'Yes. It's a very old grave and so on. There won't be anything in it but bones. And this treasure.'

'Maurice Allington, have you gone totally and completely out of your mind?'

'No, I don't think so. Why?'

'You can't be serious. Digging up a grave.'

'I assure you I am serious. I want that treasure. As I say, there may be nothing there at all, or something quite worthless, but you never know. I asked you to help because I must have somebody to hold the torch and lend a hand generally, and you're the only persoon I can ask who won't be shocked out of their mind.'

That went down very satisfactorily, but she still had a piece of finessing to do. 'It's not true, though, is it, about lending a hand? You want company. You're afraid to do it on your own.'

I nodded with pretended ruefulness. The last bit was not true either: if there was going to be anything out of the ordinary to see in that graveyard, I just wanted somebody else on hand to see it too. But I had not lied when I said that Diana was the only one I could ask. That was something substantial in her favour.

'Has it got to be at night?'

'Well, yes, I think so, don't you? with people passing by on the road all day long, and sterling chaps doing things to the soil. It shouldn't take more than half an hour or so.'

'There's no curse or anything on it, is there?'

'Oh, good God, no, nothing like that. The fellow was just after a safe place to stow a few things.'

'Oh, very well, then. I'll come along. It might be quite fun.'

'Out of the ordinary, anyway. What about tonight? No point in hanging about. Can you get away?'

'Of course I can. I do as I please.'

We had reached the corner. I arranged to pick her up at half-past midnight at a spot nearer her house. On the way back home, I stopped at the graveyard and looked Underhill's grave over with some care. I could foresee no special difficulty later: there was nothing in the way of a stone to lift, and the soil, when I prodded it, seemed to be as light as elsewhere in the area. Whatever the place might feel like in the dark, at five o'clock on a summer afternoon it was solidly un-eerie, giving no impression of age or decay, merely of rankness and dilapidation, heavily overgrown for the most part (though not in Underhill's corner), and littered with more ice-cream wrappers and beer-cans than fragments of headstone.

I drove to the Green Man, went upstairs and started on a quick drink before bathing and changing. I sat in a nondescript but comfortable armchair beside the fireplace, facing the window in the front wall. This had its curtains drawn, but there was plenty of light from the other window to my left, where the French girl stood. Amy's gramophone was playing some farrago of crashes, bumps and yells from her room down the passage. As I listened, or endured hearing it, the noise stopped abruptly. Sipping my Scotch, I waited half-consciously for another record to go on. How quiet it was by contrast; totally quiet, in fact. And that was not just odd, it was impossible. No inn is silent for more than a couple of seconds at a time, except for four or five hours between the last departure to bed and the stirrings of the first servant. I went to the door and opened it; there was no sound whatever. When I turned back to the room, I found that it looked different in some way, different, at any rate, from how it had looked when I entered it five minutes before. It was darker. But how could that be? Sunlight was streaming in as brightly as ever from the side window. Ah: it was the other window that was darker. There was no light at all showing between the curtains and at their edges. That was impossible, too. Feeling for the moment nothing but a great curiosity, I hurried over to those curtains and threw them apart.

Outside, it was night, absolutely dark it seemed at first, as if I had opened my eyes thousands of fathoms under water, at the sea bed. Then I saw it was not really as dark as all that: there was a three-quarter moon low in the sky, and no cloud to speak of. The horizon and the distance were the same as any night, except that a plantation of conifers just below the sky-line was missing. In the middle distance, small fields under cultivation replaced the areas of grassland I had always seen before. And in the foreground, immediately below me, the hedge lining the road had gone, and the telegraph-poles—of course—had gone, and the road itself had dwindled to a rough track. Although nothing moved, it was a living scene, not the equivalent of a still photograph.

I turned back to the dining-room, which was quite unchanged. My five sculptured people looked into space as ever, but for the first time I thought I found something slightly malignant in their impassivity. I crossed to the side window, and looked out on the familiar daytime landscape. As I watched, a light-blue sports car, a TR5 by the look of it, emerged from the direction of the village and moved, accelerating sharply but in complete silence, up the road towards the house. It did not—of course—come into view at the front window.

I stood and thought. There was an obvious case for rushing along to Amy and bringing her here, in the hope of proving to myself and everybody else that I was not seeing things, or rather that what I saw was really there, or at least that I was not insane. But I could not subject that child to the terror of either seeing what I saw, or finding that she and I were seeing differently. And, if I did go down the passage to her room, I was far from sure that I would find her there, or anything there that I knew.

At this point of irresolution, I heard voices below me, male and female, and then an outside door shutting at the front of the house, but it was not the sound of my front door. The woman I had twice seen on the landing came into view carrying a small lantern and set off towards the village—I caught the merest glimpse of her face, but her general outline and her gait left me in no doubt. Very faintly, the man's voice was again audible from the floor beneath, this time with a different intonation, one of a peculiar monotony, one I could identify, or, if I tried, name a close parallel to. Yes, a parson, a priest, intoning a part of the service that is best got over quickly.

The woman was almost out of my view; I could just see the swaying light of her lantern. Then I picked up a movement on the other side, from the direction of, among other things, what at this stage I need only call the wood. A tall and immensely broad figure came stumping awkwardly along the track, massive legs, apparently of not quite the same length, pounding away with the implacable vigour of machinery, long arms pumping in an imperfectly synchronized rhythm. If it had been human, it would have weighed twenty-five stone at least, but it was not human: it was made up of lumps of timber, some with thickly ribbed bark, some with a thin glistening skin, of bundles of twigs and of ropes and compressed masses of green and dead and rotting leaves. As it drew nearer, laboriously quickening its pace, I saw that its left thigh, the one nearer to me, was encrusted with a plate-like fungus, fragments of which fell off at every stride, and I heard the creaking and rustling of its progress. When it was exactly level with me, it turned its lumpish, knobbled head towards the house, and I shut my eyes, having no more desire to see its face now than when it had appeared to me before, in my hypnagogic vision of two nights ago. At the same moment, a cry of alarm or loathing came from beneath my feet; I knew that Underhill was at that very moment (whenever it was) watching from the window of the dining-room, which was now (my now) closed and empty.

When I opened my eyes again, the creature was beginning to move out of sight at a grotesque, lurching trot. I waited, wondering what I would do if this show simply went on and on, leaving me poised somewhere between Underhill's time and mine. If I could manage to get myself into the view I could still see by way of the side window, perhaps its sound would come back and I should be all right. But how was I to get there? I had listened, not looked, when I opened the door a moment earlier, but I had no doubt at all now that this room was the only part of the house that had not reverted to what it had been nearly three centuries previously. Through the side window and down the wall seemed the only possible route. I was beginning to be worried by the thought that that version of reality might turn out to be a visual hallucination, but then I heard screaming, not near by, perhaps two hundred yards away, but very clear in the utter silence, and very loud, and accompanied by another sound, also loud, a wailing or an unsteady hooting, like something quite often heard but inappropriate in the context, like a high wind, through trees. I put my fingers in my ears and went on staring at the now deserted nocturnal landscape in front of me. How long could I stand its going on being there?

Then, slightly to left of centre, and almost dazzlingly bright, and instantaneously, a light or flame sprang up, a yellowish green in colour. After a few moments another switched itself on, apparently in the sky and of tremendous size, like a sun, only jigsaw in shape and of a deep blue. There was a longer pause before two more such flared into being almost together, a second yellowish-green one near the first and another, larger blue one on the opposite side of the sky. The former of these, shaped like a fat, slightly jagged pillar, had a thin dark vertical bar running up nearly through the middle of it. I recognized this, at first without being able to name it, then saw that it was part of a telegraph-pole. Further lights appeared at short, irregular intervals, like splotches of molten metal thrown on to a dark photographic plate. Three of them coalesced to give me a view of some yards of sun-lit metalled road. I took my fingers out of my ears. More rapidly than any physical approach would have made possible, the noise of a car grew in volume outside. I heard men's voices and the sound of a front door being opened and shut—my front door. When there were only a few isolated patches of darkness remaining, the door into the room opened behind me.

I turned sharply. Victor galloped up, threw himself at my feet and fell on to his side. Behind him was Amy. I hurried to her and put my arms round her.

'What's happening, Daddy?'

'Nothing. It's all right. I was just feeling a bit sad.'

'Oh. Didn't you hear the screaming?'

'The what?'

'The screaming. Somebody in the street, it sounded like. A long way off, but sounding sort of as if it was near. Didn't you hear it?'

'Yes.' Trying to look and sound calm was such a severe effort that I could hardly speak. 'But ... weren't you playing your...?'

'I was between records and it was all quiet.'

'It wasn't dark outside, was it?'

'Dark? No. How could it be?'

'What sort of person was it who screamed, do you think?'

'You said you heard them.'

'Yes,' I said, picking up my whisky and draining it, 'but I want to hear what you thought.'

'Oh. Well ... it was a lady. She sounded very frightened.'

'Oh, I don't think it was that, darling. More like just one of the village girls having a lark.'

'It didn't sound like that to me.'

'Did you hear any other sort of noise?'

'No. Ooh yes. A sort of ... calling-out howling noise, or like someone singing without any words, just going on and on. And going up and down all the time. You heard it, didn't you?'

'Oh yes. Just people fooling about.'

Amy said nothing for a moment, then, 'Would you like to come and watch Pick of the Hits with me? It comes on at five forty.'

'I don't think I will, thank you, Ame.'

'You said you enjoyed it last time.'

'Did I? Yes, but I'm going to be busy tonight. I'll have to change and get downstairs as quick as I can.'

'Okay, Dad.'

'I'll look in later.'

'Okay.'

She went off quite pacifically. For once, I should have preferred an outbreak of temper. Amy was not reconciled, only preoccupied, and not in any comfortable way: she knew I had not told her the truth. But how could I say that there was no need to worry about what she had heard, because it had happened in 1680-something?

Despite this, and despite feeling fairly thoroughly shaken up by what I had witnessed and how, I was much relieved. Few people are tough enough to rest solely on an inner conviction that, in the face of what might be impressive evidence to the contrary, they are not going mad. In celebration, as much as anything else, I drank two brimming tumblers of Scotch and water in two minutes and with no effort. Then I went to have my bath.

Lying torpidly back in the hot water, I felt almost all right. It was certainly true that heart and back had kept themselves to themselves since first thing that morning. Jack Maybury would have had something to say about that, though I could hardly tell him what had formed a substantial part of the day's distractions from egotistical brooding. I felt sober, or rather, since feeling completely sober had been disagreeable to me for some years, fairly sober. Very nearly completely all right. The green man. The Green Man. Dozens, perhaps hundreds, of English pubs and inns bear the name, in reference, I remembered reading somewhere, either to a Jack-in-the-green, a character in traditional May Day revels, or merely to a gamekeeper, who would formerly have worn some kind of green suit. Was it possible that my own house, which had been so called from its beginnings in the late fourteenth century, was a different case, that Underhill's supernatural employee had existed even then? If true, to christen the place after such a creature was an odd way of inviting custom. But an interesting speculation.

I grew more torpid. Staring in an unfocused way towards the junction of wall and ceiling, I saw a small scarlet and green object moving slowly from right to left. First lazily, then as alertly as I could, I tried to decide what it was. A fly of some sort, or a moth. But surely there were none of either coloured like that, not in England. And the thing was not travelling with a fly's quick darting motion, such that wings and legs disappear into a round or roundish dark blob, nor in the unsteady, fluttering style of a moth. The wings of what I saw—two of them—were beating the air in an easily perceptible slow rhythm, and, not so easy to make out, its legs—two of them—were tucked up underneath the body, and there was a neck, and a head. It was a bird. A bird the size of a fly, or small moth.

I splashed to my feet and looked more closely. The thing was still a bird: I could see the sheen on its plumage and, by straining my eyes, the separate claws of its feet, and I could just hear a tiny beating of wings. I put my hand out to grab it, and it disappeared for a moment, then came into view again, flying out of the back of my hand. I picked up my towel, rolled it into a ball and screamed into it with my eyes shut for perhaps two minutes. When I opened them again, the bird had gone. I whimpered and sobbed into the towel for another two or three minutes, then dried myself with it as quickly as possible, counting in my head, and ran to the bedroom. If I could get dressed before I had reached four hundred and fifty thousand, I would not see the bird again, or not for some time. I kept my eyes shut whenever I could, and got my evening bow tied without once having to open them, but had to look at myself in the glass to do my hair, and caught sight of a small fly circling silently round my head. Although I was absolutely certain it was only a fly, I found I could not stop myself falling on to the bed and screaming and sobbing into my pillow for a time, still counting. I gave myself an extension of a hundred thousand for that period, which was fair, because I had not allowed for it when I set my original figure, and it could not have gone on for less than a minute and a half. I had my dinner-jacket on and was out of the door at the count of four hundred and twenty-seven thousand, so that there was a chance I would not see the bird again for a time.

I had no trouble getting to the landing with one eye shut and the other mostly shut. Here I ran into Magdalena, and sent her off to find Nick, or, failing him, David. Then I went back into the dining-room, mainly by feel, sat down, avoiding the chair that faced the front window, and kept both eyes shut. After less than a minute, I heard hurrying footsteps and opened my eyes again; I stopped counting, which I had gone on doing with no particular purpose in mind. By now I was breathing normally.

Nick hurried in with Jack Maybury. They both looked concerned, Nick in Nick's way, Jack professionally, but with no hint of censoriousness. He came close and peered at me.

'What's the trouble, Maurice?'

'I saw something.'

'Not more ghosts?' He glanced at Nick and then back at

me. 'I've been hearing about your encounters with the spirit world.'

'Why are you here, Jack?'

'I dropped in for a drink on the way back to my surgery. Just as well, it appears. Nick, would you ring Diana and tell her I'll be late?' He gave the number and Nick went. 'Now, Maurice, let's have your story,' he went on, gently for him.

I told him enough about the green man, and about the woman's screams, and that Amy had said she had heard them too. I did not mention the other noise we had both heard.

'So you think Amy shared your experience, or part of it? I see. When was this? I see. But there's more, is there?'

'Yes. I saw a bird flying round the bathroom. Very small, it was.' At this point I began sobbing again. 'But it was flying like a big bird. Beating its wings slowly. It went away quite soon. I'd had a big drink not long before, because I was so relieved that Amy had heard the screams, that somebody else as well as me had, I mean. I expect that had something to do with it.'

'Well, possibly, yes, but it's a much longer-term thing than that. You need a slow build-up normally.'

'I suppose it was . . .'

'It does sound like a little D.T., certainly, whereas your wooden chap on the whole doesn't much. Have you had that sort of dream before, Maurice?'

'I told you, it wasn't a dream. I never dream.'

'Couldn't you just have nodded off in your chair? Surely you——'

'No, I saw it.'

'All right.' He started to take my pulse.

'What will that tell you?'

'Very little, probably. Still sweating a lot?'

'Not today.'

'Had the shakes at all?'

'No more than usual.'

'Right. Now, whatever you see in this way can't harm you. I can understand your being frightened by these things, but try to remember that that's as much as they can do. Delirium tremens is a warning, not a disaster in itself, and we can deal with it. It's usually brought on by emotional strain, plus drink, of course, and I'd put all this down to your father's death. I think these ghosts of yours were a sort of prelude to the business in the bathroom, and your general idea that there are sinister and hostile characters around is very common in these cases. Are you with me?'

'In the sense that I understand what you mean, yes.'

'Okay. What you need is some time off. Now, young David's a very competent lad, and Joyce——'

'I'm not going inside, Jack.'

'It's not *inside*, for Christ's sake. It's a nursing home that deals with all sorts of things, with a very nice——'

'I'm not going. There's too much to see to here. I've got my father's funeral tomorrow, for one thing. Later, perhaps. You've got to tide me over. Tell me what I ...' I heard returning footsteps and speeded up. 'Keep your mouth shut and get me some pills. There are pills, aren't there?'

Nick came in.

'Of a sort. All right. But I disagree.' Jack turned to Nick. 'Okay?'

'Yes. Sorry, it was engaged all the time.'

'Yes, I know. Well, the verdict on your father is that he's been hitting the bottle a bit too hard. So he's going to cut it down, with medical help.'

'Cut it down, hell,' I said. 'I shan't want another drink for the next fifty years.'

'No, Maurice. That's the surest way to, uh, run into trouble. You're to cut down your intake by half in the first instance, and I mean half, not more. Take things as easy as you can. Lean on young David. And talk to Nick and Joyce about this. That's medical advice. Well, I'm not going to be as late as I thought. Nick, if you like to pop round in about half an hour there's some stuff for him I'd like you to pick up, if you would. Ring me any time you like, Maurice. This'll pass off in a couple of days, provided you do as I say. Goodbye now.'

'I'll see you out, Jack,' said Nick.

'Oh, there's no ... All right. Thanks.'

As soon as they had gone, I shut my eyes. Just a precaution: I was already feeling better, or less bad. Except under the immediate threat of death, life can never be only one thing. Bird or no bird, I was going to pick up Diana later and find out what Underhill had had buried with him. The doing of that would probably be frightening, but so much the better. I would not be able to be frightened of seeing the bird while I was frightened of what might happen in the graveyard.

Nick came back and pulled up a low chair next to mine.

'He didn't drop in by chance, Nick, did he?'

'No. I asked him to. Just as well, as he said.'

'What did you ask him a minute ago?'

'Whether he thought you were going off your head. He said some things did point that way, but on the whole he thought not.'

'Well, that's cheering, I must say.'

'What's wrong, Dad? I mean really wrong.'

'Nothing. Hitting the bottle. You heard all that. Jack's a terrible puritan about drink. It's his way of——'

'Balls. With the greatest disrespect along with a lot of respect, balls. You've decided not to tell me. And you think that's pretty marvellous of you. Heroic sensitive Maurice Allington keeps his mouth shut as to what's weighing on his heroic sensitive soul. But it isn't like that. You're just too lazy and arrogant and equal to everything (you think) to take the trouble to notice people like your son, and your wife, and deem them bloody well worthy of being let into the great secret of how you feel and what you think about everything, in fact what you're like. Sorry, Dad, it wasn't the time to say it, I know, but there's nothing good about being self-sufficient except over things that don't matter or when you've got to be because there just isn't anybody else around, but that isn't so in your case—it's bad that *you* don't depend on other people, especially the ones that depend on you. I can see you're feeling rotten, but if anything really crappy happened and it could have been prevented by you telling someone like me, or Joyce, what was going on beforehand, then you'd only have yourself to blame, or rather I'd blame myself too for not going on at you about it. Which I'll stop doing now, but I'll go on with it when you're feeling better. Sorry, Dad. Forget it for now.' He put out his hand and I gripped it. 'You just say how you want things to be this evening, and I'll see to it that's how they are.'

I stated some vague preferences about everything being normal, and about perhaps a look at television. Without giving any reason, Nick said that he would move the (family, non-Amy) set from the drawing-room, where it spent nine-tenths of its time, and plug it into its sockets here in the dining-room. He did all that, and shortly afterwards went off to pick up my pills at Jack's, leaving me watching, rather in Amy style, a programme about rehousing schemes in (I think) Salford.

As soon as Nick had gone, I picked up a hammer, a chisel and some sort of steel bar from the tool-box in the utilities cupboard, collected a couple of torches from their drawer in the office, went outside to the hut where the very idle and disagreeable old man (all I could get) whom I paid to do the gardening spent his time drinking tea and, no doubt, pulling his wire, found a spade showing no signs of recent use and stowed all these implements in the back of the Volkswagen. Doing this cheered me, and also helped me considerably to shove beneath the surface of my mind any question of what the hell I thought I was doing. It must have been at about this point, in fact, that I became finally committed to following the Underhill thing through, in the sense that afterwards I never once considered turning back until it was too late.

Another distraction, of course, was the problem of how to introduce to Joyce the topic of the orgy project. I was determined to talk her into this with the least possible delay, without at the same time having any idea at all about how to start, or how to go on either. If other things had been normal, to get, or seem, very drunk might have looked like an obvious preliminary, but getting so would not do now, seeming so would quite probably not fool Joyce, who knew me well, at least in such areas as this, and neither was likely to make the right impression, whatever that might be. I turned it all over in my mind while, accompanied by David, I made a sketchy round of bar, kitchen and dining-room, but could think of no solution. This did not worry me, perhaps because before I started I had opened Jack's package and swallowed two parti-coloured transparent cylinders containing some sort of coarse brown powder and very roughly resembling dolls' egg-timers. I would have to trust to the inspiration of the moment, in other words put my head down and charge full tilt.

The moment came shortly before nine o'clock, after I had had a desultory chat with Amy in her room and come upon Joyce and Nick in the dining-room. No sooner had I mixed myself a water and Scotch—ten to one—and given Joyce a glass of Tio Pepe than Nick said, staring at me rather, that he felt like going down to the bar for a bit and would see us at dinner.

Joyce asked me how I was and I soon satisfied her curiosity, which had not seemed to be of the burning sort in the first place. Then I said,

'I ran into Diana this afternoon, on my way back from Cambridge.'

'Ran into her?'

'She was just coming out of the post office as I went by, so I stopped and gave her a lift. She had a shopping-bag or so.'

'And?'

'Well, it was all rather curious. Would you say she got tight at all? I don't mean on my scale, but at all?'

'No.'

'No, neither would I, but she did seem a bit tight this afternoon. Or something, from the way she went on. Anyway, she started saying how marvellously attractive she thought you were, wonderful colouring, terrific figure and everything, so much so that it began to dawn on me that she wasn't just paying compliments, she had something particular in mind. So, after a bit it all began to come out.'

'Go on.'

'She went into a great kind of thing about how dull life was in Fareham, for people like her and you and me, and of course I agreed with that, and how we ought to do something about it, get some excitement from somewhere. Such as where? Well, what was wrong with the idea of the three of us having a little romp together?' Joyce said nothing, so I went on, 'She meant all going to bed. I thought she was joking at first, but evidently not. I said I wasn't sure I could satisfy two ladies all by myself, and she said I needn't worry, that wouldn't be necessary.

'What did she mean?'

'Well, I suppose she meant, in fact I'm sure she meant you and she could have fun together between times. It would be all sort of mixed.'

'I see. What did you say?'

'I said I thought she had something, but naturally I couldn't commit myself until I'd talked to you about it. Oh, there was one other thing she said. We needn't worry about the Jack side of it, because it turns out she hates him.'

Joyce looked at me for the first time since we had started talking. 'Diana hates Jack?'

'That's what she said.'

'You mean she had to tell you?' (At this point it was I who said nothing.) 'The first time we met them Diana couldn't bear Jack, and she's gone on not being able to bear him ever since. How funny you've never noticed.'

'Why didn't you mention it to me?'

'I thought it was so obvious it wasn't worth mentioning.'

'That's not how things work. In the ordinary way you'd have been bound to bring it up some time, just casually. Why have you been keeping it to yourself for so long?'

'Pretty good deduction,' said Joyce, apparently with genuine mild admiration, though I was on the alert about appearances, at any rate for the moment. 'I haven't mentioned it because I was waiting to see if you'd ever notice it on your own, and you haven't. That's typical, both bits, I mean you not noticing and you seeing straight away that I'd not mentioned it on purpose. That's how you are. You sort of observe all the time, and do it bloody well, often, and yet you don't see. Do you see what I mean?'

'Yes, and you may be right,' I said, trying not to sound impatient. 'But let's get back to Diana's idea. She seemed to think we could——'

'She meant that you'd, well, do her, for instance, and then she and I would work each other over for a bit, until you were ready again, and then you'd do me from behind, I don't mean, you know, just *from* behind while she sort of did the front of me, and then she and I would go on together again until perhaps you could do the same thing again only the other way round, or else you and I could divide her up and take different bits of her, and then you and she could take different bits of me, and so on. Is that the kind of thing?'

'Roughly, yes.' Listening to Joyce's outline had been not altogether unlike having the plot of *Romeo and Juliet* summarized by a plasterer's mate. At the same time I was swallowing hard with the effort not to want to laugh. 'Of course, we'd find plenty of——'

'All right.'

'What?'

'Let's do it, then.'

'Are you sure?'

'Yes. We might just as well. Why shouldn't we? You fix it up with Diana and let me know. Now I must go and find Magdalena. There's the chef's *gazpacho* tonight, and then lamb cutlets Reform. Ought to be damn good.'

With Victor in a loose ball on my lap, I sat and tried, not very hard, to watch *Friday Playhouse*, one of those two-character efforts which nevertheless seem marred by the excessive size of the cast. I was puzzled by the sensation that Joyce had let the situation down in some way: having wished beforehand for nothing better than her ready acceptance of the orgy project, I was now wishing she had put up objections for me to beat or wheedle out of the way. There was material here for a mental discussion about sex and power, but I shelved this. Perhaps it was Joyce's reaction that had—against all the odds —made me feel less than totally triumphant about the replacement of orgy project by orgy prospect, or perhaps it was just Jack's pills. If the latter, then there was a problem looming.

Dinner came and went; so did further television, culminating, or ending, in a discussion about God that made God seem comparatively immediate and to be reckoned with, as if God's sphere of influence might reach out to within a few light-years of the Solar System any millennium now, or traces of God's activities had been proved to extend as late as the beginning of the Devonian Age. Joyce went silently off to bed before it was over. Nick sat on for a while over a journal of French studies, then told me I was to wake him at any time if I felt like some company, and retired in his turn.

It was exactly midnight. I washed down two more pills with the puny draught I must habituate myself to, and left the apartment, picking up a lightweight raincoat on the way. This —camouflage, not protection from the weather—I put on and buttoned up to the chin before hurrying downstairs and out at the side door. In the open, there was plenty of movement to and fro, and plenty of standing about, too; as I waited in the shadows for a clear moment, I congratulated myself on having allowed plenty of time. At last a man half-lifted a girl into a car I considered he was much too young to own, and drove off, leaving the car-park empty of people. I scuttled across to the Volkswagen and got away without being seen, feeling light-headed in a more literal sense than I would have imagined possible, had I ever considered the matter: the parts of my brain usually reserved for thinking seemed to have been invaded by some gas, of low atomic weight but not otherwise tricky to handle—helium, perhaps, rather than hydrogen.

To use up spare minutes, I drove rounnd the village a couple of times. It was deserted and showed hardly a light. Diana was waiting at the place we had agreed; I picked her up with most of the swift efficiency of somebody on TV mounting a robbery or an assassination. This parallel obviously occurred to her too, and for the next few minutes she interrogated me about the sense of adventure, and whether its appeal to men rather than women did or did not go to show that men were really frightfully school-boyish at heart, in all sorts ... of ways. I probably said it did.

We reached the graveyard. I parked the car off the road in

the deep shade of a pair of elms; there was a thin but clear moon. Diana stood and waited, hands in the pockets of her rather schoolmistressy cardigan, while I collected the tools out of the back.

'Don't you feel scared, Maurice?'

'Not at the moment, no. Why should I?'

'But you told me you knew you were going to be, and that's why you insisted on me coming along.'

'Oh yes. I was really thinking about when we actually start. Take this, would you? Keep the light pointed away from the road.'

We moved off through the thick grass, halting and standing still for a quarter of a minute or so while the headlights of a car, no doubt full of drunken diners from the Green Man, swept towards and across us, or near us. The corroded iron gate of the graveyard leaned open. We entered, the torch Diana held making odd bits of greenery, at our feet or at head height, flare up like a mild and miniature firework display. One after the other, we stumbled over minor obstructions.

'Careful,' I said. 'Round here by the wall. A bit more to your left. Yes, that's it, there.'

'So here we are ... Maurice, don't you feel a frightful sense that one's about to do something one really wasn't meant to do? Oh, I know this Christianity thing's pretty well on its last legs these days, but surely there's a kind of basic thing about not interfering with last resting-places and all that, you know, superstition and primitive fear and the rest of it. Do you honestly think it's worth it?'

'That remains to be seen. Hold the torch steady. The next part is going to be totally boring.'

I was understanding it. Even a dry, sandy soil yields very slowly to the spade, and it must have been an hour at least before, soaked with sweat and unsteady on my feet, I had uncovered most of the top of the long oaken box I was after. Diana had behaved very creditably in the interval, taking time and trouble to wedge the torch into a crevice in the wall, initiating no discussions, hurrying to shield the light whenever a car approached on the road, falling asleep once for ten or fifteen minutes. She was awake when I finished digging and held the torch again—the reserve one, the battery of the first having given out—while I got going with the hammer and chisel. I had the latter muffled with sacking, but the noise was still considerable in the silence. However, that silence was otherwise unbroken by now, we were a hundred and fifty yards at least from the nearest houses, which were all in darkness, and a dozen taps and some creaking while I levered away were as much as was unavoidable.

When I opened the coffin, there was an odour of dry earth and of what I can only describe as powerful clean sheets; nothing in the least disagreeable. I took the torch from Diana, who bent closer while I ran its beam up and down. Underhill was totally and securely wrapped in linen, rather flattened about the abdomen and below, with the sharpness of bone showing through at knees and feet. At first I saw nothing but all this, then caught a gleam of dull metal at the end by the head. My fingers closed on something and I pulled it out and shone the torch on to it. What I held was a rough leaden casket, rectangular, about the size of a box of fifty cigarettes or a little thicker through. There was a lid, but the metal of this had been crudely fused with that of the casket itself, the whole forming a serviceable damp-proof container. I shook it and it rattled in a muffled, impeded way. I thought I knew what was rattling and what was impeding.

'Is that all?' asked Diana.

I shone the torch up and down and across. 'This was all I expected there to be here. I'll unwrap him if you like, but I don't——'

'No. Never mind. Let's get the lid on again.'

This too took a long time, and so did shovelling the earth back into an approximation of where it had been. It would obviously be years before the signs of interference ceased to be noticeable, but I could not imagine the Fareham constable, a chubby young man who spent as much time as was relevant at Newmarket races and the rest of the time talking about these and such matters, in the role of inquirer into the possible despoliation of some old bugger's grave from way back.

'Well, that's it,' I said.

'Aren't you going to open that thing you found?'

I considered. As I moved the earth and roughly levelled it off, I had been thinking of almost nothing beyond the prospect of opening the casket, but had visualized total seclusion. On the other hand, after something like two hours of unstinted and largely silent co-operation, Diana was entitled to some return, or at least would be expecting it. Fair enough. And yet, if I really was right about the thing that had rattled ... But the possibility of antagonizing Diana at this stage ...

I found the hammer and the chisel. 'Yes. Why not?'

In a couple of minutes I had made enough impression along the line of the original lid to prise the soft metal out of the way. I up-ended the casket and a small object fell into the palm of my hand. It was intensely cold, so much colder than the lead of its container that I nearly dropped it. Diana shone the torch. There it was, just as described; a silver figure about three inches tall and half that from one extended hand to where the other had been, with a smile of sorts on its face. I am no judge of silver, but I knew that the thing was much more than three hundred years old.

'What an ugly little creature,' said Diana. 'What is it? Do you think it's valuable? It's only silver, isn't it?'

I hardly heard her. Here was Underhill's proof. If I had thought to show what I had found this morning in my office notebook, to Nick or anyone else, before starting on tonight's expedition, I would now have had something to show the world—something, but not a proof, perhaps a case of extra-sensory perception, perhaps just a curious coincidence, an interesting story, an oddity. It was a proof only for me, and even I could not have said how much it really proved. Not yet, at least; but I felt a kind of hope I had never felt before.

'Maurice? Is it a charm or something? What do you think it is?'

'I don't know. I must try to find out. Hold on a minute.'

The expected sheets of paper could be seen inside the casket. I drew them out and unfolded them. They too were cold to the touch, but whether owing to true cold or to damp I did not know or care. The handwriting, the first words were enough, but for a few moments I read mechanically on.

'AVE, O MI AMICE SAPIENTISSIME. As thou see'est, thou hast understood mee aright. Count thyself the most fortunate of mankind, for shortly the veritable Secret of Life shall be reveal'd to thee. But mark curiously what follows, & thou shalt possess what is more durable than Riches, more to be envy'd than a Crown . . .'

'What does it say? Anything about this charm thing?'

'Not that I can see. Most of it's in Latin. Legal stuff, probably. I'll have a go at sorting it out some time.'

Well, I had been right about the papers too, but there was nothing supernatural in that. I folded them up again, slipped then and the silver figure back where they had been and managed to fit the casket into the side pocket of my dinner-jacket. Then I started picking up the tools.

'Is that the lot? Not much of a show, was it?'

'Oh, we did find something, didn't we? Not too bad.'

'I don't call that treasure.'

'That thing may be worth a bit, we don't know. I'll find somebody in Cambridge who'll tell us.'

'Where are you going to say you got it from?'

'Leave that to me.'

As we were leaving by the churchyard gate, a gust of wind, unexpected on such a still night, stirred the branches and leaves above our heads. I must have sweated even more than I had thought, because the air struck chill. At the same moment, the light of the torch in Diana's hand dimmed abruptly. We made our way back to the Volkswagen by almost unassisted moonlight. Down the empty road, the Green Man was in complete darkness, and there was no sound but that of our own progress until I opened the back door of the car and stowed the tools. Diana, a shifting, breathing shape, faintly illuminated at temple, shoulder and elbow, turned to me.

'Where does Joyce imagine you are tonight?' she asked, with something of her husband's accusatory tone.

'If she happened to wake up, which she never does, she'd think I was sitting up reading or drinking or brooding. But listen, I asked her about our little get-together idea and she was all for it. Any time to suit us.'

Diana reacted to this, but for a couple of seconds I could not have said how. Then she came forward, pressed herself against me and began a steady to-and-fro wriggle.

'Maurice.'

'Yes?'

'Maurice, do you think I might be the most terrible sort of kinky pervert type without knowing it?'

'Oh, I doubt that. No worse than me, anyway.'

'Because ... the moment you said that about Joyce and us I suddenly started feeling frightfully randy. I mean as regards straight away, not just for when we have the get-together. Is that absolutely unspeakable and depraved of me? I wonder whether it's anything to do with what we've been——'

I had been about to plead tiredness outwardly, and blame Jack's pills inwardly, when I realized that nothing like that was called for. Diana's interestingness had started taking more and more interesting forms. In something less than a quarter of a minute we were kneeling face to face in a patch of shadow.

'We can't really——'

'No, let's just take our——'

'Okay, yes, fine.'

In another quarter of a minute we were at it again. I had about the least sense possible of another person being there at all; there was a lot of wool and other material, some cheek, some panting, some movement, some pressure, and what was I doing. Even that was set at a distance by the lack of everything else, for a time. Suddenly it all turned very immediate and as much as anybody could deal with. Diana's body lifted and seemed enormous, then sank back and became slender and powerless again.

This was not an occasion for lingering. I was just going to move away when my heart gave a prolonged vibration and Diana screamed—no ladylike squeak, either, but a full-throated yell of fear.

'There's somebody watching us. Look, there, in the . . .'

As quickly as I could, I disengaged myself and turned, still on one knee. The moon was less bright than it had been, but I could not have missed any creature or movement. There was none.

'It was . . . He was standing in the middle of the road, looking at me. Oh God. Ghastly. Staring at me.'

She had struggled to a sitting position. I knelt beside her and put my arm round her.

'There's nobody there now,' I said. 'It's all right.'

'There was something awful about him. Something wrong with the shape of him. Not like proper arms and legs. I only saw him just for a second, but he was sort of deformed. Not really deformed, though, not the way people are. He was the wrong shape. Too thick in some places and too thin in others.'

'What was he made of?'

'Made of?' she asked in renewed fear. 'How do you mean?'

'Sorry, I . . . What was he wearing?'

'Wearing? I couldn't see. He was only there for a moment.'

'What colour?'

'You can't see colours in this light.'

True, but no matter: there had been no real need to ask. Diana had justified her inclusion in tonight's party; though not quite in the way I had hoped, by seeing what I saw when I saw it. Another thought struck me. 'Did he move at all, make any——?'

'No. I told you. He was just standing there, and the next

minute he'd gone.'

'You mean vanished?'

'Well ... I didn't see him go.'

'He must have gone pretty bloody quick to be in the middle of the road when you screamed and nowhere in sight when I looked.'

'Yes ... I suppose he must. Who could it have been?'

I was trying to reason, or at least to be relatively rational. The ghost of the green man, as ghosts were supposed to do, as Underhill's ghost was apparently accustomed to do, had appeared in an instant and disappeared in an instant, called into brief being, it might be, by our activities at its master's grave, perhaps by the disturbance or removal of the silver figure, which must in that case be associated with it in some way, though the one was certainly not the image of the other. At any rate, while there was plenty of excuse for alarm, I could see no reason for it. All my instincts confirmed Lucy's pronouncement that a mere phantom cannot inflict direct harm on anyone, and that (like those Underhill had conjured up in the case of the Tyler girl) the most it can actually do is terrify. And any terror that was not of the kind inspired by a fly-sized scarlet-and-green bird ... No, any such terror could be faced, or could be fled from; must always be less terrible than a portable, infinitely adaptable demon living and acting in the mind.

I pulled myself together. 'Sorry. Who was it? Some farm boy on his way home from a drunk. They come in pretty odd shapes and sizes round here. Anyway, he couldn't possibly have recognized you, so don't worry about it. It's ... good God, it's nearly three o'clock. I'll take you home.'

Like Amy earlier, Diana went through the motions of acquiescence while making it plain that my proffered explanation did not satisfy her. She said almost nothing on the way back. I parked the car off the road and walked her towards the house.

'I'm very grateful to you for coming along tonight.'

'Oh ... it's nothing.'

'About the get-together with Joyce—can I telephone you? What would be a good time?'

'Any time.'

'Let's make it soon. What about tomorrow?'

'Isn't it your father's funeral tomorrow?'

'Yes, but that'll be all over by lunch-time.'

'Maurice...' She rejected the shoddy pseudo-psychological question I had been preparing myself for. 'That ... just now. It wasn't a ghost I saw, was it, Maurice? Because it did vanish, I thought.'

For this one I was about half prepared. 'Yes, I was thinking along those lines. I suppose, well, it could have been, granted there are such things. Rather a funny place to find a ghost, though, isn't it? in the middle of a country road. I just don't know.'

'Then ... when you said it must have been a farm chap you were sort of trying to put my mind at rest, were you?'

'Yes. Of course.'

'Or your own mind at rest?'

'That too.'

'Maurice ... one of the things I like about you is that you're completely honest.' She kissed me on the cheek. 'Run along now. Give me a ring about Joyce as soon as you like.'

She ran vivaciously off, doubly puffed up, I assumed, at having got me to admit to needing to put my own mind at rest and at the thought—unconfided to me, which was odd—that she had demonstrated a fresh superiority by seeing a ghost when I had not. Did she now think she had really seen a ghost? What would she think if and when Jack should tell her that I had claimed to be seeing ghosts? Never mind; I was genuinely tired now, so tired that I staggered as if from drink (which for once could not be) when I walked from the garage to the house.

I washed down two more pills with heavily watered Scotch and went straight to bed, having locked up the casket in the office. I needed what sleep I could get, with a funeral and an orgy ahead, and, no doubt, something more.

'Death's an integral part of life, after all. We settle for it by the mere act of being born. Let's face it, Mr Allington, it is possible to take the end of the road a bloody sight too seriously.'

'And you don't mean because we ought to think of it as the gateway to another mode of being and part of God's purpose and so on.'

'Good God, no. I don't mean that at all. Not at all.'

The Reverend Tom Rodney Sonnenschein, Rector of St James's, Fareham, sounded quite shocked. He did not really look shocked, because he had one of those smooth, middle-aged-boyish faces that seem unfitted, even at moments of warmth or concern (if any), to express much more than a mild petulance. In the church and at the graveside, I had supposed him to be showing indignation at the known godlessness of all those in attendance, or perhaps to be suffering physically; now, in the bar of the Green Man, it was becoming deducible that he had been merely bored. I found it odd, and oddly unwelcome too, to meet a clergyman who was turning out to be, doctrinally speaking, rather to the Left of a hardened unbeliever like myself; but no doubt he would soon be off to some more spiritually challenging parish in London, and anyhow I did not proposed to see the man again after today.

'Not at *all*?' I asked.

'You know, this whole immortality bit's been pretty well done to death. One's got to take the historical angle. Immortality's just a passing phase. Basically, it was thought up by the Victorians, especially the early Victorians, as a sort of guilt thing. They'd created the evils of the Industrial Revolution, they could sense what kind of ghastly bloody monster capitalism was going to turn out to be, and the only refuge from hell on earth they could think of was a new life away from the smoke and the stink and the cries of the starving kids. Whereas today, of course, now it's beginning to get through people's heads at last that capitalism just won't do, that the whole bloody thing's simply not *on*, and we can set about changing society so as to give everybody a meaningful and organic existence here on earth, well, we can put immortality back in the junk-room along with, oh, mutton-chop whiskers and Mr Gladstone and the Salvation Army and evolution.'

'Evolution?'

'Surely,' stated the rector, simultaneously smiling hard and frowning hard and dilating his nostrils and blinking rapidly, one for each, perhaps, of his pieces of junk-room furniture.

'Oh well ... But what I don't quite see is why these Victorians of yours were so keen on the idea of an after-life when they were so eaten up with guilt about what they'd been doing in this one. They'd have thought they'd be much more likely to end up in hell than in any sort of——'

'Oh, but, my dear, that's the whole *point*, do you see. They were mad about hell—it was going to be just like their public school, where they'd had the only really intense emotional experiences they were capable of. Caning and flogging and fagging and cold baths and rowing and slip-practice and a terrifying all-powerful old man always telling you what utter shit you were and how you were polluting yourself. They were off their heads about it, I promise you. You don't imagine it's a coincidence, do you, that this was the great age of masochism, chiefly in England but by no means confined to here?'

'No,' I said. 'An age of masochism couldn't be a coincidence.'

'Well, hardly, could it? The whole thing's absolutely basic to the capitalist psyche, love of pain and punishment and misery generally, all the Protestant qualities. If you wanted to be smart without being *too* superficial, you could say that the immortality of the soul was invented by Dr Arnold of Rugby—bit unfair on the old love, but there we are.'

'Could you? But isn't there a lot about it in the Bible? And a lot of stuff about pain and punishment in the Middle Ages? And hasn't the Catholic Church always taken personal immortality very seriously?'

'Let's just take those points in order, shall we? There's virtually nothing about it in the Old Testament, which has come to be generally recognized as the more uncompromising and more unsentimental of the two. Quite frankly, the Jesus of the Gospels can be a bit of a wet liberal at times, when he's not taking off into flights of rather schmaltzy Semitic metaphor. As regards the Middle Ages, their devils and red-hot pincers and so on represented nothing more than a displaced enactment of what they wanted their enemies to suffer on earth. The Catholic Church, well ... Simple pie in the sky, isn't it generally agreed? I mean, you don't think it's an accident, do you, that they invariably give their support to backward and reactionary if not actually vicious régimes, like in Spain and Portugal and Ireland and——?'

'Yes, I know the ones you mean. Well, I don't know what I think. But you've certainly given me a most interesting exposition, Rector.'

'Which I might advise you, Mr Allington, to think over at some more favourable time. It's never pleasant to have one's unquestioning beliefs put in their historical context, as I know from experience, I can assure you.'

'What would you say if I were to tell you that I had evidence seeming to show that an individual had actually survived death in some form or other?'

'I'd say you were off your . . .' On the Rev. Tom's unworn face, the inbuilt look of petulance gave momentary place to a kind of wariness; over the last few days, I had seen something like it on most of the faces I knew well. 'Uh, you're talking about ghosts and so on, are you?'

'Yes. Specifically, a ghost that gave me information, accurate information, that I couldn't otherwise have known.'

'Mm. I see. Well, off the top of the head I'd say that was a matter for your medical adviser rather than someone in my position. Uh, where is Jack? I don't see him——'

'He's gone off to a patient. You mean I must be mad if that's what I think has happened?'

'Mm—no. But we are talking about, let's say non-normal states of consciousness, aren't we, by definition?'

'Because by definition people don't survive death. Of course.'

'I say, do you think you could possibly get me another drink? I mustn't get too pissed because I'm going to a rather exciting barbecue tonight in Newnham garden, but I think perhaps just one more shot, if I may.'

'What are you drinking?'

'Bacardi and Pernod.' He got a tacit 'you *fool*' into the intonation.

'Anything in it?'

'Sorry?'

'Tomato juice or Coca-Cola or——'

'Good God, no. Just ice.'

I passed the order to Fred, who closed his eyes for a moment or two before setting about it. He was having a deservedly unstrenuous time for once, the house being shut until the evening and the present party confined to Diana, David, three or four neighbours and my own family group, plus the rector, now staring into his glass and rotating it furiously before he risked a sip.

'Is that all right?'

'Sure. You mentioned God's purpose just now,' he said, showing a power of recall I disliked having to attribute to him. 'Interesting point, in its way. I'm going to tell you that there's more fantasy-building about God's purpose, in the sense of people letting their unconscious drives come out into the open in a socially accepted way, than in any other belief area, except martyrdom, of course, which is more blatantly sexual. God's purpose. Huh. I'm no more qualified than the next man to tell you what that is, or even if there is such a thing, which a lot of the younger people in the Church today would put a *big* bloody question-mark to. The trend undoubtedly is for a committed God to go the same way as the immortality of the soul, with a twenty- or perhaps a twenty-five-year consciousness-lag. Now, if you'll excuse me, I must go and have a word with those two smashing-looking dollies over there. It's been a most——'

'I'll come with you.'

By chance (presumably), Joyce and Diana had put on virtually identical outfits for the funeral: black barathea suit, white *broderie anglaise* shirt, black fish-net stockings, black straw hat. This made them look more than ever like sisters, even fraternal twins. While the rector dismantled Christianity for my benefit, or just as likely for his own, I had been observing them as they sat and talked together on the window-seat, and wondering if one or the other of them had brought up the impending orgy. It occurred to me now that I had forgotten to tell Diana that I had told Joyce that the idea had come from Diana in the first place, but I had hardly begun to move over to them, the rector slouching surlily at my side, before I saw that all was well. Well and to spare: their shoulders and knees were touching, each was slightly flushed in the face, and, in their different fashions, each gave me a glance of complicity, Joyce's straight and serious, Diana's with a little pretended shock and shame round the edges.

'Mr Sonnenschein has been explaining to me about God's purpose,' I said.

The rector gave a quick wriggle of one hip and the opposite shoulder. He said deprecatingly, 'Oh well, you know, that sort of thing's bound to come up from time to time in my field.'

'What is God's purpose?' asked Joyce, using the interested, far from unfriendly, wholly reasonable tone that I had learnt to recognize as a warning.

'Well, I suppose one might start to answer that by saying what it isn't. For instance, it's nothing to do with getting hot and bothered about the state of one's soul, or the resurrection of the body, or the community of saints, or sin and repentance, or doing one's duty in that state of life into which it has pleased——'

I had been looking forward to an exhaustive list of what God's purpose was not; Joyce, however, cut in. 'But what is His purpose?'

'*I* should say, *I* would say that what ... God wants us to do'—there were sneer-marks round the last phrase—'is to fight injustice and oppression wherever they are, whether they're in Greece or Rhodesia or America or Ulster or Mozambique-and-Angola or Spain or——'

'But that's all politics. What about religion?'

'To me, this is ... religion, in the truest sense. Of course, I may be wrong about the whole thing. It isn't up to me to tell people what to think or how they ought to——'

'But you're a parson,' said Joyce, still reasonably. 'You're paid to tell people what to think.'

'To me, I'm sorry, but that's a rather outmoded——'

'Mr Sonnenschein,' put in Diana, chopping it up so sharply that it sounded a bit like one of those three-monosyllable Oriental names.

The rector waited quite a creditable length of time before saying, 'Yes, Mrs Maybury?'

'Mr Sonnenschein ... Would you mind frightfully if I were to ask you a rather impertinent question?'

'No. No, of course not. It's a——'

'What- ... 's-the-point of somebody like you being a parson when you say you don't care about things like duty and people's souls and sin? Isn't that just exactly what parsons are supposed to care about?'

'Well, it's true that the traditional——'

'I mean, of course I agree with you about Greece and all these places, it's absolutely ghastly, but everybody knows that already. You must simply not take offence, please not, but lots of us would say it's not up to you in your position to start sounding like, well ...'

'One of those chaps on television doing a lecture on the problems of today and freedom and democracy,' said Joyce, even more reasonably than before.

'We don't need you for that, you see. Mr Sonnenschein . . .'

'. . . Yes, Mrs Maybury?'

'Mr Sonnenschein, don't you perhaps think that when everybody's so tremendously, you know, ahead of everything and knowing it all and everything, then it's a *bit* up to you to be jolly crusty and jolly full of hell-fire and sin and damnation and *jolly* hard on everybody, instead of, you know . . . ?'

'Not really minding anything like everybody else,' said Joyce. She drained her sherry, looking at me over the top of the glass.

'But surely one must tell the truth as one sees it, otherwise one——'

'Oh, do you really think so? Don't you think that's just about the riskiest thing one can possibly do?'

'You can only think you know it, probably,' finished Joyce.

'Yes. Well. There we are. I must go and see the major,' said the man of God, so rapidly and decisively and so immediately before his actual departure that seeing the major (even though there was a retired one actually present) might have been a Sonnenschein family euphemism for excretion.

I turned back to the two girls. I had never seen them behave in concert like this before. 'Well, that was a marvellous seeing-off, and no mistake. I wish I'd said all that. Can I get you both a drink?'

As I spoke, they looked at each other in a brief thought-exchanging way, then at me without much warmth. Diana, wide-eyed, leaned forward.

'Maurice, why did you bring that ghastly little dog-collared drip over here like that?'

'I didn't bring him over; he insisted on coming to chat the two of you up, and I thought it would be less painful if I——'

'Couldn't you have stopped him?' asked Joyce.

'I suppose I could have, yes, if I'd realized it was so important.'

'Surely, Maurice, you could see we were having a chat.'

'Sorry. Anyway, talking of having a chat . . .'

'You mean about us and you going to bed together,' said Joyce, not dropping her voice much, and speaking as if we had turned to a less stimulating and sufficiently familiar topic.

'Ssshh . . . Yes. Well, what do you——?'

'We thought four o'clock this afternoon would be a good time,' said Diana.

'Splendid. We might——'

'Where?' asked Joyce.

'I thought we could use number eight in the annexe. No booking there until Monday. I'll mention it to David and he'll see we're not disturbed.'

'What will you say to him?'

'Leave that to me.'

Mention it to David I did, in the same fashion as several times before when about to entertain a lady in my house, though without asking him, as several times before, to have a bottle of champagne and an ice-bucket and glasses ready in the room, an omission made less out of economy than inability to think what to say about the number of glasses required. This brief exchange came just after an unenjoyable luncheon in the main dining-room. The rector was in attendance, fully recovered from his drubbing at the hands of the girls, in fact quite exuberant, making an untentative verbal pass at Nick over coffee (as Nick told me later) and going off last and adequately pissed with three glasses of my Taylor 1955 inside him. I wished him ill for his Newnham garden barbecue. When he had finally departed, I went to the office, locked myself in, turned off the telephone and tried to think about my father.

It was a case of trying, more than succeeding, because it had been so hard to connect anything about his burial with anything about him, or because I had four o'clock on my mind (though it did not feel like that), or because the recently living take so long to start seeming really dead, or because of something to do with Jack's pills. Cold and unmeaningful phrases circled in my brain: he had gone off easy, he had given me life, he had been a good age, he was at peace, he had done his best for me, he had seen his son and grandson settled, he must have known it would come (as if that were a comfort). And he had gone to a better place, he was dead in the body but not in the spirit—not easy to find more of the same to add, nor even to try to find a meaning in anything of the sort, not nowadays. It sounded as if, it felt as if, for every imaginable wrong reason, that fool of a rector had been right. And yet I had meant what I had said to him about evidence of survival in Underhill's case. A different case, then, a far-off one, concerning a man who was not a man at all, only a name and words and bones and perhaps, no, certainly, an apparition. Immortality seemed either too exotic or too crude a concept to be fitted into somebody one had known for so long in the flesh. It might be possible to work on this from the other end, so to speak—try to make Underhill more real to myself, more of a person, more of a presence, however remote, in the same kind of way as my father was a presence.

I unlocked a drawer in the desk and, from under a pile of bank statements and cleared cheques, pulled out the casket containing the silver figure and the manuscript. I had been too tired to examine these the previous night, and had had no time, nor much inclination, so far that day. Now I was eager to do so. I took the figure to the window and turned it over in the strong sunlight there. Except round the neck and crotch, it was not much corroded, but other parts of it appeared to have been worn smooth. Both trunk and limbs were roughly cylindrical, with little representation of waist, elbow or knee, and the surviving hand, although disproportionately large, showed no knuckles or finger-joints. In the same fashion, the head did not taper appreciably towards the chin, the top of the skull was almost flat and the features were to a large extent matters of token; only the mouth, set in a wide straight grin that revealed a dozen or more teeth of roughly equal size, had been treated in any detail. I was certain the thing had not come from anywhere in western Europe, and felt strongly that east was the wrong direction to consider. Africa, possibly, though very unlikely, I thought, in view of Underhill's date, if nothing else. The New World, the pre-Columbian cultures—yes: I had seen just that kind of joyful, greedy ferocity on the faces of Aztec sculptures. There would have been plenty of time—a century and a half, in fact—for such an object to make its way from conquered Mexico to the England of Underhill's day, however hard it might be to imagine a plausible route; the capture of a Spanish treasure-ship was one obvious and not too unlikely piece of guesswork. But from whatever source and by whatever way it had reached Fareham, it was by far the most disagreeable work of human hands I have ever seen, as I had been aware the moment I looked at it closely. It was also unpleasant to the touch, being hardly less cold, or clammy, than when I had first handled it, twelve hours or so previously, and not being appreciably warmed now by several minutes' contact with my fingers; no doubt the result of some impurity in the metal. All in all, it seemed just what Underhill would have chosen, probably from a collection of such images of man's beastliness, to have buried with him and to serve as proof of his survival.

I put the figure down on the desk and picked up the journal, which turned out at the first glance to be written on the same kind of paper as the notebook I had inspected in the Hobson Room at All Saints'; it had perhaps lain originally between the same covers. The writing on these sheets had faded very markedly, to a kind of washed-out mid-brown, but was still quite readable. It was a thin sheaf of papers, no more than fourteen or fifteen in all, and the first dozen carried nothing but agonizingly vague injunctions to the unearther of the manuscript; stuff like

'Bee not impacient: all things shall be deliver'd to thee in time. Put thyself under my Will, & thou shalt see a great Wonder. Prepare; abstain from all spirituous Liquors & Cordials [here at least I had already started to do my best to cooperate], takg only such Wine & small Beer as may conduce to health. Bethink thee, that altho' Philosophy be amiable in herself, her Aspect is upon occasion full strange & stern ...'

And so on. The only entry that stood out in any way from this kind of thing, inset from the margin as though to differentiate it, to mark it perhaps as a note from Underhill to himself (a type of communication I have shown I understand) rather than a memorandum to me, ran as follows:

'The name, Fareham village. Cf. Fareham Haven in Southhamptonshire. No knowledge of this. Quasi, far Home, sc. distant habitation, or, fair Home. Or, from the Saxon & Gothick, feor, sc. fear. So, feorhame, quasi, the Place of Fear.'

Whatever the rightness or wrongness of Underhill's etymology, I found this making a kind of sense, the same kind as my conjecture about the derivation of the name of my house. But such theorizing belonged to an impossibly vast and remote field of thought; I put it by and went dispiritedly on through the journal. On its last leaf were half a dozen lines of writing, in a tumbling, scribbled hand barely recognizable as Underhill's.

'My time is nearer than I had thought. Dismiss thy Servants at once; send all from home save thine own Family. Go not abroad thyself; see no one & keep thy chamber, that I may find thee alone when I come to thee. Have our small Freind of Silver by thee AT ALL TIMES—or everything will be in vain, Now, fare well, until I shall return.'

There was only one of these instructions that it would not be difficult to obey, but that one was evidently the most important. Unhesitatingly, unreasoningly and with revulsion, I picked up the figure and placed it in my left side coat pocket, where it made an ugly bulge. That was that; what now? Separatory to gathering the papers together, I turned the last one over and laid it on top of the others, noticing as I did so that it bore a couple of lines of writing. They were in the firm, un-hurried hand of the earlier pages, and read:

'I will wait upon thee in my Parlour at twelve of the clock, the night following thy Discovery. See thou art alone.'

What made me stare and rise to my feet and start trembling was not the content of this message, but the quality of the ink: dark blue or black, not faded at all, as if it had been put on paper that day. But how could that be?

A powerful but (again) unreasoning sense of urgency came upon me. I must find Lucy at once. I had heard her say that she was going to spend the afternoon ... how? Where? Yes—reading, sunbathing, in the garden. I snatched up the paper and rushed from the office, across the hall, out of the front door and along to the south-east corner of the house. Lucy, with Nick near her, was sitting on an outdoors chair in the middle of the lawn. Slipping clumsily about on the thick dry grass, and with the silver figure bumping against my hip, I ran over to her.

'Lucy, look at this. The ink.'

'What is it?'

'Look at the colour of the ink. New, fresh. Isn't it?'

'I don't see——'

'No no, the other side, that one. That's fresh ink, isn't it?'

She hesitated, finally saying, 'It doesn't look fresh to me,' and handing the paper back.

Of course she was right. The writing on both sides was brown and faded. No amount of hurrying, presumably, would have made any difference. He had caused it to fade, or, more likely, he had caused it to look unfaded a minute ago. I noticed that Lucy was wearing a navy-blue bathing-dress with the shoulder-straps pulled down, and had a brightly-jacketed book on her lap, and was looking slightly dazed with sun. Nick took the paper from me, glanced at it, then started to read it. He was just wearing trunks and sandals.

'No, it doesn't,' I said, 'now I look at it again. I don't know what made me ... It must have been the light. It's not very good in the office. The light. Unless you have the light on.'

'What's all this about, Dad?' asked Nick.

'Well, it's ... part of a letter or something, I suppose. I found it.'

'Where?'

'Oh, I was turning out an old cupboard and this had got sort of shoved underneath a lot of stuff.'

'How could it have been written in fresh ink, then?'

'I don't know. I just thought it looked like that.'

'What does it mean, this friend of silver thing, and this discovery?'

'I don't know. I've no idea.'

'Well, why all the excitement? You were——'

'It doesn't matter.'

A car I recognized was turning in at the main entrance to the house, a green Mini-Cooper belonging to the Mayburys. For a moment I thought I was going to have Jack on my hands, with more pills and unwelcome advice; then I saw Diana in the driving-seat, and remembered.

'Never mind, Nick,' I said, recovering the paper. 'Sorry to have bothered you. Forget it.'

I went back to the house, put the papers together, half dropping them in my impatience, and locked them up again. By the time I re-emerged from the office, Diana was coming in by the front door and Joyce descending the stairs into the hall. Both had changed their clothes since lunch—Diana into a tan shirt and green trousers, Joyce into a short red dress of some faintly glossy material—and both were groomed and earringed and necklaced as if for a garden party. When, with precision no rehearsal could have improved, we had converged in mid-floor, neither girl made any move to kiss the other as they usually did on meeting, an odd omission in the circumstances. Joyce seemed as tranquil as ever, if not more so, Diana nervous or nervy, her eyes widened and blinking a lot. There was a brief silence.

'Well,' I said bluffly, 'no point in hanging about here, is there? Let's go. I'll lead the way.'

I did so. We crossed the empty sunlit yard to the annexe and went upstairs and along a passage hung with my second-best prints. Number eight was at the end; I unlocked it and bolted the door after us. The bed was turned down, but without any personal belongings to be seen the room looked official and public—I remembered waking up in that same bed one afternoon the previous summer and thinking that it felt like lying about in a model room at a department store. I drew the curtains. Outside there was sun and sky and the tops of trees, everything quite motionless. I was feeling not so much excited as grateful, even slightly incredulous, that nothing had come up to prevent our getting this far.

The two girls looked communicatively at each other and then at me in the same way as they had done in the bar before lunch, preparatory to accusing me of interrupting their chat. I smiled at each of them while I tried to sort out priorities in my mind.

'What do you want us to do?' asked Diana, with just a hint of impatience in her voice and demeanour.

'Let's all take everything off for a start,' I said.

A woman can always beat a man to the state of nudity if she puts her mind to it, and here were two women evidently doing so. Despite earrings and necklaces, Joyce and Diana were embracing naked beside the bed while I was still working urgently on my second shoe. By the time I was ready to join them, they had thrown the covers back and were lying side by side in an even closer embrace. I climbed in behind Diana and started kissing her shoulders and available ear and the back of her neck, none of which seemed to make much special difference to anybody. I found it difficult to slide my arm round under her arm, because Joyce's arm was thereabouts too, and impossible to touch more than the outer side of Diana's breast, because Joyce's breast was against the remainder of it. When I tried the same sort of thing at a lower level, I came across the top of Joyce's thigh. After that, I tried to alter the girls' positions with a view to setting up one of the triads of lovemaking Joyce had mentioned the previous evening in her unvarnished way. That meant her thigh would positively have to shift, but it stayed where it was. To get Diana on to her back was not even worth attempting, with her inner thigh between both of Joyce's. It is never easy to move people about bodily unless they co-operate a bit, and neither of these was doing so at all.

What were they doing? Kissing repeatedly, in fact almost continuously, pressing themselves against each other, breathing deeply, though not particularly fast. What more? I had a totally obstructed view from where I was, but both Joyce's hands were in sight, one behind Diana's head, the other at the small of her back, and anyway their embrace had been so tight from the beginning that neither could have been caressing the other in any way; they would have had to draw a little apart for that, which would have afforded me an opportunity, but I doubted very much whether either of them had bothered to think of such a point. I told myself I was not going to give up, said so aloud, said a lot more things, managing to stay just this side of whining and abuse, moved round the bed to behind Joyce, and got no change there either.

There it was, then. I stood and looked at them while they went on exactly as before, neither speeding up nor slowing down, like people unable to foresee ever doing anything else, even of the same general sort. How well I could remember that feeling! Just then Diana's hazel eye opened, moved across the drawn curtains and me and more of the curtains without the least self-consciousness in paying the same attention to me as to the curtains, and shut again. The thought of two women making love can be an exciting one, but let me tell you that, when they are as totally absorbed in each other as these two were, the actuality is sedative. Indeed, for the moment I felt calmer than at any time during the past few days. I blew them a kiss, rejecting the idea of kissing each of them on the shoulder or somewhere as more trouble and no more likely to be noticed, picked up my clothes at leisure and carried them into the bathroom.

When I emerged dressed, Joyce was holding Diana's head against her bosom, but everything else was unchanged. I found the DO NOT DISTURB notice hanging on a hook on the door and left it on the outside doorknob. When I arrived back in the main building, it was deserted. I went into the office and stood there for a time without being able to think of anything I wanted to do or would ever want to do. Then I went upstairs to the dining-room and stood looking at the titles of my books, wondering what the hell had ever possessed me to buy any of them. Poetry, any poetry, seemed then as poignant and meaningful as a completed crossword puzzle or Holy Writ. Books or architecture or sculpture were books on mindless lumber, large or small. I could not imagine feeling differently about these matters. I turned my back and reviewed my own pieces of statuary. There was lumber all right, and in the round. I would chuck them all out the following morning.

The house was quiet, apart from the affected chattering of Amy's TV set, which was bringing her news and views of to-day's sport, perhaps even highlights therefrom, before getting to grips with space monsters or the yelling of pop idols and their idolaters. The curtains were drawn back; the sunlight from outside seemed unusually harsh and yet almost without colour. Through the side window I could see and hear a tractor, with some red-and-green painted piece of farm equipment in tow, approaching from the village, surrounded by a thin cloud of the dust and small soil that had drifted across the road, together with plenty of smoke. It passed out of view below my line of sight. As it did so, the noise it made, while still growing louder, started slowly descending in pitch. No doubt the driver was planning to halt directly outside my house and tinker with his engine while he raised more noise and smoke. But something odd was happening simultaneously to the television voice from along the passage: it too was falling in pitch, and it was slowing down in the same ratio. This sort of thing could happen with a gramophone whose motor had been switched off, and with a tape-recorder; I did not think it could happen with a TV set. I stood still and attended to the action of my heart while tractor and voice, in exact step with each other, disappeared below the threshold of audibility and a total silence supervened. I walked slowly to the front window.

The tractor and its tow had come to rest just about where I had predicted, almost immediately opposite me. The driver, however, had not dismounted, nor had he made any other significant move. He had one hand on the wheel and the other was passing a coloured handkerchief across his forehead, or rather had stopped in the act of doing so. Round him and the vehicles there hung stationary veils of smoke and dust, with individual motes shining minutely and steadily in the sun. I went to the side window. Down to the left, forty or fifty yards away across the grass, a couple of waxworks cast their shadows, the seated one with a hand stuck out in the direction of something, probably a cup of tea, that the standing one was offering it, and were Lucy and Nick. This time, the view from both windows had the exact quality of a very good photograph, frozen hard but also full of potential motion. This time was going to be different from last time in other ways too, because I was not going to stay here and just watch whatever it was I had been intended to watch.

I hurried over to the door and opened it and was about to make off down the passage when something made me halt abruptly—a subliminal sound-effect or air-movement. I put my hand forward and the finger-tips touched an invisible barrier, hard and totally smooth, like plate-glass but without any trace of reflection. It filled the doorway. Uncertain what to do next, I turned aside, looked up and saw that somebody was sitting in the armchair on the far side of the fireplace. This person, a young man with silky fair hair and a pale face, could not (of course) have come into the room without my knowing it.

'Very good,' said the young man heartily. He was watching me with a faint down-turned smile. 'A lot of people, you know, would have gone walking straight into that thing. Shows you've got good reflexes and all that. Now, if you'd like to sit down there, we can have a bit of a talk. Nothing too serious, I assure you.'

At the outset I had let out a girlish shriek of alarm. The alarm was sincere enough, but it immediately passed, to be replaced by an intensification of the charged-up feeling I had had the previous morning before setting off for Cambridge: nervous energy with nervousness but without nerves. Perhaps my visitor had brought this about. I came forward and seated myself in the opposite chair, looking him over. He was, or appeared to be, about twenty-eight years old, with a squarish, clean-shaven, humorous, not very trustworthy face, unabundant eyebrows and eyelashes, and good teeth. He wore a dark suit of conventional cut, silver-grey shirt, black knitted silk tie, dark-grey socks and black shoes, well polished. His speech was very fully modulated, like that of a man interested in discourse, and his accent educated, without affectations. Altogether he seemed prosperous, assured and in good physical shape, apart from his pallor.

'Are you a messenger?' I asked.

'No. I decided to come, uh ... In person.'

'I see. Can I offer you a drink?'

'Yes, thank you, I'm fully corporeal. I was going to warn you against making the mistake of supposing that I come from inside your mind, but you've saved me that trouble. I'll join you in a little Scotch, if I may.'

I got out the glasses. 'I suppose I couldn't get into the passage because all molecular motion outside this room has stopped?'

'Correct. We're not subject to ordinary time in here. Makes us pretty safe from interruption.'

'And all radiation has likewise ceased, outside?'

'Of course. You must have noticed the way the sound packed up.'

'Yes, I did. But in that case, why hasn't the light packed up too, outside? And in here as well, for that matter? If all wavelengths are affected, I can't see how the sun can get to us, any more than the sound of the tractor can. Everything would be dark.'

'Excellent, Maurice.' The young man laughed in what was clearly meant to be a relaxed, jovial way, but I thought I could hear vexation in it. 'Do you know, you're almost the first non-scientist to spot that one? I'd forgotten you were such a man of education. Well, I thought things in general would just look better if I arranged them like this.'

'You're probably right,' I said, holding up glass and water-jug and starting to pour. 'Is this a test of some sort?'

'Thank you, that's fine ... No, it isn't a test. How could it be? What do you suppose would happen to you if you passed a test I'd set for you? Or failed it? You of all people know I don't work that way.'

I moved back with the drinks and held one out. The hand that came up and took it, and the wrist and lower forearm that disappeared into the silver-grey shirt-cuff, were by no means complete, so that the fingers clicked against the glass, and at the same time I caught a whiff of that worst odour in the world, which I had not smelt since accompanying a party of Free French through the Falaise Gap in 1944. In a moment it was gone, and fingers, hand and everything else were as they had been before.

'That was unnecessary,' I said, sitting down again.

'Don't you believe it, old boy. Puts things on the right footing between us. This isn't just a social call, you know. Cheers.'

I did not drink. 'What is it, then?'

'More than one thing, of course. Anyway, I like to make these trips every so often, as you're well aware.'

'Keeping in touch?'

'Don't fool about with me, Maurice,' said the young man, with his downward smile. His eyes were a very light brown, almost the colour of his hair and his thin eyebrows. 'You know I know everything everybody thinks.'

'So you haven't come because you're particularly interested in me.'

'No. But slightly because you're particularly interested in me. In all my aspects. You'd agree, wouldn't you?'

'I'd have thought only in the one you demonstrated to me a moment ago,' I said, drinking now.

'I'll be the judge of that. Whether you like it or not, and whether you're aware of it or not, being interested in one means being interested in them all. You're in quite a common situation, actually.'

'Then why pick on me? What have I done?'

'Done?' He laughed, altogether genially this time. 'You're a human being, aren't you? Born into this world, and so forth. And what's so terrible about my popping in to see you like this? Worse troubles at sea, you know. No, I picked on you, as you rather ungraciously put it, partly because you're, uh ...' He paused and rotated the ice in his drink, then went on as if starting a new sentence, in the way he had. 'A good security risk.'

'Drunk and seeing ghosts and half off my head. Yes.'

'And not what anybody in their senses would take for a saint or a mystic or anything. That's it. I have to be careful, you see.'

'Careful? You make the rules, don't you? You can do anything you like.'

'Oh, you don't understand, my dear fellow. As one might expect. It's precisely because I make the rules that I can't do anything I like. But let's leave that for now. I want to talk for a moment, if I may, about this chap Underhill. Things have been getting a bit out of hand there. I want you to be very careful with him, Maurice. Very careful indeed.'

'Steer clear of him, you mean?'

'Certainly not,' he said, with emphasis and, it seemed, in complete earnest. 'Quite the contrary. He's a dangerous man, old Underhill. Well, in a mild way. A minor threat to security. If he's left to himself, it'll be just that much more difficult to keep going the general impression that human life ends with the grave. A very basic rule of mine says I have to maintain that impression. Almost as basic as the one about everything having to seem as if it comes about by chance.'

'I see that one, but you must admit that impression about the grave is comparatively recent.'

'Nonsense. You only know what people said they believed. There's never been any real difficulty from that direction. Now then, I want you to stand up to Underhill and, uh ... Put paid to him.'

'How?'

'I can't tell you that, I'm afraid. Sorry to be a bore, but I'll have to leave the whole thing to you. I hope you make it.'

'Surely you know? Whether I will or not?'

The young man sighed, swallowed audibly and smoothed his fair hair. 'No. I don't know. I only wish I did. People think I have foreknowledge, which is a useful thing for them to think in a way, but the whole idea's nonsense logically unless you rule out free will, and I can't do that. They were just trying to make me out to be grander than I could possibly be, for very nice motives a lot of the time.'

'No doubt. Anyway, I don't much care for doing what you want. Your record doesn't impress me.'

'I dare say it doesn't, in your sense of impress. But all sorts of chaps have noticed that I can be very hard on those who don't behave as I feel they should. That ought to weigh with you.'

'It doesn't much, when I think of how hard you can be on people who couldn't possibly have done anything to offend you.'

'I know, children and such. But do stop talking like a sort of anti-parson, old man. It's nothing to do with offending or punishing or any of that father-figure stuff; it's purely and simply the run of the play. No malice in the world. Well, I think you'll take notice of what I've said when you turn it over in your mind afterwards.'

I could hear my watch ticking in the silence, and thought interestedly to myself that it was the only one on the planet still going. 'The run of the play can't be going all that well for you if you have to keep taking these trips of yours.'

'The play is all right, thank you. In fact, I've been able to cut the trips down a good deal in the last hundred or two hundred years. It's still patchy, mind you. Nothing for nearly three months, and now today, besides you, in fact at this very moment, if I can use the expression, I'm dropping in on a woman in California who's got the wrong idea about something. Just —how shall I put it?—saving myself a bit of sweat. Oh, and don't waste your time trying to get in touch with her, because she won't remember anything about it.'

'Shall I remember?'

'I don't see why not. I've been assuming so, but it's really up to you. We can leave it until just before I go, can't we? See how you feel.'

'Thanks. Would you like another of those?'

'Well, yes, I think perhaps just one more, don't you? Marvellous.'

I said from the drinks cupboard, 'But you must be able to save yourself sweat without having to turn up in the flesh like this. Distance and time and so on are no object with you, after all.'

'Distance agreed. Time's another matter. Oh, there's a lot in what you say. The truth is, I enjoy my trips for their own sake. Self-indulgent of me, which is why I try to limit their number. But they are fun.'

'What sort of fun?'

He sighed again and clicked his tongue. 'It's difficult without denaturing the whole thing. Still. You're a chess-player, Maurice, or you were in your undergraduate days. You remember, I mean you must remember wishing you could be down on the board among the pieces, just for two or three moves, to get the feel of it, without at the same time stopping running the game. That's about as near as I can get.'

'The whole thing's a game, is it?' I had returned with the drinks.

'In the sense that it's not a particularly, uh ... edifying or significant business, it is, yes. In other ways it's not unlike an art, an art and a work of art rolled into one. I know you think that's rather frivolous. It isn't really. It's entirely a matter of how it's all grown up,' said the young man, lowering his voice and staring into his whisky. 'Between ourselves, Maurice, I think I took some fairly disputable decisions right at the start, not having foreknowledge. Honestly, this foreknowledge business is too absurd. As if I could carry on at all if I had that! Well, then I was stuck with those decisions and their results in practice. And I couldn't go back on them; one thing nobody's ever credited me with is the power of undoing what I've done, of abolishing historical fact and so on. I often wish I could—well, occasionally I do. It's not that I want to be cruel, not that so much as finding that's what I seem to be turning out to be. Not an easy situation, you know. I just realized that I was there, or here, or wherever you please, and on my own, and with these powers. I must say I wonder how you'd have managed.' He sounded slightly cross. 'You can't imagine what it's like to be faced with a set of choices that are irrevocable and also unique.'

'Well, you're supposed to be brighter than I am, though one would hardly think so, judging by results. But I had no idea you hadn't always been ... wherever you are. And whatever that means.'

'It means everywhere, if we're going to go into it, as you know perfectly well, though not everywhere equally all the time, of course. As for my always having been around, I have. But there have been developments. You could put a date to the point at which I found out I was around, so to speak. Quite a while ago, that was. It was at the same stage, in fact it was the same thing, as my discovery of what I was and what I could do.'

'All that part of it, the doing, must be pretty satisfying.'

'Oh yes, very, in a way. But it does go on rather. An awful lot of it's not much more than duty, these days. And I keep thinking of things it's too late to do. And things I oughtn't to do, but which have a certain appeal. Sweeping changes. Can you imagine the temptation of altering all the physical laws, or working with something that isn't matter, or simply introducing new rules? Even minor things like cosmic collisions, or plonking a living dinosaur—just one—down in Piccadilly Circus? Not easy to resist.'

'What about making life a little less hard on people?'

'No prospect of that, I'm afraid. Much too tricky from the security point of view. I daren't take the chance of coming that far out into the open. Some of your chaps have found out quite enough already. Your friend Milton, for instance.' The young man nodded over at my bookshelves. 'He caught on to the idea of the work of art and the game and the rules and so forth. Just as well it never quite dawned on him who Satan was, or rather who he was a piece of. I'd have had to step in there, if it had.'

I looked at him, noticing again how pale he was.

'Well . . .' He turned his mouth down. 'A little heart attack, perhaps. Paralytic stroke. That kind of thing.'

'You must have plenty of less crude methods than that up your sleeve.'

'Well . . . There's such a lot that's ruled out if you've got free will, you see. It makes life difficult for everybody, I know, but you can't do without it. And it isn't as if there weren't still a very great deal that isn't ruled out in the least. I must be off; I've been self-indulgent enough. But let me give you one piece of advice. Use the Church where appropriate. Oh, I don't mean go and listen to that posturing idiot Sonnenschein making me out to be a sort of suburban Mao Tse-tung. But remember that he's a priest of the Church, and as such he has certain techniques at his disposal. You'll see what I mean when the time comes. Just remember you're getting this from someone who, whatever you think his shortcomings may be, does indisputably know more than you do. Now, in return for putting up with me, and for the whisky, you can ask me one question. Want a moment to consider?'

143

'No. Is there an after-life?'

He frowned and cleared his throat. 'I suppose there's nothing else you could call it, really. It's nothing like here or anything you've ever imagined and I can't describe it to you. But you'll never be free of me, while this lot lasts.'

'Isn't it going to last for ever?'

'That's a further question, but never mind. The answer is that I don't know. I'll have to see. I mean that. Do you know, it's about the only absolutely fascinating, first-class, full-sized problem I've never started to go into? Anyway, you'll find out. Do you want to remember what we've been saying, and everything?'

'Yes.'

'All right.' The young man, moving like a young man, got to his feet. 'Thank you, Maurice, I really have enjoyed it. We'll meet again.'

'I'm sure we will.'

'When I'm in my ... executive capacity. Yes. You'll come to see the point of that part of me in the end, you know. Everybody does. Some more than others, of course.'

'Which sort am I?'

'Oh, the sort that's more inclined to appreciate me, obviously. You think about it, and you'll find I'm right. Ah.' He felt in a waistcoat pocket of the conservatively tailored suit, and brought out a small bright object, which he handed to me. 'A little keepsake.'

It was a slender and very beautiful silver crucifix of (I would have guessed) late Italian Renaissance workmanship, but as new as if it had been fashioned an hour before.

He nodded in confirmation. 'Nice, isn't it? Though I say so myself. I wish I could find a way of making it genuinely difficult for somebody in my position to run up stuff like that.'

'Is it you? I mean the ...'

'Oh yes. A piece of me.'

'That was coming out into the open, wasn't it?'

'Mm. I must have been bored, I suppose. I thought, why not? Then I thought I was heading straight for disaster. I needn't have worried, need I? He hasn't made much difference to anything, as you see.'

'But you were telling me just now that the Church was important.'

'Well, in a way. It can't help being. After all, it was me He was a piece of. Goodbye, Maurice.'

The crucifix jerked and spun in my hand, twisted itself away before I could close my fist on it, fell non-perpendicularly to the floor and twirled off towards a corner. As I scrambled in pursuit I heard his genial, sincerely amused laugh, and then, just after the flash of silver had disappeared into a crack between wainscot and floor, a deep ascending grumble which presently resolved and separated itself into the sounds of tractor and TV set rising towards normal pitch. I was at the front window long before they had reached it, in time to see the unique sight of reality moving from slow motion to ordinary motion, dust particles and wisps of smoke accelerating, a man engaged in coming to life, his arm circling at an increasing rate as he returned the handkerchief to his pocket. Then everything was as it should have been.

I left the window, but with nowhere in particular to go. My heart beat twice in a fraction of a second, stopped while I plunged forward and grasped the back of a dining-chair, then gave such a slam inside me that I bent in the middle and at the knees and nearly pulled the chair over. The pain in my back came while I was in the act of moving my hand to the spot, and began steadily expanding and contracting in a new way. I felt sweat spring out on the palms of my hands and my chest and face, and my breathing quickened. All the fear I had escaped during the young man's visit was upon me now, or its symptoms were. I found the whisky-bottle, drank a little, prevented myself from drinking more and washed down three pills with water. I realized there were two things that had to be done at once.

At the doorway I could not control a momentary hesitation, but then was out and hurrying down the passage. I found Amy, with Victor diagonally across her lap, looking at a cricket scoreboard on the screen.

'Darling, what time is it?'

She said without moving, 'Twenty past four.'

'Please look at your watch. No, show it to me.'

The small clock-face she wore at her wrist said four twenty-two. I looked at my own watch: four forty-six. A huge reason for fear departed, and left me feeling much as before. I started clumsily shifting the hands of my watch.

Still looking at the screen, Amy said conversationally, 'So I tell lies about the time now.'

'But you didn't tell a lie. It was——'

'You thought I had. You wouldn't believe me when I told

you. You had to see for yourself.'

'Well, you hadn't looked at your watch.'

'Just before you came in I had.'

'Sorry, darling, but I didn't know that, and I wanted to make sure.'

'Okay, Dad.'

'Sorry.'

'I don't suppose you want to watch Pirate Planet with me, do you?' she asked in the same tone as before. 'It comes on at five five.'

'I'll see. I've got a lot to do, but I'll try.'

'Okay.'

Next, I went to the office and collected the still-active torch of the two Diana and I had used in the early hours of that day, fetched from the utilities room the same hammer and chisel as before, plus a jemmy, and returned to the dining-room. It took me only a few minutes to get a fair-sized section of the carpet up, but the floor-boards were of solid timber, and in the excellent repair my predecessor had put them in. I made a good deal of noise, did some damage and sweated copiously getting the first one up. There was nothing but whorls of dust and streaks of cobwebby material on the laths and plaster beneath it, or as far as my weakening light would reach between the joists. On the assumption that the crucifix had gone on behaving supernaturally after disappearing, it might be anywhere in the area generally beneath me, if indeed it had not passed altogether beyond my reach. But I could see no alternative to going on as I had started.

Time went unprofitably by. I was working on my fourth floor-board when Nick and Lucy arrived.

'Hallo, Dad, what's going on?'

'Just . . .' I looked up at them, and was aware of how much like a husband and wife they seemed. 'I dropped something down a crack in the floor. Rather a valuable thing. I thought I'd see if I could find it.'

'What sort of thing?' Nick sounded sceptical.

'Well, it's a kind of heirloom. Something Gramps gave me.'

'Can't you, I mean, which crack did it go down? You seem to be——'

'No, it rolled, you see. I don't know.'

Nick glanced at Lucy. 'Are you sure you're all right, Dad?'

'Fine. Bit hot.'

'This isn't part of all the ghost stuff and everything that's

146

been going on, is it? I wish you'd say if it is.'

'No, honestly. Just this——'

'Because you know you can tell us and it'll be all right,' said Lucy. 'We won't think you're mentally disturbed, or tell anyone else if you don't want us to. It'll be all right.'

'No, really,' I said, thinking that her use of the plural stretched the facts a little. 'Don't worry; if I can't find it soon I'll pack up.'

When I turned back to my work, I was aware of a brief silent conference going on above my head, and ending with their departure. At the end of another five minutes or so, I had the fourth floor-board out. Nothing again; or perhaps something, an odd bulge in a joist, a small object leaning against it at arm's length. My extended fingers touched metal.

What I held in my hand a moment later was just recognizable as the crucifix the young man had given me: speckled, worn and stained almost black in places. In its present state it testified to no sort of miracle; an impartial mind would merely add it to the endless list of mildly surprising discoveries in old houses. I dismissed it from consideration, but was still overwhelmed with what felt like rage and disappointment. These and allied emotions went on showing through while I put all the energy I could into the task of relaying floor and carpet. As soon as this was done, they returned in full.

I left the tools and the torch where I had dropped them, and walked round the room trying to master myself, which meant, or must be prefaced by, discovering what it was that oppressed me. As if in answer, my visitor's empty glass, standing on the low table between the armchairs, presented itself to my eye. I snatched it up and saw the marks of a human hand on its surface and of a human mouth at its rim. Well, what of it? Was I to take it to a spiritualist medium, a forensic scientist or the curator of the Vatican museum? I threw it hard into the back of the fireplace, breathing fast and starting to cry. Yes, it was disappointment all right, with him for his coldness and his lightness, with myself for my failure to have brought forward any question or accusation of the least significance, and also with the triviality of the ultimate secrets I had supposedly learned. And there was fear besides. I had always thought that personal extinction was the ultimate horror, but, having taken in those few dry hints about an after-life, that pronouncement that I would never escape from him, I now knew better.

An overwhelming desire to get out of the house took hold of

147

me and helped me to stop crying. There were more things to be done before I could leave. A quick shower and a change of underclothes took off the sweat and grime of my exertions with the floor-boards. When I had dressed I went in search of Lucy, and by good luck found her alone in the great bedroom, brushing her short head of hair with surprising energy.

'Lucy, I'm going out now and won't be back till late. Will you tell the others? I'll talk to David before I go.'

'By all means.'

'And there's something else I'd like you to do for me. I want everybody in bed and preferably asleep by midnight. Well, I know you can't put them to sleep, but Joyce is never any problem, and if you could try to get Nick off in good time, that would be a great help to me.'

'I'll do everything I can, of course. Uh, Maurice, is this something to do with your ghosts, or is it, you know, somebody you want to see privately?'

She made this allusion to my amorous activities (I had not known that—or not bothered before now to wonder whether— she knew about them) with commendable tact of manner. 'It's my ghosts,' I said.

'I see. Would you like me as a witness?'

'Thank you for offering, Lucy, but I'm sure he won't come if there's anyone else apart from me about. You believe I saw him before really, don't you?'

'I still think you thought you saw him, but I may be wrong. Did you find that thing you were looking for under the floor?'

'Yes.'

'Was it any good?'

'No.'

'Like the writing on that piece of paper?'

This was an inspired guess or feat of deduction. 'Very much like that.'

'Well, let me know what happens tonight, if anything does.'

'I will. Thanks, Lucy.'

The last thing was getting hold of David and asking him to see to it that the few expected outside diners and drinkers were similarly off the premises by midnight. The resident guests could not actually be sent to their rooms, but they were un- likely to feel like prolonged carousing in the bar the night after a funeral so close by. I supposed, at least, that talking to David would be the last thing, until I almost literally ran into Joyce and Diana in the car-park.

148

They had their jewellery and their garden-party look on again, and were unfeignedly sorry to see me. I thought at first that they were (as they might well be) nervous of possible embarrassment, then I thought that they were simply resentful at the intrusion of any third party, and then I saw that they were even more simply annoyed because I had turned up.

'Hallo,' I said brightly. At that moment I could not devise any other utterance that seemed absolutely free of irony and/or obscenity.

They exchanged their now familiar glance of consultation, and Joyce said, 'We thought we'd go and have a drink in the village.'

'Good idea. I'm going out myself. Don't wait up for me.'

'Do you want me to leave you something to eat?'

'No thanks. See you, then.'

While they got slowly into the Mini-Cooper, I got quickly into the Volkswagen, reflecting on Diana's silence during the last exchange. I had never before known her to be content with less than about a two-thirds share of any conversation, however brief. And her whole demeanour over those dozen seconds had been docile, almost subservient. Whatever had happened between those two had had plenty of time to happen, I decided when I looked at my watch and found that the time was exactly eight o'clock.

My spirits, which had been improving a little, fell again sharply when I contemplated the four hours that had somehow to be filled in. I still had no idea where I was making for, and the mere action of driving at speed towards no destination had the effect of emphasizing to me my anxiety to escape, which soon started to make me feel as if I were being pursued by some malignant person or thing. Only as if; I was perfectly clear in my mind that nobody and nothing was pursuing me; but I have never known a powerful illusion of this kind to be appreciably weakened by being recognized as an illusion. I had touched eighty on the A595, and missed a head-on collision with a petrol tanker by a few seconds, before it occurred to me that no speed is great enough to permit a man to escape from himself. I found the banality of this idea soothing, and was able to drive less furiously thereafter.

I stopped at the George on the outskirts of Royston, ate some tongue sandwiches, drank a pint and a half of bitter, took a pill, bought a quarter-bottle of White Horse and drove on. In Cambridge I went into a cinema, and sat through forty minutes of a wide-screen Western (in which, apart from much talk and even more dead silence, one man shot at another and missed) before deciding that I felt too tense and jittery to continue. On bad days, sitting in a cinema can give me a curiously strong foretaste of dying, out of some fortuitous combination of the darkness, the felt presence of unseen strangers, the vast, unnaturally-coloured, ever-changing images, the voices that are not quite like voices. I walked the streets for a while, counting my footsteps and telling myself that something interesting was going to happen between three hundred and three hundred and fifty, and that this would show everybody that Allington was a good judge, whose predictions could be relied on. By the three hundred and forties nothing remotely interesting had turned up, not even a passable woman, so I settled for the stand of paperbacked novels I could see through the window of a supermarket. The place was still open; I went in and bought something I had never heard of by a writer whose first book, a satire on provincial life, I remembered had been commended at the time. In the little cocktail bar of the University Arms, I got through about forty minutes' worth of this too, before going out and dropping it into a rubbish basket on the way back to my car. To the endemic unreality of all fiction, the author had added contributions of his own: an inability to leave even the most utilitarian sentence unadorned by some verbal frill or knob or curlicue, recalling those savage cultures whose sacred objects and buildings are decorated in every square inch; a rooted habit of proceeding by way of violent and perfunctory transitions from one slackly observed scene to the next; and an unvaried method of characterization whereby, having portrayed a person as one sort of cliché, he presently revealed him as a predictable different sort of cliché. Oh well, what had I expected? The thing was a novel.

On the road again, and in the dark this time, I very soon felt panic settling upon me. I had reason (of a sort) to feel afraid of encountering Underhill; this was nothing to do with that, a pure, unmotivated, objectless fear that, in my boyhood, had sent me running out of the house and across the common that it faced until I could literally not run any more, and, later, had caused me to read the entire contents of a newspaper aloud to myself as fast as possible while I tapped first one foot and then the other as fast as possible. This is a poor frame of mind in which to drive a car among traffic moving at between thirty miles an hour and sixty-five or more on a not particularly wide road. Each time, as I pulled out to overtake in the face of a column of oncoming headlights or at the approach to a blind corner, rational fear seemed as if it would drive out irrational fear for ever, to recede unnoticed and unremembered as soon as the danger was past.

The accident took place on a bend of the A595 about three miles south of Royston and four from home. I caught up with a largish car, a Humber Hawk or something similar, which was ambling along at about forty, and started to pass it a couple of hundred yards from the start of the bend, not an outstandingly dangerous manoeuvre provided the Hawk maintained its original speed. No doubt spurred by an idiot resentment at being overtaken by a car half the size of his, its driver accelerated instead. As, more or less side by side, the two vehicles began curving round to the left, an immense articulated lorry, chains of red lights outlining its extra wide load, appeared from the other direction. I had not the m.p.h. to pass the Hawk, and could not predict what it might do; so, trusting to my memory of a road I had travelled four times a week for seven years, I swung to the right across the front of the lorry and into the wide grass verge I hoped very much was there. It was there, but rougher and more sloping than I had thought. These features slowed me down, at any rate, and I was not going very fast when I drove into the brickwork of a culvert (as I learned later) and hit my head on something.

'Are you all right, mate?' asked a voice.

'Yes, thank you.'

'Well, you bloody well oughtn't to be. You daft or something? Double-banking on a bend like that? Pissed, I suppose, like 'em all.'

'No.'

'Flat pissed, you must be, if you aren't off your rocker. Yeah, he's okay. No call to be, but he is, so he says.'

Another voice spoke then, but I never remembered to what effect. I know only that, after some lapse of time, I was standing in front of my house while a car—a Humber Hawk, perhaps—receded into the distance. I felt like a man on the moon, almost weightless, or as if on the point of disembodiment, like myself after a heavy night and a heavy lunch, like a child, observant without expectation, curious and disinterested.

It was eight minutes to midnight. Just nice time, I said to myself. Indoors, everything was quiet and in darkness. Splendid. I went to the bar and fetched a tumbler, a siphon of soda and a bottle of Glen Grant, took a weak drink and a pill, and settled down in the public dining-room to wait the remaining two minutes. I sat at a corner table in the part where Underhill's parlour had been, with just the one heavily shaded light in front of me turned on, out of consideration to him. I was almost directly facing the window at which he was accustomed to make his appearances, with the hall door diagonally opposite. The night was warm, but not humid.

Very faintly, I heard the church clock in the village begin striking midnight. I could not remember whether, with clocks that do not strike the quarters, the first note or the last signified the hour. Nothing happened, at any rate, while the clock was striking. And nothing happened after it had finished, either. I waited. The clock must be fast. But my own watch said two and a bit minutes after twelve.

By ten past I had decided that I had got the whole thing wrong, I had misunderstood Underhill's message, it had not been a message at all, I had been mistaken about the freshness of the ink, he had just been seeing if I could be fooled into keeping this appointment, he had been joking. But I was not going to give him up yet. I sat there, unable to find any way of helping the time to pass. Through my mind went thoughts of Joyce, and Amy, and Diana, and my father, and Margaret, and the young man, and death, and ghosts, and drink, and Joyce again, and Amy again. In my current (perhaps precarious, but remarkably durable) state of detachment, all these topics struck me as very interesting but of no personal moment whatever, like, say, the New England whaling industry in the nineteenth century being considered by an intelligent and imaginative Grimsby trawlerman of our own time.

I went on not looking at my watch for much longer than I would have thought was possible. Then I did. It was three minutes to one. Fine. To wait an hour was as much as politeness and sanity demanded. I poured a short weak drink and sipped it deliberately. As faintly as before, but, it seemed to me, more distinctly, the church clock sounded, and I got up to go.

'Stay. I am come as I said I would,' said somebody, somebody standing in the shadows of the corner directly opposite the door.

'You're late, Dr Underhill.'

'Not so, I've been most punctual. Now to the purpose. Have you our silver friend about you?'

I had not thought of this for hours, but when I felt in my pocket the thing was there. 'Yes.'

There was a sort of sigh from the corner. 'That's well. Be so good as to place it on the table before you.'

I did as I was told. 'There. What now?'

'Now I'll entertain you.'

'Before you do, may I ask a question?'

'Assuredly.'

'When did you write that note asking me to meet you to-night?'

'This morning, by your reckoning, the morning of the day just past. But yours was the hand that writ, mine merely the hand that guided yours.'

'I don't remember that.'

'Not to remember is your quality, Mr Allington.'

'Is that why you chose me to . . . assist you, or whatever it is you want me to do?'

'How have I chosen you, when it is you that have each time come in search of me? But now, pray you, have done for the moment. There are many marvels in store.'

I had time to admire the justice of my own description of the voice—sounding as if artificially produced, with a kind of Gloucester-cum-Cork accent—before Underhill's show began. The room was suddenly and brightly illuminated, only it was not the room any more, but a cave, or a cave-mouth. A group of naked women flashed into apparent existence, in mid-performance of some sort of slow, writhing, vaguely Oriental ballet. Their voluptuousness was extreme, and also theoretical, like the fantasy-drawings of a prurient but talented schoolboy: enormous breasts, nipples that in proportion were even more enormous, tiny waists, spreading hips and buttocks, sexual organs displaced forwards into the V of the crotch, as in Indian sculpture. There was monotonous music and a strong scent of roses. I would have grinned at all this, had it not been for something two-dimensional about the dancers and their movements that gave me the uncomfortable sensation of watching them through an invisible telescope. And I did not feel happy about the pair of red eyes, apparently belonging to some small creature like a snake or a rat, that were watching me from farther back in the cave.

The music grew louder, the smell of roses became insufferable and a troop of naked black men, of physical endowment so immense as to outdo the proportions of the women, leaped among them with loud yells. An orgy soon developed, cast and directed with a crudity that again might have made me want to laugh, but by now I had noticed the pallid, glistening coils of fungus that clung to the walls and roof of rock, and the second, larger pair of red eyes in the darkness of the cave, also fixed on mine. By their size and position, these might have belonged to a being about the size of a tall man. They did not move or blink.

With a rippling, sticky jerk, as if what I saw were being magic-lanterned on to a thick sheet of gelatin, the orgy scene gave place to an encounter between two black girls and what I supposed was a white adolescent boy, though he was equipped on the same scale as his black predecessors and had long fair hair like a woman's. This was even less to my taste than what had gone before, but before it disappeared in its turn the girls' faces struck me as not resembling, even in colour, those of any black people I had ever seen—they were much more like the handiwork of someone who knew them only from descriptions. Behind the music, which had become lumpishly repetitive, a man's voice, not Underhill's, was calling, too faintly for any words to be distinguishable, though seemingly familiar.

The new manifestation was two white girls making love, and went on for only a few seconds: an outstandingly abortive attempt to entertain me. When I looked again at the cave-mouth background, which had remained constant throughout, it was empty. I hoped very much that I had made some grimace or gesture by which Underhill had been able to read my discomfort; I did not want to think that he had seen it in my mind—still less that, just before, he had come across a buried memory of the afternoon and misread it as desire. By now the music, abandoning, so to speak, any attempt at rhyme and reason, had degenerated into an irregularly pulsating noise, and the smell was of decaying roses. But the two pairs of eyes were fixed on me as before.

It was from hereabouts that the next development came. There was a stirring of some sort, and two obscure shapes started to emerge, moving with the foreshortened effect I had noticed earlier, so that the sideways component of their progress was unnaturally emphasized. As they moved, the illumination died down, but enough remained for me to be able to make out a sort of quadruped about the size of a small pig, and secondly a biped creature with the same kind of skin. It was of the rough general shape of a man, but it was not a man, nor any kind of ape or monkey. I could not name what it and its companion were. The flesh of both looked soft and loose, and was indeed becoming softer and looser, was beginning to disintegrate and at the same time form itself anew. Limbs, if they could any longer be called limbs, dwindled and disappeared while fresh appendages came bulging, bursting, twisting out of the main trunk, which itself continuously changed shape in both cases. At one moment the two entities were united by a swelling rope of what could have been living matter, at the next the larger of the two started to divide about its longer axis. Either the whole sight was a reproduction, by another intelligence, of the hypnagogic hallucinations I was subject to, or I was imposing it on top of whatever illusions were now being directed at me, this while fully awake and with my eyes open. I felt my equanimity wearing thin.

The accompanying noise, though as before destitute of pitch or any rhythm, still retained the capacity to vary in volume. In the quieter moments I could just make out Underhill's voice, speaking in a monotone—the liturgical monotone I had heard coming from this part of the house during my night-vision of the previous afternoon. I looked down at the table in front of me. The silver figure had gone.

This was much worse than anything that had happened so far. It was time to make a move. When I got to my feet, immediate and complete darkness descended, and at the same moment the noise changed to the beating of many wings and a shrill, cawing clamour, and the smell changed to that of an aviary or hen-house, though intolerably intensified. After a few seconds, the air round my head was full of tiny scarlet-green birds, scores of them, evidently phosphorescent, for they were as bright as if the sun had been shining on them, and yet there was no external source of light. Clacking their tiny beaks, they wheeled and plunged and dived at my face, striking me head-on in the cheekbone, at the point of the chin, over the eye, though I felt nothing, and then vanishing, winking out like a snuffed flame, though their number did not grow less. I closed my eyes, and they were there as before, put my hands over my closed eyes, and they were there, stuck my fingers in my ears, and the cawing and clacking went on. I had no breath to scream; from moment to moment I strove to work out where the door was, but each time one of them flew into my face I had to stop and start again. With my orientation hopelessly lost, I heard, through it all, Underhill laughing, and instantly found myself standing next to the ripped-up area of floor in my dining-room upstairs, putting the crucifix in my pocket (an action I had at once forgotten). The next instant I was back among the birds, but with my hand still, or again, holding the crucifix. With the birds redoubling their attacks and positively shrieking, I threw it where Underhill's voice had seemed to come from, and heard it strike wall or floor.

Slowly and steadily, what was happening to me changed. The birds began to confine themselves to the middle and left-hand side of my vision, and were growing oddly flattened, though they flew at me as before, while their noises progressively deteriorated in quality, with the precise effect of a wire-less receiver being detuned a little at a time. Now the birds were gathered in a narrow and narrowing sector to my left, becoming wafer-like, as though the screen on which they were projected were being turned away from me towards the end-on position, and I could hear only a faint and undifferentiated roaring. Soon I was looking at a vertical line of flecked scarlet-and-green light, which faded to nothing in the silence. I was standing alone in the middle of the room, in darkness but for the moon through the windows.

I realized that I must have turned off my table-lamp at some earlier point, and started to move to the switches by the door. On the way, my eye was caught by a gleam of metal on the floor in the corner where Underhill had first appeared. I picked up, not the crucifix, but the silver figure, and at once heard, from outside, a faint but familiar and dreadful rustling sound off to the right, and Amy's voice calling me from the opposite direction.

I ran out into the hall, to the front door, not stopping to turn on any lights, but my fingers knew the bolts, and I was out of the house almost immediately. Amy was about a hundred yards away down the road, wearing white pyjamas and carrying something in her arms: I assumed it was Victor. As she walked slowly towards the village, she was looking about her—in search of me? From the other side, that bizarre, rough-hewn, malformed shape was approaching, stiffly and clumsily, but steadily, with reserves in hand, and I remembered how I had seen its phantom quicken up as it drew near the house, and with what eventual result. This, however, was the reality, not the phantom, and I knew now, had known before I reached the front door, what Underhill's second purpose had been—not merely to survive death, nor to subdue a living person to his will, but to reach from beyond the grave to bring about what I would see enacted within a minute, unless I could prevent it.

The creature was jolting along at this stage in a version of a brisk walk, crackling as it moved, It looked larger than before, but also less compact, perhaps even yet not having achieved its final form. Evidently it had so far not seen me. I had lost three or four seconds already: I started forward and ran at top speed towards Amy along the grass verge, as silently as I could, but she heard me before I was within twenty yards of her, and began to turn. I shouted to her not to look round—in vain: she saw me, and then the green man, and her face went stretched and rigid. I reached her.

'What's that, Daddy?'

'It's somebody bad. Now you put Victor down and run into the village as fast as you can and just shout and shout till people come.'

'What will you do?'

'Don't worry about me,' I said, with a rustling, creaking jog-trot behind me. 'Off you go at once. Run.'

I faced about. The thing was coming up fast now, its legs driving powerfully and arms crooked, still accelerating. If it were left to itself, Amy would never reach the village. I stood in its path and marked out a place in the left groin that seemed made only of twigs and creepers, so perhaps vulnerable to a fist. I saw its face now for the first time, an almost flat surface of smooth dusty bark like the trunk of a Scotch pine, with irregular eye-sockets in which a fungoid luminescence glimmered, and a wide grinning mouth that showed more than a dozen teeth made of jagged stumps of rotting wood: I had seen a version of that face before. Then the green man was upon me, its dissimilar arms held out before it, and that cry as of wind through foliage issuing from its mouth, exultant as much as menacing. Before I could close with it, it swung a forearm without breaking its stride and dealt me a blow across the chest that flung me to the ground a couple of yards off. I was not knocked out, but for the moment all strength had left me.

Amy had retreated a little way, then stopped and turned, and between her and the pounding bulk of the creature stood Victor in a posture of defiance, his back arched and tail swollen. A kick from a wooden foot smashed into him, with a snapping of twigs or bones, and he went skidding, a lifeless bundle, across the road and into the ditch. Then Amy turned again and ran, ran in earnest, in long-legged strides, but even when she reached her best speed, she was not gaining on the green man. By now I was aware of what I still held in my hand, and saw what it was I must do, and pushed myself to my feet and ran in my turn down the road towards the graveyard. Ahead of me, the pursuit continued; from where I was I could not judge the distance between the one and the other, and did not try, but drew back my arm and hurled the silver figure over the graveyard wall. I heard it touch ground, and immediately that misshapen being came lurching to a halt, did more than halt, was bowed down, was borne backwards by some immense force, step by step, shaking and flailing, while portions of it detached themselves and came whirling towards me, around me and over my head, leaf, twig, bough, stump, so that I crouched down and crossed my arms over my face, ducking instinctively as a stout length of wood swished past, and again when a thorny tendril scored my wrist, eyes screwed up and ears filled with a drawn-out, diminishing howl of inhuman pain and rage.

Silence fell, broken only by some heavy vehicle speeding towards London on the A595. I got up slowly, walked a few paces, then ran on towards the village calling Amy's name. She was stretched out at the edge of the road with blood on her forehead, one knee and one hand. I carried her back to the house, laid her on her bed and telephoned Jack Maybury.

5: A Movement in the Grass

'Physically, there's nothing to worry about,' said Jack just after midday. 'That's a perfectly healthy sleep she's in now. No evidence of concussion. No fever. And those cuts and bruises are quite minor. Psychologically, well, I doubt if there's much grounds for anxiety there either, not immediately anyway, though I must admit I'm a bit out of my depth with sleepwalking. Are you sure it was sleepwalking?'

I turned from the window of Amy's bedroom. 'I don't know. I just assumed it was.' I had decided it was, as the most flexible rough version of what had really happened. 'The front door woke me up, I saw her passing the window, so I went and——'

'So you said. What exactly happened when you got to her?'

'I called out to her, which was probably a mistake, only I didn't think, and she gave this great start and half turned round, and tripped.'

'And hit her head on the road hard enough to knock her out, but ... I just wouldn't have thought a bang that caused such a comparatively minor contusion would be enough to knock a healthy person out. Still. Why were you in the public dining-room instead of your own place up here?'

'I go there sometimes. Less chance of being interrupted.'

'Yeah. Just as well you did, this time. Right, well I'll look in again this evening. Keep her in bed meanwhile. Light lunch. We'll see how it goes. There's a very good kids' headshrinker bloke at the hospital I can get hold of tomorrow. Personally, I doubt whether she was sleepwalking at all.'

'What do you think she was doing?'

'Pretending to sleepwalk. She'd read about it.'

'What would be the point of that?'

'Oh, to get herself a bit of attention from someone,' said Jack, with a full dose of his censorious look. 'Anyway, I'll be off now. How are you?' he added grudgingly.

'Fine. A bit tired.'

'Get some rest this afternoon. No more little birds?'

'No. Would you like a drink?'

'No thanks.'

As he started to leave, I asked without premeditation, 'How's Diana?'

Jack stopped leaving. 'How is she? She's all right. Why?'

'No reason.'

'I'll just say this much, Maurice. I like things the way they are. I don't like turmoil or upsets or letting one part of your life interfere with the other. I'm not against people enjoying themselves in any way they happen to fancy, provided they don't start behaving like bloody kids. Okay?'

'I'm for that too,' I said, wondering what Diana could have said to him, but, as a mere ex-lover of hers since yesterday, not wondering very hard.

'Good. See you tonight.'

Then he did go. Very soon afterwards. Amy opened her eyes in the manner of someone waking up with tremendous reluctance after a tremendously deep sleep. She smiled at me, then felt the taped bandage on her forehead and traced its outline. We hugged each other.

'Have I been sleepwalking, Dad?'

'Well . . . you might have been. All sorts of people do.'

'I had a funny dream, Dad,' she went on immediately. 'You were in it.'

This was the first time that day she had spoken more than a couple of words. 'What happened?'

'Well, I dreamt I was lying in bed here, and you were calling to me. You told me to get up and come downstairs, so I did. I took Victor with me, because he was here. You didn't tell me to, but I thought you wouldn't mind. Then when I got downstairs, you said I was to go outside into the road. I still couldn't see you, but that was what you said. So I went outside, but you weren't there, so I started looking for you.'

'Go on.'

'I'm trying to, but it gets harder to remember after that. You gave me a fright, but you didn't mean to. You came up and told me I was to put Victor down and run into the village, so I did. I started to, anyway. Then I really forget what happened. But I do sort of remember that you were being very brave, Dad. Was there a man chasing me?'

'I don't know. You were dreaming.'

'I don't think I was. I wasn't, was I?'

She was looking hard at me. 'No,' I said. 'It was real.'

'Well done, Dad,' she said, and took my hand.

'What for?'

'Not pretending. And being brave. What happened to the man?'

'He ran away. He won't be back.'

'What happened to Victor? The man killed him, didn't he?'

'Yes. But it was over in a moment.'

'He was brave too. It wasn't really you telling me to get up and come downstairs, was it? Then what was it really?'

'I think that part of it must have been a sort of dream. You imagined it. No, not quite that. There was a spell on the house, so that people saw things and heard things when there wasn't anybody there.'

'You mean like that screaming the other day?'

'That was part of it. But it's all over now, I promise you.'

'Okay, Dad. I mean I believe you. I'm all right. Where's Victor? He's not just still lying there, is he?'

'No. I've got him safe. I'm going off to bury him in a minute.'

'Good idea. Come and see me again when you've got time.'

'Would you like me to get Joyce or Magdalena to sit with you?'

'No, I'll be all right. Could you pass me that magazine about Jonathan Swift there on my dressing-table?'

'Jonathan Swift? Oh, I see.'

The front page of the publication carried a colour photograph of a young man (or so I assumed him to be) who had yet to undergo his first haircut or shave; it had been deliberately worsened in quality by a no doubt advanced fuzzing process, and had evidently been taken from some sunken chamber or hole in the ground at its subject's feet. I handed the thing to Amy, who immediately opened it and started reading.

'What would you like for lunch?'

'Hamburger and baked beans and chips and tomato sauce and tinned cherries and cream and a Coke ... uh, please, Dad.'

'Won't that be too much for you? Dr Maybury said you were to just have something light.'

'Oh, Dad. I'm so hungry. I'll eat it slowly.'

'All right, then, I'll fix it.'

I went downstairs in search of David and found him in the front bar, an all-too-popular rendezvous on Sunday mornings. It was full of middle-aged men in Caribbean shirts drinking pints of bitter, and less straightforwardly middle-aged women in floral trouser-suits drinking Pimm's. They were all talking as if from one side of a busy street to the other, but quietened down and stared into their drinks when they saw me, out of respect for the bereaved, or the insane. David was in the middle of taking an order from a party of six that included a pair of identically dressed identical twin queers, and looked as though he had had trouble getting that far. He greeted me apprehensively, no doubt hoping, with some justification, that I was not about to ask him to do anything along the lines of preparing a room for Count and Countess Dracula, and cheered up a good deal when I did no more than tell him Amy's wishes and say I would be resuming charge at 6 p.m. (I had determined to finish everything by then.)

With this out of the way, Nick and Lucy not yet emerged and Joyce nowhere to be seen, I picked up the hammer and chisel I had used on my dining-room floor and dropped them in the passenger's seat of the trade truck. Then I fetched Victor from the gardening hut, where he had lain wrapped in sacking since I stowed him there before breakfast. I also took a shovel and a scythe. The least unsatisfactory plan I could think of was to drive up as close as possible to the graveyard gate, unload and then re-park the truck at an inconspicuous distance. In the event, nobody saw me; at this time everyone was in the pub or the kitchen.

First, Victor. I soon found him a pleasant, secluded spot near the wall, out of sight from where Underhill lay, and in that soil it was not difficult to open a trench eighteen inches deep or so. In he went, and I shovelled the earth back into place, thinking how much I would miss his total lack of dignity and of ill nature. A couple of days earlier, I should probably have considered taking his body to the vet, in the hope of establishing something about the force that had killed him, something objectively factual that would support my story. But by now I had given up all such notions: I had seen what I had seen, and there would never be a way of convincing anyone else that I had. I smoothed the earth flat with my hands.

The second task was a far more formidable affair. I had some idea of direction, but very little of distance, and I spent over an hour and a half, and had cleared something like twenty square yards of ground, before I found the silver figure in a tuft of couch-grass; I suppose even then I was lucky. Laying it on a triangular piece of somebody's headstone, I went at it with the hammer and chisel and, aided by the softness of the metal, quickly had it in half a dozen not easily recognizable pieces, which I buried in different parts of the graveyard. Having done this I felt a lot safer, but by no means

162

safe. More effort was going to be necessary before that state could be attained.

I was just about to move on to the next job when a thought struck me. I went over to where Underhill was buried, dropped the tools and pissed on his grave.

'You bastard,' I said. 'You tried to pretend you hadn't chosen me, out of all the people who've lived in that house since you. You just waited until Amy was the age you liked, and then you set to work to arouse my curiosity. And in your present form you couldn't do to her what you did to those other poor kids, so you tried to kill her instead. For fun. Very scientific. Some purpose.'

Again without being seen, I returned to the truck and drove through the village, which under the bright sunshine had a look of spurious significance, as if its inhabitants were known to be the wisest and happiest in England. I drew up outside the rectory, a small but beautiful Queen Anne house across the road from the church. Its garden was overgrown and littered with rubbish, including a number of framed pictures, mostly of country scenes, which had presumably come with the house. Music was rampaging away inside it. I tugged at the rusty iron bell-pull and an electronic chime sounded from within. After about a minute, a rather better-kempt version of Jonathan Swift opened the door. He looked at me while he chewed something.

'Is the rector at home?' I asked.

'Who are you?'

'One of his parishioners.'

'His what?'

'Parishioners. People who live in his parish. Round here. Is he at home?'

'I'll see.'

He turned away, but the advancing shape of the Reverend Tom Rodney, clad in a turquoise tee-shirt and skin-tight black denim trousers, was now to be seen over his shoulder.

'What is it, Cliff? Oh ... Mr Allington. Do you want to see me?'

'Well yes, I was hoping to. If you've got a minute.'

'Uh ... of course. Do come in. I'm afraid everything's in a bit of a mess. Oh, Mr Allington, this is Lord Cliff Oswestry.'

'Ch-do,' said Lord Cliff.

'Hi there, man,' I said, not sure whether he had adopted the title for some trade reason, or had acquired it willy-nilly.

Judging by his manner so far, I favoured the second of these.

'I haven't had a chance to clear up all the crap,' said the rector. 'We got back about three this morning, and I just made morning service with a big low on. Oh, Cliff dear, could you turn it down a bit? I'm afraid Cliff and I are sort of hooked on Benjie again. He does get to one, doesn't he?'

By now we were in a sort of drawing-room with black wall-paper on three walls and gold on the fourth, a squat bamboo screen enclosing nothing in particular and a lot of suède-topped stools. I could not see much crap, apart from some broken crockery that looked as if it had been hurled rather than dropped, and an object resembling an aerial sculpture that had made a forced landing. An invisible singer with a bad head-cold was doing his best to reach some unreasonably high notes among a lot of orchestral fuss. Very soon this faded to a murmur, presumably by the agency of Lord Cliff, of whom I saw no more.

'Well, what's the trouble?' asked the rector, almost like a real rector. This kind of thing must be an example of the dead weight of tradition he was constantly on guard against, some-times, as now, with inadequate vigilance.

'No trouble,' I said, squirming about on my stool in search of some tolerable position. 'There are two things I'd like to bring up. The first is that the seventh centenary of the found-ing of my house, the Green Man, comes round next month, as you probably know.'

'Oh yes, somebody was telling me about it the other day.'

The somebody must have been the Father of Lies himself, since I had just made up the centenary idea. In the same im-provisatory vein, I went on, 'Anyway, I was thinking of throw-ing a rather special party to mark the occasion. It's been a very good summer for me, financially that is, and if this weather keeps up I could put on quite a show in the garden there. I get quite a lot of, well, prominent people at my house from time to time, show business, television, fashion, even the odd politi-cian, and I thought I'd just invite the lot. You never know who might turn up. Anyway, I was wondering if you'd like to come along. Plus any chums you might care to invite, of course.'

People's eyes do not actually glisten unless they are weeping, but the rector put up a convincing simulacrum of it without recourse to tears. 'Could I bring my bishop? The old sweetie would adore it so.'

'You can bring the Moderator of the Free Church of Scotland if you like.'

'Oh, how super.' His eyes stopped glistening. 'What was the other thing?'

'Oh yes. I expect you've heard that my house is haunted. Well, it's been getting quite troublesome recently. I'd like you to perform a service of exorcism to get rid of the spirits, or whatever they are.'

'You've *got* to be joking.'

'I'm perfectly serious.'

'Oh, come on. You mean you've actually been seeing ghosts? *Really*.'

'Yes, really. Otherwise I shouldn't have bothered you.'

'You don't suppose a lot of religious mumbo-jumbo could have the slightest effect, do you? On *anything*?'

'I don't know. I'd like to give it a trial. It would be a great favour to me if you'd just run through the service, Rector.'

I was fully prepared to go on and tell him in the plainest terms that no exorcism meant no invitation to the party, but he was ahead of me. No doubt the course of his career had trained him to recognize a *quid pro quo* as soon as he set eyes on one, or rather overtrained him, because he would never get any kind of *quo* from me. With the irritation which his face was so well constructed to express, he asked, 'When?'

'Now. I can drive you there in three minutes.'

'Oh, *honestly*,' he said, but without heat, and was busy in calculation for a moment. My bet is that he had spotted the annoyance-potential to Lord Cliff of going off with me on such an eccentric errand. 'Oh, very well, but I think it's shaking to find a person of your education falling prey to gross superstition like this.' But he got off his stool nimbly enough.

'You'd better put on your regalia for this do, I think.'

'Oh, for ...' Lord Cliff (on my reading) entered his thoughts again, and he cheered up a little. 'Might as well do the thing properly while one's about it, I suppose. Amuse yourself. Have some fruit. Back in a trice.'

There was a bunch of bananas on a table-top of an untrimmed chunk of slate, I ate a couple and told myself I was having lunch. But, in my experience, even a lunch as light as that needs washing down. I went to a likely-looking (also very nasty-looking) cupboard I had spotted on first entering the room. Apart from what might have been sticks of incense and what almost certainly were marijuana cigarettes, it contained gin, vermouth, Campari, white port, a variety of horrible drinks from the eastern Mediterranean, a siphon of soda and no glasses. I rejected the idea of mixing myself a dry Martini in a near-by ash-tray, and took a swig from the gin-bottle. Warm neat gin is nobody's nectar, but I managed to get some down without coughing much. I chased it with soda-water, taking this perforce from the nozzle of the siphon, a different kind of feat, then swallowed a pill. As I did so, it crossed my mind that, if Underhill had been able to manufacture a hundred scarlet-and-green birds, he could certainly have manufactured one. It was true that he had produced something like my hypnagogic visions, which I had had for years, since long before moving into his house, but his version of these had been a passable copy, a counterfeit, whereas (I realized for the first time) the birds had been exact replicas of the original one I had seen in the bathroom—how like him to have tested a weapon before using it in earnest. Well, when I had had time to forget just how much the solitary bird had frightened me, there was going to be a case for going back on the bottle: the half-bottle, at least.

Time went by. There was a large book-case full of books across the room, but I left them quite alone, knowing how angry they would all make me. I had begun to contemplate pretty steadily another assault on the drinks cupboard when the Rev. Tom returned, in clerical rig-out and carrying a suit-case covered with what looked like white corduroy. He seemed in top form now, toned up by whatever had taken place while he was changing. 'Shall we go?' he asked me, twitching his eyebrows and shoulders. I agreed that we should.

At past three o'clock on a Sunday, the public dining-room was empty. We went in by way of the kitchen without being observed, and I at once locked the door to the hall. In quite a businesslike fashion, the rector put his suitcase on a serving-table, took out his vestments or whatever one calls them, plus some other odds and ends, accoutred himself with them and produced a book.

'A bit of luck I happened to have this,' he said. 'It's not the sort of thing one's asked to produce every day.'

'Good. You can start as soon as you're ready.'

'All right. I still think this is a lot of balls, but anyway. Oh *no*,' he added after finding his place in the book.

'What's the matter?'

'One's meant to have holy water for this business.'

'Haven't you got any?'

'What would I be doing with a whole lot of holy water? You don't imagine I keep it round the place like gin, do you? Wait a minute—it tells one here how to make it. You have to ... Look, you don't want me to go through all that, surely to God. It'll take——'

'If it says holy water, you use holy water. Get on with it. What do you have to do?'

'Oh, *hell*. Okay. I'll need some water and some salt.'

I fetched a jugful from the kitchen and poured some salt on to a plate from a cellar on one of the dining-tables.

'Evidently one has to sort of cleanse the stuff for some reason.' He pointed his first two fingers at the salt and read, 'I render thee immaculate, creature of Earth, by the living God, by the holy God,'—here he made the sign of the cross—'that thou mayest be purified of all evil influences in the name of Adonai, who is the lord of angels and of men ...'

I went to the window. It occurred to me to have another look for the crucifix, which I had vainly tried to find round about dawn, but I was sufficiently sure that, having fulfilled its purpose, it had been taken back by its giver. Instead, I waited. After a minute or two a very faint voice spoke to me, so faint that it could not have been heard more than a few feet away.

'What are you about? Would you destroy me?'

Cautiously, my eyes on the rector, I nodded my head.

'I'll put you in the way to acquire great riches, you shall take any woman on earth to be your paramour, you shall have all the glory war affords, or peace too, so you but cease.'

I shook my head.

'I exorcize all influence and seeds of evil,' read the rector. 'I lay upon them the spell of Christ's holy Church that they may be bound fast with chains and cast into the outer darkness, until the day of their repentance and restoration, that they trouble not the servants of God ...'

When the tiny voice returned, there was fear as well as pleading in it. 'I shall be nothing, for I am denied repentance for ever. I shall be a senseless clod to all eternity. Can one man do this to another? Would you play God, Mr Allington? But God at least would have mercy upon one who has offended Him.'

I shook my head again, wishing I could tell him just how wrong he was on that last point.

'I'll teach you peace of mind.'

Now there was an offer. I turned my back on the rector and

stared out of the window, biting my lips furiously. I imagined myself not noticing myself for the rest of my life, losing myself, not vainly struggling to lose myself, in poetry and sculpture and my job and other people, not womanizing, not drinking. Then I thought of the Tyler girl and the Ditchfield girl and Amy and whoever might be next: deprived of the green man, Underhill would surely devise some other way of harming the young and helpless. It was convincing, it was my clear duty; but I have often wondered since whether what made up my mind for me was not the unacceptability of the offer as such, whether we are not all so firmly attached, in all senses, to what we are that any radical change, however unarguably for the better, is bound to seem a kind of self-destruction. I shook my head.

Across the room, the rector sprinkled water on the floor and continued, 'In the name of the Father and of the Son and of the Holy Ghost, by the token of the life poured out in the broken body and blood of Jesus Christ, and by the seven gold candlesticks, and by one like unto the Son of Man, standing in the midst of the candlesticks, and under the sign and symbol of His holy, bloodstained and triumphant cross, I exorcize thee...'

At that point I heard, no less faintly than before but with complete distinctness, a single, drawn-out, diminishing scream of abandoned terror and despair. It did not quite die away, but was cut off abruptly. I shivered.

The rector looked up. 'Sorry, did you say something?'

'No. Please get it over.'

'Are you all right?'

'Of course I'm all right,' I said savagely. I had had enough of this query in the last few days. 'How much more to go now?'

'Oh, very well. There's only another couple of sentences. Visit, O Lord, we beseech thee, this room, and drive from it all the snares of the enemy: let Thy holy angels dwell herein to preserve us in peace, and may Thy blessing be upon us evermore, through Jesus Christ our Lord, amen. There. I hope you're quite satisfied?'

'Perfectly, thank you.' I assumed that what had just been done would have no effect on the appearances, upstairs, of the red-haired woman, and was content: I had no wish to put an end to that timid, evanescent shade. 'That's it, then. I'll run you back.'

A couple of minutes later, I was about to get into the truck beside the rector when Ramón came up to me.

'Excuse, Mr. Allington.'

'What is it?'

'Mrs Allington like to see you, Mr Allington. In a house.'

'Whereabouts? Where?'

'Down estairs. In a office.'

'Thank you.'

I told the rector I would be back in a minute. Joyce was on the office telephone. She said she had to go now and rang off.

'Ramón told me you wanted to see me.'

'I'm sorry, Maurice, but I'm leaving you.'

I looked at her wide, clear blue eyes, but not into them, because, turned in my direction though they were, they were not on me at all. 'I see. Any particular reason?'

'I just can't go on any longer. I can't go on trying any more. I'm fed up with trying.'

'Trying to do what? Run your part of the house?'

'I don't like doing that, but I could do it if things were different, I wouldn't mind it at all.'

'What things?'

'I've tried to love you, but you won't let me, ever. You just have your own ideas about what to do and when and how, about everything, and they always stay the same, doesn't matter who you're dealing with or what they say to you. There's no use trying to love someone when they're always doing something else.'

'These last few days I've been having a——'

'These last few days have been exactly the same as any other few days as far as that's concerned. More so, I mean with your father and this ghost business and everything, and now Amy, it would have been the time for anyone else but you to sort of be around.'

'I've been around today, but I haven't seen much of you.'

'Did you try and find me?—no. And don't say you've got a job to do, because everybody has. If you hadn't got a job you'd make up things to do. I don't know what you think about people, which is bad enough, but you certainly go on as if they're all in the way. Except for just sex, and that's so that you can get them out of the way for a bit. Or else you just treat them like bottles of whisky—this one's finished, take it away, bring me another one. It's only all right for you to do things and you to want things. How could you ask your wife to come to bed with you and your girl-friend? A little experiment, eh? Why not fix it up? Easy enough. It needed two girls and there were two girls, so fine. Why not? You might have had the decency to go to a prostitute or somebody for a thing like that.'

'You seemed to enjoy it all right.'

'Yes, I did, it was wonderful, but that was nothing to do with what you'd had in mind. Diana's coming with me.'

I understood now what Jack had been talking about that morning; he had merely not been told the basic facts—predictably enough. 'It sounds rather as if you've been wasting your time with me all along.'

'I knew you'd say something like that. That's how it would strike you: just sex. Just sex is all you know about. But it isn't just sex with me and her. It's not a hell of a lot to do with sex at all. It's being with someone. Who hasn't always got somewhere more important to be in the next two minutes. Amy won't miss me much. I couldn't do enough about being her mother, because you never did anything about making her be my daughter. I'm not going straight away. I'll stay on until you've found someone to help housekeep. We can talk about the divorce in the meantime.'

'Supposing I made a real effort?'

'An effort's no good. And you'd soon forget to make it.'

That was about that. I looked at her eyes again, and her thick yellow hair, not fine, not coarse, simply abundant, with a very slight but firm wave from broad forehead down to strong shoulders. 'I'm sorry, Joyce.'

'That's all right. I'll aways come and see you. Do you think you could possibly go now?'

I went. I heard the key scrape in the lock and a smothered sob from behind the door. It was impossible to think about any of it now, except for one small part which it was impossible not to think about, for a moment at least, the part to do with experiment: 'a little experiment, eh? Why not?' Was I really capable of thinking—inclined to think—like that about things, and about people? If so, there might have been more to Underhill's selection of me as his instrument than the co-presence of Amy in the house: something to do with an affinity. I hated that idea, and tried to suppress it as I walked slowly back to the truck and the rector.

That divine looked at me with more emphatic and specific

petulance than usual when I joined him. 'Nothing of any great gravity, I hope?'

I started the engine and steered out of the car-park. 'Tom, I can't say how much I appreciate your taking time to come along here. On a Sunday, too.'

'What's so special about Sunday?'

'Well ... aren't there things like services? Sermons to prepare?'

'You don't imagine I'd prepare *sermons* for a bunch of swedes like I've got here, do you? You've got to realize the whole sermon thing has gone now, along with antimacassars and button boots.'

'And evolution.'

'And evolution, quite so. Anyway. I've got Lord Cliff preaching tonight. Not that any of that lot will ... Hey, where are we going?'

I had turned uphill instead of down towards the village and the rectory. 'I'm afraid we've got one more call to make.'

'Oh *no*. What is it this time?'

'Exorcism again. In a wood along here.'

'You positively *have* to be joking. It'll take——'

'What were you saying about Lord Cliff?'

It worked: I saw the corners of his mouth turn up (for once) as he visualized whatever deeply satisfying reaction to his prolonged absence he visualized. When we got to the copse, I handed him a cut-glass vinegar bottle from my kitchen into which I had, without his knowledge, poured half a gill or so of holy water. He accepted this, kitted himself up again and started on the service with what was, for him, a good grace. I walked to and fro, looking for signs of the green man's embodiment and subsequent disembodiment, and finding them: a fresh scar where the limb of an ash had been torn from the trunk, at a point well above arm's reach; a scattered heap of bruised leaves from half a dozen kinds of tree and shrub. Such had been the constituents of his form here, in an English wood; he must originally have come to birth, have first been called into being, in some place where the prevailing vegetation consisted of trees with rather uniformly cylindrical trunks and boughs; so at any rate, the lineaments of the now shattered silver figure had seemed to testify. But it, and its power, had proved remarkably adaptable to a radical change of location.

It was very quiet and shady and sunny in the copse. The

rector's voice pursued its slightly irritable, perfunctory course.

'By the emblems of the eye of the angel, the tooth of the dog, the claw of the lion and the mouth of the fish, I charge thee to depart, enemy of joy, child of perversity, and in the sign of the spirits of the black waters and the white mountain and the wilderness without end, I command thee, in the authority of Christ, to go now to the place of thy choice...'

Suddenly, ten yards off, I saw and heard a shivering among the grasses and bushes, a violent local movement of air too shapeless and multi-directional to be called a whirlwind. At first the disturbance was confined to one spot; then it seemed to spread; no, it was not spreading, it was shifting, at first almost imperceptibly, then at a slow walking pace, then faster, straight for where the rector was standing. I ran past it in a curve and pulled him out of its path. He staggered, almost slipped, steadied himself against the trunk of an oak and glared at me.

'What the devil is the matter with you, Mr Allington? Have you gone out of your mind? I've had just about all I can take...'

While he continued to expostulate, I turned my back on him and saw the disturbance, still accelerating, pass over the place where he had been and out of sight behind a holly-bush. Perhaps, once launched, it was powerless to change direction; perhaps that direction had been a matter of coincidence; perhaps it had no hostile properties; but I was very glad I had acted as I did. I hurried to a position from which I could track its course. By now it had almost reached the edge of the wood.

'Come here, quick,' I called.

'I'll do no such thing.'

Once out in the open, the phenomenon spread, became diffused, was soon a minute trembling of grass over an area the size of a tennis-court, and then was nothing. I felt the tension ebb away from my muscles, and walked back to the rector, who was still holding on to the oak tree.

'Sorry about that. But didn't you see it?'

'See it? I saw nothing.'

'Never mind. Anyway, we can pack up now.'

'But I haven't finished the service yet.'

'No doubt, but it's taken effect already.'

'What? How do you know?'

I realized that, under the peevishness inseparable from his expressing any emotion, the Rev. Tom was frightened of me, but I could think of no explanation that would not frighten him more, and reasoned anyway that a spot of fear, from whatever source, could not fail to do him good. So I mumbled something about intuition, got him on the move and endured, first his continued protests, then his huffy silence, while we went back the way we had come. Outside the rectory, he said in a conciliatory tone,

'You'll give me a bit of notice about the party, won't you?'

'Party? *Party?* Have you gone out of your *mind*?' was what I longed to say, ramming it home with Grand-Guignol-style bafflement, and had started on an ape-man frown before relenting, or deciding it would be more fun to have him wake up to the deception by degrees. Anyway, I said I would do as he asked, thanked him for his trouble and drove home.

In the car-park, I saw Nick's Morris with its boot-cover lifted, and a moment later he appeared carrying two suitcases and closely followed by Lucy.

'We're off, Dad. Got to pick up Jo and get her to bed.'

'Sure. Well ... thank you for coming. For your support.'

Nick glanced at his wife and said, 'Joyce told us. We're both very sorry. But I never thought she was right for you.'

'It's more that I wasn't right for her.'

'Well, anyhow ... Come up and see us as soon as you can. Get shot of this place for a bit. Give old David a taste of responsibility.'

'Thanks. I'll try.'

'Don't just try,' said Lucy. 'Do it. You know you can. We'd love to see you. The spare room's really nice now, and Jo sleeps right through till eight most mornings.'

I kissed her for the first time since their wedding, and that had not been a real kiss. Nick and I kissed and the two of them got into the car. Before he drove off, he rolled down his window to say, out of her hearing,

'I was going to ask you about that ghost business of yours. Is it still, you know ...?'

'All taken care of. All over. I'll tell you the full story some day.'

'Not *some* day. The next time we meet. So long, Dad—I'll ring you tonight. Oh: Amy was asking where you were. Said she had something to say to you. And you listen, whatever it is. And you say something to her. Please, Dad.'

I found Amy sitting up in bed, while the TV screen showed a pair of unengaging candlesticks and an octogenarian voice said, 'They're very beautiful, aren't they? I should say *late* eighteenth century, not English, of course ...'

'Turn it off, Dad, please.'

I turned it off and settled down on the edge of the bed.

'How are you feeling, Ame?'

'Fine, thank you. Joyce is going away, isn't she?'

'How do you know?'

'She told me. She came in to see if I wanted anything and we had a chat, and I asked her if we were going to Eastbourne for the week-end before I go back to school like we did last year, and she said you and I might be, but she wouldn't be with us then. Then she told me. She was upset, but she wasn't crying or anything.'

'How extraordinary. Just telling you like that.'

'Not really. You know how she tells you things without thinking what you're going to think about them.'

'Yes, I know.'

'You don't seem to have much luck with your wives, do you, Dad? Perhaps you don't give them enough treats. Anyway, I started thinking about what we ought to do. Now I'm thirteen now. I shan't want to get married until I'm about twenty-one. That's eight years, at least that, because I might not find the right man straight away. And I can help you all that time. I'm quite good at cooking already, and if you don't mind me being in the kitchen when we're not busy I can learn a lot more just by watching. And I can take telephone messages and things like that, and when I'm older I'll be able to do other things, like seeing to the accounts. I'll be very useful.'

'That's sweet of you, darling,' I said, and made to embrace her, but she drew back and glared at me.

'No it isn't. I'm not saying it just to make you feel better. That's what you do. I've been thinking about it very seriously, and making plans. To start with, I think you ought to sell this place, because of Gramps dying and Joyce going away and the man last night. We ought to go somewhere where I can go to a good school and live at home. Cambridge or Eastbourne or somewhere like that would be the sort of place. Don't you think that's what we ought to do?'

'Yes. You're right. We've got to get away. Of course, it depends on what hotels and inns and so on are on the market, where we go, I mean.'

'It'll all be up to you, that part of it. Then when we think we've found a place, we can go and look at schools.'

'I'll start making inquiries tomorrow.'

'If you've got time.'

'No, I'll have time.'

She reached out to me, and I kissed her and held her. Soon afterwards I left, after having my offer to turn the TV set on rejected: she said she wanted to go on thinking. It was time to go and shower and change for the evening. As I started on this, I reflected that things had sorted themselves out after a fashion. Or some things had. I was feeling tense again, and my heart was beating heavily, moving towards the point where it would begin to flutter and stumble. Also, as had been happening increasingly of late, I noticed how clumsy I was getting, knocking my shoulder against the bathroom door-jamb, barking my knuckles on the shower-taps when I reached for them, slamming the soap down in the holder with unwilled violence, as if I were drunk, which I certainly was not, or as if my powers of co-ordination were progressively deteriorating. That thought wearied me unendurably, and so did the thought that tomorrow was another week, and I must telephone the insurance company about the Volkswagen, and see the solicitor about my father's will, and fetch the meat, and bank the takings, and make new arrangements about fruit and vegetables, and prepare for another week after that. And Joyce, and selling the house, and looking for another, and finding somebody to go to bed with.

Much sooner than I could have expected (I had not really had any such expectation), I found I had begun to understand the meaning of the young man's prophecy that I would come to appreciate death and what it had to offer. Death was my only means of getting away for good from this body and all its pseudo-symptoms of disease and fear, from the constant awareness of this body, from this person, with his ruthlessness and sentimentality and ineffective, insincere, impracticable notions of behaving better, from attending to my own thoughts and from counting in thousands to smother them and from my face in the glass. He had said I would never be free of him as long as the world lasted, and I believed him, but when I died I would be free of Maurice Allington for longer than that.

I put on my dinner-jacket, swallowed a strong whisky and went downstairs to begin the evening round.